Raves for Selma Eichler and the Desiree Shapiro mysteries

Murder Can Upset Your Mother
"Eichler scores again. . . . [A] delicious cozy."
—*Publishers Weekly*

Murder Can Spoil Your Appetite
"Desiree Shapiro is a shining creation."
—*Romantic Times*

Murder Can Singe Your Old Flame
"Witty dialogue . . . charming New York setting . . . hilarious characters." —*Publishers Weekly*

Murder Can Spook Your Cat
"A very realistic character. . . . The mystery is creatively drawn and well plotted."
—*Painted Rock Reviews*

Murder Can Wreck Your Reunion
"Another wildly hilarious mystery." —*The Snooper*

Murder Can Stunt Your Growth
"Poignant and satisfying. . . . The real pleasure of this book is spending time with Desiree Shapiro . . . just plain fun to read." —*I Love a Mystery*

Murder Can Ruin Your Looks
"Highly entertaining." —Carolyn Hart

Murder Can Kill Your Social Life
"A tasty treat combining the best of humor, food, and just plain good writing. I laughed till I cried; then I made myself a sandwich."
—Tamar Myers

Also by Selma Eichler

MURDER CAN KILL YOUR SOCIAL LIFE
MURDER CAN RUIN YOUR LOOKS
MURDER CAN STUNT YOUR GROWTH
MURDER CAN WRECK YOUR REUNION
MURDER CAN SPOOK YOUR CAT
MURDER CAN SINGE YOUR OLD FLAME
MURDER CAN SPOIL YOUR APPETITE
MURDER CAN UPSET YOUR MOTHER

MURDER CAN COOL OFF YOUR AFFAIR

A Desiree Shapiro Mystery

Selma Eichler

A SIGNET BOOK

SIGNET
Published by New American Library, a division of
Penguin Group (USA) Inc., 375 Hudson Street,
New York, New York 10014, U.S.A.
Penguin Books Ltd, 80 Strand,
London WC2R 0RL, England
Penguin Books Australia Ltd, 250 Camberwell Road,
Camberwell, Victoria 3124, Australia
Penguin Books Canada Ltd, 10 Alcorn Avenue,
Toronto, Ontario, Canada M4V 3B2
Penguin Books (N.Z.) Ltd, Cnr Rosedale and Airborne Roads,
Albany, Auckland 1310, New Zealand

Penguin Books Ltd, Registered Offices:
80 Strand, London WC2R 0RL, England

First published by Signet, an imprint of New American Library,
a division of Penguin Group (USA) Inc.

First Signet Printing, March 2002
10 9 8 7 6 5 4 3

To my husband, Lloyd Eichler, again,
for his help and remarkable patience—again.

ACKNOWLEDGMENTS

I'm very grateful to—

Major Alan G. Martin of the New York State Police, who, as he has so many times before, came to my rescue with this book, too,

my editor, Ellen Edwards, for recommendations and guidance that went even beyond this manuscript,

Lexi Adams, Ellen's assistant, for all of that Internet sleuthing on Desiree's behalf,

Helen Eichler, Attorney-at-Law, for her time-consuming legal research,

and, certainly not least,

my friend Joe Todaro, for his assistance with this new computer of mine. Without Joe's help, the next couple of hundred pages might have been blank.

Chapter 1

I could only keep my fingers crossed that Mr. and Mrs. Lander would turn out to be a couple of very skinny people.

Not that I have anything against those who are comfortably built, you understand, being of not insubstantial poundage myself. But my cigar-box-of-an-office just wasn't meant to accommodate more than one visitor at a time. So if even a few inches of either Lander's seat should extend beyond the chair's seat, we were facing the possibility of busting through the walls here.

But I needn't have worried. When they arrived for their one o'clock appointment that Friday—and on the dot, incidentally—John and Trudie Lander were all I could have hoped for.

Trudie was tall, maybe five-six (well, from my five-feet-two perspective, that's tall), with the long, scrawny neck, sunken chest, and—happily—bony hipbones of a once-upon-a-time fashion model. That time, if it existed, having been about thirty years in the past.

John Lander had at least half a foot on his wife. A slightly balding fellow with a pleasant face and warm brown eyes, he wore an ill-fitting navy suit that hung so loosely on his spare frame that he seemed almost gaunt.

As soon as they settled themselves across the desk from me—with John in a chair schlepped in from an office across the hall—the phone rang. And while I was confirming Monday morning's gynecologist's appointment, I gave my prospective clients a quick once-over.

They were fairly attractive individuals, I decided, although as a couple they did strike me as slightly mismatched.

In sharp contrast to her husband, Trudie was very fashionably turned out. Her red-linen suit—the ideal choice for a temperate spring day—might have been custom tailored. Her black patent pumps had a beautifully shaped, up-to-the-minute heel. And if that quilted leather bag wasn't a Chanel, I'd eat it.

They were dissimilar in another, more basic way, too. Even during the brief time I was on the line, Trudie was extremely animated, her eyes darting here and there, her hands fingering first her skirt, then her tawny shoulder-length hair. Actually, *edgy* might be a more accurate description of the woman. John, on the other hand, I took to be a quiet, laid-back sort of man, appearing so relaxed he could have been mistaken for a disinterested party. Well, they (whoever "they" are) do say that opposites attract. And, of course, it's not hard to figure how this kind of difference might, in fact, wind up being a good thing.

Finally, there was the disparity in their ages. In spite of Trudie's unusually taut facial skin (evidently the work of an overzealous and not particularly talented plastic surgeon), I estimated the woman to be on the seasoned side of fifty. This would make her easily ten years her spouse's senior. And good for her, I say. I can remember when it was almost *written* that the man had to be older than the woman (and no one seemed overly concerned about how much older, either). As for the other way around, though, that used to be practically *verboten*. Still, while I really do feel things are a lot fairer these days, I suppose I'm not quite as accepting as I like to believe I am. I mean, now that I think about it, why else would I be dwelling on the age business like this?

Anyway, once the phone call was over I began the interview with, "Your wife said when she contacted me this morning that you may be in danger."

Obviously, I was addressing John, but it was Trudie who responded. "Yes, I certainly did."

Oh, it's going to be like that, is it? Okay then, I'd just skip the middleman. "What makes you think so?" I put to the woman, who was fidgeting with her hair again.

"Before I go into it, it would probably be best if we gave you a little background. Don't you agree, dear?"

Dear, who apparently recognized this for the rhetorical question it was—owing, no doubt, to years of experience—didn't so much as nod before Trudie plowed ahead.

"Last month John's extremely wealthy uncle was told he had an inoperable cancer. You may have heard of him, Ms. Shapiro—Victor Lander? No? He's really quite well known—a pioneer in the plastics industry. Poor Victor. His illness is so-o tragic. He'd always been such a strong, vital man, in spite of being well into his eighties. But, sadly, in the fall he began to deteriorate, and now the doctors are saying that he has only a few months to live. At any rate, two weeks ago this past Tuesday—nine days after Uncle Victor revealed his diagnosis to the family—John's cousin Edward, Victor's principal heir, was *murdered.*" As she uttered the word, Trudie shuddered, after which she swallowed a couple of times. When she spoke again there was an urgency in her tone. "What we're here about, though, is that this Monday there was an attempt on my husband's life, too. He had been at the office until quite late that night, and when he got home at around eleven-thirty, someone took a shot at him right in front of our building. John could actually hear the bullet whiz past his ear, couldn't you, dear?"

John knew better than even to attempt an answer.

"It appears, however," Trudie went on, "that he was

the only one who did hear anything. The gun must have been equipped with one of those silencers."

At that moment Trudie took a couple of seconds out to pick some imaginary lint off her skirt, and I used the opportunity to slip in a few words. "Have you spoken to the police about this?"

She looked up, eyes blazing. "The police!" she spat. "The morning after it happened—before my husband went to work—we stopped in at the station house to report what had occurred. We saw one of the detectives who's investigating Edward's death, and he wrote down the information and promised they'd follow up. But I'm sure they've merely been going through the motions. I don't believe that fellow gave any credence at all to what we had to say."

"Why do you think that?"

"You could tell from his attitude that he regarded the whole thing as a ploy to divert attention from the fact that John had a very good motive for wanting Edward out of the way. And, unfortunately, there were no witnesses."

"What motive are we talking about?"

"Oh, didn't I tell you? John is next in line."

"For what?"

Trudie eyed me rather pityingly. I got the impression she'd concluded that I was more than a little slow-witted.

"Why," she informed me, "to inherit Uncle Victor's millions, of course."

Chapter 2

I was curious to learn what had brought the couple to me—I mean, to *me* specifically—and I started to pose the question. But Trudie aborted the attempt.

"I should tell you this before we go any further," she said as she slid over to the edge of her seat. And now she leaned so far in my direction that there was a good chance of her falling. If there'd been any room for her to fall, that is.

"Tell me what?"

"John isn't the only one who had reason to kill Edward. There are others who, under certain circumstances, would also profit from Edward's death." She sat back in the chair again to deliver her next sentence, according it the slow-paced, dramatic reading she felt it warranted. "Those circumstances being that John has to be disposed of first."

"Trudie," her husband admonished. It was the only time since we'd introduced ourselves that he'd uttered so much as a peep.

"Well, who do you suppose shot at you, darling—the tooth fairy?" And dismissing him with a wave of the hand, Trudie returned her focus to me. "If John should die before Uncle Victor does, John's twin cousins Shawna and Scott Riley would split the inheritance between them. And if, in turn, anything were to happen to *them,* the estate would pass to David Hearn, the nephew of Victor's deceased wife."

"And in the highly improbable event that David, too, should meet with an untimely end?" I asked.

"Charity. I think Uncle Victor specified that the bulk of the money would be divided among five charities. I can't remember which ones at the moment."

I was startled when John jumped in and rattled off, "American Cancer Society, Heart Association, Make-a-Wish Foundation, Lighthouse, and Alzheimer's."

"How certain are you that these are the terms of the will?"

"I'm *absolutely* certain," Trudie assured me. "That Sunday when Uncle Victor had us all to his home to give us the terrible news about his health, he also revealed his decision to leave the bulk of his estate to Edward. He'd made Edward his principal heir, he said, because the two of them had such a special bond. You see, Edward was orphaned at thirteen, and Uncle Victor had practically raised him. If anything should happen to Edward, however—and, of course, Uncle Victor had no expectation that it actually would—he wanted John to have the money. John and Uncle Victor were never that attached really, except for a short period about ten years ago, right after Aunt Bella— Uncle Victor's wife—died."

"What happened then?"

"John would go over to his uncle's once or twice a week in an effort to console him. Mostly they'd spend a couple of hours just sitting around and talking. Sometimes my workaholic husband would even let Uncle Victor prevail upon him to leave the office early enough to make it there in time for dinner. John would always try to take him to a restaurant instead— you know, to get the poor man to leave the house. On occasion he actually managed it, too. At any rate, apparently Uncle Victor hasn't forgotten John's kindness to him."

"Did you accompany your husband on these visits?"

I asked for no real reason except that I'm pathologically nosy.

"No, I decided Uncle Victor would feel freer to pour out his heart about Aunt Bella and their marriage—or whatever—if it was only he and John."

And besides, consoling a grieving widower is hardly your idea of a gala evening out, isn't it? I thought. Immediately after which my nicer, more tolerant self admonished me. I was hardly being fair to the woman; I didn't even *know* her, for heaven's sake. But in all honesty, Trudie Lander wasn't easy to take. I mean, I'd had people dominate a conversation before. But this tomato was in a class by herself.

At any rate, I swear she sneaked into my head just then because, her chin out to *there,* she declared firmly, "Listen, Uncle Victor *had* to be more comfortable with John alone."

"You're probably right," I conceded diplomatically. And now, momentarily forgetting myself, I put a question to John. "You and your uncle didn't remain that close, though?"

"No, eventually things tapered off a bit. With the hours John spends at work, he barely has time for *me,* much less his uncle." This, of course, from Trudie.

"I want to make sure I have everything straight," I said. "If your husband is eliminated, his share is divided between the twins. And if by some quirk of fate they, too, are out of the picture when Uncle Victor departs this world, Aunt Bella's nephew becomes the primary beneficiary. Correct?"

"Yes. And the whole business is totally bizarre, if you ask me."

"I gather those conditions took you by surprise."

"You gather right. Until Uncle Victor outlined his intentions, John and I had more or less assumed that most of the money would be apportioned among the four cousins. And while we were virtually certain that the largest chunk would be going to Edward, we figured there'd be plenty left over for the rest of us. Trust me, it isn't that there aren't enough assets here to go around. I believe the others had also been under this impression, don't you, John? However, the way Uncle Victor explained it that day, the remaining relatives had been allotted only token amounts."

"Uh, you said something about the *four* cousins," I pointed out while frantically having a second go at totaling relatives on my fingers.

"We never considered that David Hearn would be included in the will. I doubt very much if Uncle Victor has been in any sort of regular contact with him. John and I hardly know the boy—he rarely even bothered to attend Uncle Victor's family gatherings."

"Maybe my uncle didn't invite him," her husband threw in dryly.

"I don't remember seeing him at the house that frequently when Aunt Bella was alive, either," Trudie retorted sharply.

"He was a *kid* then, for Christ's sake. Besides, your memory's letting you down. Before David's parents moved to Florida, the three of them used to show up fairly often."

Trudie gave him a positively lethal look, and I quickly changed the subject to forestall the twins' ending up the big winners in the Uncle Victor sweepstakes. "Is there anyone else who might have had reason to harm your husband?" I asked.

"No one."

I glanced at John. "No one," he agreed. "I don't seem to excite that much passion in people, one way or the other." And for the first time he smiled. It was a really appealing smile, too.

"It could be that the shooter wasn't actually aiming at you," I offered tentatively. "There's always the possibility it was one of those drive-by things."

"Oh, sure," Trudie scoffed. "Not even two weeks

after John becomes heir to a fortune, some disinterested party just *happens* to come close to getting him out of the way. You're not big on coincidence, are you, Ms. Shapiro?''

Now the truth is, I'm not at all big on coincidence. In fact, it wasn't until fairly recently that I was even willing to concede that there *is* such a thing. "I agree that it's highly unlikely," I said, trying not to sound defensive, "although at this point I wouldn't rule it out completely. And please call me Desiree—both of you. But listen, there are a few more things we should cover.''

Trudie nodded her permission.

"Are you able to account for your whereabouts at the time your cousin was murdered, Mr. Lander?''

Trudie actually allowed the man to reply. "It's John, Desiree," I was informed. "And as far as my whereabouts, Edward was killed at approximately eight o'clock in the evening. I was—''

"The police were able to pinpoint the time of death like that?" I broke in.

"Well, from what I've been told, Edward's wife phoned him at a little after seven—she had a class that night—and during their conversation, he mentioned that he was about to stick a casserole in the oven. The dish takes a half hour to bake, and the medical examiner's report indicated that he'd consumed the meal just before he was shot. Plus, when a friend of Edward's called the apartment at a few minutes past eight, there wasn't any answer. And a short while later, at eight-fifteen, a neighbor rang the bell to return a book he'd borrowed, but no one came to the door.''

"That seems to do it, all right. Anyway, before you were so rudely interrupted, I had the idea you were about to tell me where you were when your cousin died.''

"I was at work.''

"Is there anyone who can verify that?"

John smiled sheepishly. "I'm afraid not—the police asked me the same thing. My secretary went home at five-thirty, so no help there. For the most part I concentrated on catching up on my paperwork that night, although I did get in touch with a few prospective buyers—I'm in real estate. I tried to reach one of them at just around eight o'clock, too. But the party wasn't in; I didn't even get an answering machine."

"Nobody telephoned *you*, I take it."

"Unfortunately, lately I tend to be doing most of the pursuing."

"Did anyone stop in at your office? With a food delivery, maybe? Or how about the cleaning lady?"

"Don't I wish!"

"Did you have your car with you that day?"

"Yes, I always drive to work."

"Your office is where?"

"In Brooklyn—Brooklyn Heights," John replied, naming one of the borough's more upscale areas.

"Answer this for me. About how long would it take to drive from your office to your cousin's place?"

Evidently Trudie had grown impatient with not hearing her own voice for a few minutes, because guess who jumped in. "At that hour of the evening? He could probably make it to Edward's in a half hour. Perhaps less."

Well, since she's so eager to participate . . . "Umm, I'll have to ask you the same thing I just asked your husband, Mrs. Lander. Would you mind telling me where you were at eight o'clock on the night of the murder?" Following this, I hastily threw in the same lie I've relied on too often in the past to even estimate. "I'm only asking for my records, of course."

There was a large dollop of sarcasm in the response. "That's easy. I was where I always am—at home, waiting for John to put in an appearance. He got in around ten—it was one of his early days."

"Any telephone calls? Visitors?"

"I can't be absolutely certain, but I believe I spoke to my aunt Margaret that evening. This would have been about six-thirty, though, which is when we normally phone each other."

"And you had no other calls?"

"Not that I can recall."

"How about visitors?"

Trudie shook her head. "I'm sure there weren't any."

"Tell me, who was it who discovered Edward's body?"

"His wife. She found him when she came home."

"And when was that?"

"Around a quarter to eleven. He had apparently admitted the killer to the apartment himself—from what I understand, there was no indication of a break-in. Edward was lying on the kitchen floor with a bullet in his chest." She squeezed her eyes closed as if to block out the scene.

"Just one last thing," I said, addressing John. "How did—" But Trudie had already allowed him to have his say. So reminding myself about eliminating the middleman—and with an apologetic glance at John—I redirected the question to her. "How did Edward and John get along?"

"They were buddies—right, dear? They often played golf on Sunday mornings, and they met for breakfast every Wednesday before going to their respective places of business. They belonged to the same gym, too, and sometimes they'd arrange to work out together. We even took a vacation with Edward and Sara—his wife—a couple of years ago."

"And you? How did you feel about Edward?"

"I liked him. He was a very nice man," she responded primly.

"Just one last thing," I said for the second time. "What made you decide to come to *me* with this?"

Trudie hesitated. "May I be honest?"

"Of course."

"Well, ever since John was shot at four nights ago, I'd been trying to persuade him to hire a private detective."

"*Persuade* me?" John groused. "She *hounded* me about it."

His wife ignored him. "At first he wouldn't even consider the idea." She smiled smugly. "But being an extremely determined woman, I finally managed to wear him down." *Why didn't this surprise me?* "I had inquired around a bit and gotten the telephone numbers of the top two investigative services in New York. John, however, refused to ring up either one of them—you wouldn't think it, but he can be pretty stubborn when he wants to be. He said he'd hire a detective if I insisted. But only with the proviso that the detective be you."

At this, my eyes must have grown to twice their size. I looked to John for an explanation.

"I heard about you a while ago," he said, flushing. "I wish I could remember who it was who mentioned you, but I do recall this person's saying that if he—or she—were ever in trouble, you'd be the one they'd contact, that you have a reputation for getting results. For some reason that stuck in my mind."

Well, I *have* met with a certain amount of success in recent years. But as far as this providing me with any kind of recognition, let's put it this way: *Desiree Shapiro* is not exactly a household name.

It went through my head that John might have me confused with someone else. Nevertheless, I elected to take the praise at face value. It had been a long stretch between compliments.

Soon after this the Landers supplied me with some pertinent phone numbers and addresses. After which they prepared to leave.

Trudie was already on her feet, and John was about to rise when I cautioned him, "You'll have to conduct yourself with a great deal of care until we get to the bottom of this. Keep looking over your shoulder. Be suspicious of everything. And if anything doesn't smell quite right to you, do whatever is necessary to extricate yourself from the situation. And then don't hesitate to call the police. Okay?"

"Okay," he answered.

"Is that a promise?" I persisted.

"It's a promise."

"And naturally, you'll let me know *instantly* if anything unusual happens."

"Of course I will."

In spite of these assurances, however, it was with a twinge of fear that I watched my new client walk out of the office.

I mean, over the past couple of years, I'd acquired a certain degree of faith in my abilities. So I was reasonably confident that I would be able to uncover the person who had attempted to take his life—and who, at this very moment, might be preparing to have another go at it.

But the question was, could I do it in time?

Chapter 3

The next morning the alarm clock yanked me out of a tight sleep at eight o'clock. Which on a Saturday I regard as practically a predawn awakening. But today I was motivated.

In fact, I'd never before felt the sense of urgency that I did with John Lander. I mean, when I'm involved in a murder investigation, my client is usually a friend or lover or relative of the deceased's. But in this instance my client was in imminent danger of *becoming* the deceased.

Now, I know that on Friday I'd floated the idea that the attack on John might not have been personal, that there was an outside chance it was a drive-by shooting. But the truth is, I'd have been willing to bet my entire earring collection—and this is something I hold very dear—that the incident was tied in with his cousin's murder.

So right after the Landers left me, I'd phoned Sara Sharp, widow of Edward. Her answering machine informed me that she'd be staying with her sister Dana in Richmond until next Thursday.

Immediately after striking out there, I'd tried the Riley twins, one after the other, hoping to set up a separate appointment with each of them for today. But as it turned out, Shawna and Scott were both away from their desks when I called. And, unfortunately, John and Trudie hadn't been able to provide me with David Hearn's office number, so I couldn't get in touch with him, either.

That night I had to forgo any further attempts to contact these people because I had plans for dinner and the ballet. I don't want you to think I wound up making calf eyes at some fascinating member of the masculine persuasion, however. The date was with my next-apartment neighbor Barbara Gleason, with whom I not only share a common wall but on occasion some interesting—although frequently contentious—evenings. The contentious part more often than not the result of Barbara's being one of these intractable individuals who insists the world was meant to be skinny, which leads her to monitor almost every morsel I consume. And frankly, I don't take a whole lot of pleasure in watching her watch me. As it happened, though, she was on her best behavior on Friday, allowing me to enjoy my shrimp scampi without a single *tsk-tsk.* It was a wonderful meal followed by an absolutely exquisite performance of my favorite ballet, *La Bayadère.*

But getting back to Saturday morning . . .

As anxious as I was to start my inquiries, I didn't think anyone on my list would be all that appreciative of an 8 A.M. call on a weekend. (I can tell you right now that I wouldn't be.) Actually, I reminded myself, considering the nice, warm weather—it was beach weather, really—I'd be lucky if any of these people were even in town.

At any rate, once I'd washed up, I put on the coffee, toasted an Entenmann's corn muffin, and poured some Rice Krispies and milk in a bowl. Then after shoveling down my breakfast—I was too impatient to really taste it—I remained at the table and began working yesterday's *New York Times* crossword puzzle. As usual, the daily puzzle didn't have me feeling half as

mentally stunted as one of Sunday's ego-bruising doo-
zies, and I managed to finish a decent chunk of it
before getting really antsy again.

Squirming in my seat at that point, I checked the
kitchen clock: nine-thirty. *Still on the early side,* I reluctantly conceded. So freshening my coffee—which,
incidentally, was horrendous, but since that's the only
kind of coffee I can make, I'm used to it—I returned
to the puzzle. Finally, at ten minutes to ten, I gave
myself permission to lift the receiver.

I dialed Shawna's number first. The yawn that came
immediately after the "Hello?" led me to conclude
that I'd dragged the girl out of bed, although she politely denied it. I told her my name, then explained
that I was a private investigator hired by John Lander
to find out who had taken a shot at him earlier that
week.

"You think I had something to do with *that*?" she
demanded, her soft little voice increasing considerably
in volume now.

"No, not at all. But I would be remiss if I didn't
talk to everyone who might stand to inherit from your
uncle's will."

"Listen, I like John. And so does Scott. Besides, we
would never *kill* anybody—either of us. Not for *any*
amount of money."

"I imagine that's true. But I'd really appreciate it if
you'd answer a few questions for me."

"All right, go ahead."

"It would be much better if we talked in person.
Could we get together somewhere?"

"I guess so," Shawna agreed, with a noticeable lack
of enthusiasm. But at any rate, it was arranged that
I'd stop by her West Fifty-first Street apartment at
three-thirty that afternoon.

As soon as we disconnected, I phoned her brother's
home—and reached his answering machine. I didn't
figure there was anything to be gained by leaving a

message. I mean, what were the chances of his returning the call of a woman he didn't know and, more importantly, would almost certainly not care to know?

David Hearn was next.

He picked up, at least, which I regarded as a decent start. But things immediately went into a downhill skid.

Introducing myself, I explained why I needed to see him. "I'd like to meet with you as soon as possible," I said. "When do you think you might be able to make it?"

"Never," David answered lightly in this young, bordering-on-girlish voice. I swear, he sounded as if he were barely out of puberty.

I groped around for a few words of persuasion. "I won't take up much of your time," I promised.

It didn't do the trick. "Wrong. You won't take up *any* of my time," he retorted, his tone almost playful.

I tried again. "Look, somebody wants John Lander dead. And it's possible you may be able to help prevent whoever it is from getting his way."

"I don't know beans about any shooting, Ms. Steinberg—"

"Shapiro," I corrected.

"Okay, *Shapiro.*" And then accusingly: "I'm sure you said 'Steinberg' before, though. Anyway, I really have to go now. I haven't even eaten breakfast yet, and I've got a dentist's appointment at eleven-thirty."

"A dentist's appointment? On a *Saturday*?"

"I probably found the only dentist in Manhattan who sees people on Saturdays."

I had to make one last effort. "I think I should tell you that if anything happens to my client, I'd feel compelled to relay this to the police—your refusal to cooperate, I'm talking about. That might not look too good for you, you know."

A long pause followed. "There's nothing like being threatened before your morning coffee. But you win,

Ms. Whatever-Your-Name-Is. Dr. Blake is on Seventy-eighth and Second. Can we do this somewhere around there—at a coffee shop, say? I should be through by twelve-thirty."

"Better yet, why don't you come to my apartment? I live right in the neighborhood, on East Eighty-second Street."

"Yeah, all right."

I gave David the address. "I'll even fix you some lunch."

"Okay, if you insist." And he chuckled.

"Oh, I do. Well, see you later."

The receiver was already halfway to its cradle when I heard, "But no fish, huh? I *hate* fish."

Chapter 4

"Well, can you do it today?"

There was no need to ask who was on the other end of the phone line. "Can I do *what* today?"

"We talked about starting to shop for your matron of honor gown," I was reminded.

"Oh, geez. I'm really sorry. A lot's been happening, and it slipped my mind. I already have two appointments set up for this afternoon."

"Well, we'd better start looking around soon. You don't want to leave it for the last minute, do you? Suppose you have trouble finding something you like?"

I had to smile. My niece Ellen wasn't getting married until December. And while I was absolutely ecstatic that she and Mike were going to make it permanent at last—and at the Plaza, no less—I didn't feel this pressing need to drop everything and start combing the stores for a suitable dress. Not seven months in advance, anyway.

"Listen," Ellen—a buyer at Macy's—said hopefully, "I'll be off again next Wednesday." Her tone left little doubt as to how I was expected to implement this information.

"I'll try to get together then, Ellen, but I can't tell you definitely. The thing is, I've just taken on a case that's going to require a lot of time."

"What *kind* of a case?" she asked suspiciously.

Ellen makes no attempt to hide her preference for my business activities as they once were. Some years back, you see, the worst that could happen to me in the course of an investigation was that I'd be subjected to a few blistering epithets from a missing husband who wasn't particularly grateful for the effort I'd expended in finding him. Of course, there *was* that occasion when I was on the receiving end of about a dozen scratches and three ankle bites, these administered to my person by this ill-tempered cat I'd been unfortunate enough to locate for his owner. His name was Sweetie, too (the cat's; not the owner's). Imagine!

At any rate, I didn't anticipate that Ellen would be overjoyed when she learned about my latest project. But I figured I'd fill her in now and get it over with. So, steeling myself for her reaction, I related the facts, keeping them as dry and terse as I could. But I might just as well have painted my narrative with a purple brush.

"Oh, my God!" she exclaimed when I was finished. "You're saying that someone is trying to *murder* your client?"

"I'm only saying that he barely missed being shot." Ellen's tremulous falsetto convinced me that if there was ever a necessity to resurrect my all-but-rejected coincidence theory, it was then. "I wouldn't be at all surprised if this was one of those drive-bys, though. And if so, what's the likelihood of its happening again?"

"But suppose it wasn't a drive-by? Don't you see that *you* c-could be in danger, too? If the k-killer makes a second attempt, he c-could wind up hitting you b-by mistake."

It is only in moments of extreme stress that my niece stutters—I don't think I'd heard her do it in years. So I tried that much harder to minimize her fears.

"Don't be silly, Ellen. After all, it's not as if I'm

acting as the man's bodyguard. My only job is to check into the attack on him. Besides, if he *was* actually targeted—although, as I told you, that probably isn't the case—the perpetrator is almost certainly the same person who killed his cousin. For that reason, I'll be spending the majority of my time investigating the cousin's death. Most of my contact with John Lander will be relegated to the phone, the way it normally is with my clients. Honestly, it's doubtful that I'll have more than one or two additional meetings with him. And you can be sure those won't take place on some deserted street at midnight, either."

"Still, swear to me you'll be extra careful. Okay?"

"Okay."

"You didn't swear."

"I swear," I said, irritated by then and trying very hard not to let it show. I mean, Ellen is one of my favorite people in the world. And I really am grateful for her concern. Nevertheless, sweet as she is and much as I love her, there's no getting around it: Ellen Kravitz can be a terrible nudge.

We hung up after I'd assured her—twice—that I'd do my best to leave Wednesday open for shopping. Then I got back to what I'd been working on prior to Ellen's call: making myself presentable for the first of my suspects.

Jaw set determinedly, I marched into the bathroom and picked up my hairbrush again. Today was humid, with rain predicted, and as is typical during weather like this, my glorious hennaed hair had been insisting on going its own way—which is every which way. However, almost immediately after resuming my battle with all of those nasty little clumps, I raised the white flag. I really wasn't equal to the challenge right now.

Hurrying to the bedroom closet, I got out my wig, an exact replica of my own hair but with a much more accommodating nature. I gazed down at the ratty-looking thing with genuine affection. You can't imagine how comforting it is to know that it's there for a rainy day—along with all of those other days when I just plain run out of patience.

In a matter of minutes I had the wig whipped into shape. And, for a change, it wasn't long afterward that the rest of me was clothed and shod. Then I went into the living room and deposited myself on the sofa, where for the next half hour I would wait impatiently for the downstairs buzzer to signal the arrival of David Hearn.

Chapter 5

If there was ever anyone who didn't fit his voice, I was looking at him.

I mean, from what I'd heard on the telephone I had expected a skinny little seventeen-year-old with a liberal sprinkling of acne. I'd even thrown in bad teeth when I conjured up David Hearn in my head.

The real thing, however, was well into his twenties and large. Over six feet, I guessed, and at least 180 pounds. He was also dark and muscular and good-looking. *Very* good-looking. His bright blue tee shirt had nothing on his eyes, which were an even more vibrant, deeper blue. And if you could attribute those sparkling teeth to today's dental visit, well, all I can say is that I'd trade Dr. Louis H. Lutz for David's guy in a millisecond. And, oh yes, my visitor's face was totally zitless.

Standing on the threshold, he asked hesitantly, "Ms. Steinberg?" Although the girlish tone seemed less pronounced than it had on the phone, it was jarring enough so that his hunky image took an abrupt, if transient, nosedive.

"That's right. Only it's Shapiro. But call me Desiree."

"Uh, sure," he responded, eyeing me skeptically.

It was obvious that I wasn't what David had been anticipating either. Which didn't exactly throw me. Over the years I've discovered that when most people think "female private eye" they draw from the movie version. You know, a tall, busty blonde in a tight sweater and four-inch heels, her shapely legs stretching practically to infinity.

Well, in my case, this is definitely not what they get.

Let's begin with the legs. Mine don't go very far. The truth is, being barely five-two, there are plenty of times when I'm sitting down that my feet don't even make contact with the floor. Among the other differences between yours truly and those fictional lady PIs is the fact that I'm full-figured (a term I much prefer to the alternatives)—with my chest the only part of me that *isn't* well padded. Which, I suppose, is the reason I don't have a single tight sweater to my name. Something else I don't have is blond hair, Egyptian henna being responsible for this exquisite shade of red. And don't bother checking my closet for any four-inch heels. I wouldn't be able to *walk* in those things, much less chase after the bad guys in them. (Actually, you'll never find me chasing after the bad guys in *any* height heel.) But to get back to my visitor . . .

Following me into the kitchen, David addressed my back. "Look, Ms. Shapiro, I hope this won't take too long. I have a few errands to run today."

"I'll try to keep it brief. And I thought you were going to call me Desiree."

"Okay, and you can call me Mr. Hearn." Then he laughed. "Just kidding. It's David."

The kitchen table was set with my favorite place mats—black-and-white checks to match the black-and-white-checked floor tiles. The napkins were white with black piping. And tying it all together was the pièce de résistance: my new black china. Of which—notwithstanding the insistence of my neighbor Barbara about there being something very unsanitary about black china—I am inordinately proud.

David took a seat while I attended to some last-minute preparations. Fortunately, when I'd extended that lunch invitation there was an Italian bread in the freezer, some Genoa salami, tomato, and Swiss cheese in the refrigerator, and a jar of roasted red peppers on the shelf. I'd prepared the open sandwiches close to two hours ago, so all I had to do now was toast them for a few minutes. In the meantime, I got out the potato salad, cole slaw, and Coke I'd run down to the deli for earlier. Pretty soon I joined David at the table.

"This is really delicious," he said after a large bite of the sandwich. He sounded as if he hadn't expected it to be.

"I'm glad you're enjoying it."

"What did you want to ask me about?"

Now, I couldn't see ruining a tasty little repast with business. Which I think is particularly understandable when you consider the kind of business I'm in. "Why don't we hold off until we're through eating?"

"Good idea. I'm not in *that* much of a hurry," he agreed, grinning.

We engaged in some small talk after this. I learned that David was a graduate of Yale University and Harvard Law School, that he had recently passed the bar after his second attempt, and that he was presently working for the Manhattan DA's Office.

Then it was David's turn to ask questions. And the first thing he wanted to know was how long I'd been a PI. This being some indication of my age, I chopped off a year or two—okay, five—from my answer. A short while later he wondered aloud about how a husband might react to his wife's choosing an occupation like mine for a career. I couldn't speak for anyone else, I told him, but in my case it had been no problem at all. My late husband Ed had been a private investigator, too.

We continued chatting through dessert—a Sara Lee cheesecake that had briefly resided in my freezer directly under the Italian bread. David turned down my infamous coffee, however, with a polite request for tea, making him either a very lucky young man or positively prescient. I'm not sure which.

"I understand that you were actually related to Bella, Uncle Victor's wife," I began after we had relocated to the living room. We were seated facing each other, me on the sofa, David in one of my two matching club chairs.

"That's right. She was a sweet woman, too—I was very fond of her. And by the way, Aunt Bella wasn't my aunt; she was my mother's aunt. Which made her my great-aunt."

"Hmm. That's a little different, isn't it?" I remarked.

"What do you mean—different?"

"Weren't the others mentioned in the will just plain nephews and a niece?"

"That's right. And you're curious as to why my mother isn't the one in line to inherit, is that it?"

"I suppose so."

"Both Aunt Bella and Uncle Victor had some problems concerning my father. Mostly because of his . . . uh . . . his financial misadventures."

"Are you saying he was an *embezzler*?" It just slipped out.

David took the mindless response good-naturedly. "Not quite," he told me with this little laugh that, to my ears, sounded uncomfortably close to a giggle. "See? Let that be a lesson to you, Desiree. When someone tries to equivocate like that, things usually end up appearing to be worse than they really are."

"Would you care to clarify that?"

"Okay. I'll level with you. I think Uncle Victor was worried that if my mother should by some small chance wind up his heir, my dad would just gamble the money away."

"Uh, your father's a gambler, then?" I asked—speaking cautiously this time.

"*Was*. He hasn't placed a bet in over five years. But I don't think my parents have ever been able to convince Great-uncle Victor of that."

"Incidentally, what sort of man *is* Great-uncle Victor?"

"He's a helluva guy. He was an absolutely brilliant businessman—a self-made multimillionaire. But I admire him even more for the kind of human being he is. Actually," David said thoughtfully, "Victor Lander is one of the most decent, caring people you'd ever want to meet. And very family-oriented. You can go to him with almost any kind of problem; he's never too busy to help you deal with it. And whenever there've been disagreements among the relatives, Uncle Victor has somehow managed to get them to consider one another's point of view. He seems to have a genuine knack for that type of thing.

"He's also generous. The man paid for my college and law school. And from what I gather, over the years he's done a good deal for other family members, too. I do know that he used to bail my father out of trouble—money trouble—on a pretty frequent basis. Which, since my father hasn't put the bite on him for so long, should probably have made it apparent that Dad's reformed. But I guess his past performance gave Uncle Victor reason to be skeptical of that.

"And speaking of my great-uncle's generosity, it would have been nice if he'd chosen to distribute the wealth a little more evenly." David managed a faint chuckle before adding soberly, "I can understand why Edward was his principal beneficiary. But what I can't figure out is why the bulk of Uncle Victor's assets will be going to your client now, with the rest of us only getting a few crumbs. Even worse—from my point of view, at any rate—if something happens to *him*, those snotty Riley twins hit pay dirt. Then *finally,* on the bottom rung of the ladder, there's you-know-who."

"Well, probably the reason for John's being so high on the list is that he was such a comfort to your uncle when Aunt Bella died."

"Really? I didn't know anything about that. But if that's the reason, okay. I can see it with John. *The twins,* though?"

"I'm afraid I can't help you there."

Neither of us said anything for a brief time after this. David was the one to puncture the silence. "Listen, I know all this whining about the will makes me sound pretty mercenary. But I can't help the way I feel."

"I can appreciate your disappointment. Look at it from your uncle's point of view, though. I mean, you didn't keep in very close contact with him, did you?"

"Who told you that—Trudie?" He held up his hand. "Never mind. I won't deny that I didn't see him as often as I should have. But I *was* away at school for years. And I did call him every couple of months. I could have done better, though; I admit that. I'm honestly sorry that I was so neglectful. And not just because of the money, either. Because of Uncle Victor himself.

"Even these days he's like a role model to me. In spite of his illness, he makes an effort to live his life. When I was there last time—that was when he laid that will on us—he challenged me to a game of chess. We didn't play for long—lately Uncle Victor tires pretty quickly—but what got to me was his determination not to just lie there and vegetate. He may be dying—there's no hope of his licking that cancer—but he isn't dead yet. And it's apparent that he's going to keep things as normal as he can for as long as he can."

"He sounds like quite a man."

"He is." Suddenly a worrisome thought clouded

David Hearn's handsome face. "You're not planning to question Uncle Victor, are you? Because he has no idea that Edward's been killed."

"Relax, David. The last thing I'd want to do is interrogate anyone who's that ill about the murder of a person he loves. Particularly when I don't consider it absolutely necessary—as in this instance."

"Good," an obviously relieved David responded. "I can't see how he could possibly be of help to you anyway."

"Agreed. But I'd like to talk to you about someone else now: my client. With this attack on his life, it's crucial that I find out as much as I can about your cousin John. For starters, would you mind telling me what you think of him?"

David peered at me with mock severity. "Hey! Is it conceivable that you haven't been hanging on my every word? Once again, John and I aren't cousins; we're not even related."

"That's right. I keep forgetting."

"But to answer you, I haven't actually had that much contact with John, so I can't say very much about his character. He seems nice enough, though— he's always been very pleasant to me." I was about to pose another question when David put in, "But ask me what I think of his wife, and you'll get a different story entirely."

I grinned. "All right. I'm asking."

"I could never figure out what would make a man marry someone that pushy, that overbearing. She sticks her nose into *everything*. She must be years older than John is, too." And in a show of commiseration with his noncousin, he screwed up his mouth and slowly shook his head.

"Oh, come now, David, Trudie isn't *that* bad," I protested. It was reflexive. You know, like Pavlov's dog. I mean, when a woman—especially one who is no longer of tender years—is verbally attacked, I seem to feel this compulsion to act as her champion. Never mind how obnoxious I myself consider the lady to be.

"She's a bitch," David insisted, smiling.

"Have it your way. But about John . . . do you have any idea—any idea at all—who might want him dead?"

"Only those of us on the inheritance line," he joked. At least, I took it that he was joking. "But seriously, I don't know enough about your client to have a clue about something like that."

I moved on. "There's some information I need for my records, David. First, where were you last Monday at around 11:30 P.M.?"

"You said that was when someone took a shot at him," David stated as if for verification.

"Yes."

"I was where I normally am at that hour: home in bed, watching Letterman. Alone. My girlfriend walked out on me a few months ago."

"Oh, I'm sorry."

"Don't be. I got away lucky. Suzanne's a Trudie Lander in training."

"I have to ask you something else."

"Whether I've got an alibi for a couple of weeks before that—when Edward was killed, right?" He didn't wait for my answer. "As I informed the two members of New York's Finest who came to visit me, at eight o'clock I was having dinner—all by myself—at a coffee shop near my apartment. I go to Ginger's fairly often, but I can't see why anyone should remember my being there that particular evening."

"How did you pay for your meal?"

"In cash—they don't take credit cards. Incidentally, Ginger's is on Seventh Street between Second and Third Avenues, if you'd like to check it out anyway."

I wouldn't. There really wasn't any point in it. If there had been the slightest chance someone at the restaurant could help him establish his whereabouts, David would probably be prodding me with a hot poker right now to get me over to the place. He did surprise me, however, by pulling his wallet from his pants pocket and extracting a two-by-three photograph.

"Just in case you need it for sleuthing purposes," he explained, handing it to me. I glanced at the picture, a headshot of him with a pretty dark-haired girl.

"Suzanne?" I asked.

"That's her. And by the way, don't bother returning the thing. The only reason that photo continues to exist is because I keep forgetting to tear it up."

A couple of seconds passed, then David said earnestly, "Look, Desiree, in order to inherit Uncle Victor's money, it would have been necessary for me to get rid of Edward, after which I'd still have to dispose of the others—John and both of the twins. This would make me a mass murderer, for Christ's sake! Do I strike you as being capable of something like that?"

Now, in spite of how snippy he'd been on the telephone, I was finding this man to be surprisingly ingratiating face-to-face. So much so that after a while I'd even stopped noticing that very incongruous voice of his. "No, I can't say that you do," I responded. "But I've been wrong before."

I flinched at the truth of these words. In the course of my investigations, I seem to keep leaping from one faulty perception to another. The fact is, I've pretty much come to the realization that when woman's intuition was handed out, some other girl baby got her chubby little mitts on my share, too.

So my taking a liking to David Hearn wasn't nearly as big a plus for him as one might think.

Chapter 6

David left at just after two, long before my three-thirty appointment with Shawna Riley. But if I have one major talent in this life, it's finding ways to piddle away the time.

Now, this frequently leads to my being less than punctual when it comes to social engagements—which, for your information, have hardly been making a lot of appearances on my calendar lately. Somehow, though, I almost invariably manage to be scrupulously prompt for work-related meetings.

This, however, would not be holding true today.

Of course, I did have to wash up the lunch dishes, and that must have taken at least five or six minutes. And then because I still had close to an hour on my hands—even deducting a more-than-ample thirty minutes for the taxi ride to Shawna's—I revisited the *New York Times* crossword I'd come close to finishing in the morning. But after about five minutes of further brain-taxing, I couldn't fill in a single additional letter. Irritated, I stuffed the puzzle in the garbage can, placating myself with the assurance that, for all intents and purposes (and don't ask me what I meant by this), I'd completed it anyway. It was still too early to get ready to go out, though, so I curled up on the sofa and turned on the TV, catching the last part of an ancient Joan Crawford movie. Well, being that I have a *thing* for ancient Joan Crawford movies, I got so engrossed in the story that I swear my hand froze in midair both times that I went to switch it off. Fortunately, it was over at three; otherwise, I might still be sitting there.

At any rate, now I had to rush like crazy to make myself even semipresentable, and rushing is definitely not in my nature. By three-fifteen, however, I'd made it all the way to the door. But then, when I had one foot in the hall, the telephone rang.

Forget it, I told myself, *you're late enough. Whoever it is will leave a message.*

But, as I'm sure you can appreciate, for a seriously nosy person this is a pretty impossible dictate to comply with. And I whirled around and hurried back to the phone.

It was John Lander.

"I'm so glad I caught you, Desiree. You're a very hard woman to reach, do you know that? Listen, I hope you don't mind my contacting you at home."

"No, of course not; that's why I gave you the number. Is anything wrong?"

John didn't answer the question directly. "I couldn't say anything in front of my wife—she has a tendency to overreact—" he told me, "but there's a matter you ought to be aware of, and you and I should get together again as soon as possible to discuss it. Would it be at all convenient for you to meet me for coffee or a drink or something in about an hour?"

"I was just on my way to Shawna Riley's. She's expecting me."

"I realize this is very short notice," John apologized. "I did try you at your office at around five yesterday—that was the earliest I was able to break away from Trudie for a few minutes—but you'd already left for the day. Then I called again last night. I even gave it a shot this morning."

"This morning?" But almost instantly I remembered that quick trip to the deli. Or he might have attempted to get me when I was showering. "Oh, that's right. I *was* out for a short while. But why didn't you ever leave word so I could get back to you?"

"Because that's what I was afraid of: your getting back to me. I was calling from home all those times— I'm at work now—and I was concerned about Trudie's picking up if she heard the telephone ring. But listen, when are you supposed to be at Shawna's?"

Automatically, I glanced at my watch. Following which I gulped. "At three-thirty."

"I'm really sorry. I've made you late, haven't I?"

"Actually, it wasn't you; *I* made me late. But in a way that's a good thing. If I'd left here when I should have, you would have missed me again."

"Can we have our talk after your appointment?"

"Absolutely. I should be free by five, the latest."

"I'll wait for you in front of Shawna's building."

Now, there's nothing like trying to pump information out of someone you've antagonized. So rather than just march into the twin's apartment at four o'clock or so, I figured it might be advisable to fore-warn her that I'd been detained.

"Ms. Riley?" I said when she answered the phone. "It's Desiree Shapiro. I've been held up, and I hope—"

"Held up!" The next few sentences ran together. "Oh, my goodness. Are you all right? Were you hurt?"

You'll never know how tempted I was to go along with this, but I like to think of myself as a basically truthful person—except, that is, in those rare instances when I'm absolutely *forced* to lie.

"No, no, I didn't mean it like that," I admitted. "It's just that something came up . . . uh, something of a personal nature."

"A personal nature?" Shawna echoed, perhaps not even conscious that she was doing it.

"It's . . . it's my aunt. I was at her place when she was suddenly taken ill, and I had to rush her to emergency." (Look, some sort of explanation seemed to be expected. And I couldn't see where Joan Crawford would win me any points with the girl. So, practically speaking, I *was* being forced to lie.)

"Is it anything serious?—with your aunt, I mean."

"Oh, no. She'll be fine, and thanks for asking. She just had . . . indigestion." It was the best I could conjure up on such short notice. And then, aware that the tale cried out for embellishment, I added tremulously, "But it was very scary. I thought initially that it might be a heart attack. I pleaded with my aunt to let me call 9-1-1, but Aunt Grace wouldn't even hear of it." (And, no, I don't really have an aunt Grace.)

"Well, all's well that ends well, they say."

"Yes. Anyway, I hope I haven't inconvenienced you too much. I can be over in about twenty minutes, traffic permitting."

"No problem," Shawna said solicitously. "And please. Don't hurry. You've been through enough today."

Chapter 7

Thank goodness for Mohammed—the cab driver, not the prophet.

I know Shawna had instructed me to take my time, but I could see where her patience with my travails might wear thin if I were to get tied up in traffic now. And this afternoon the streets appeared to be even more jam-packed than usual. Or maybe it was just my anxiety that was making this assessment.

At any rate, Mohammed proved to be some sort of wizard of the wheel. I mean, he wove in and out between those cars like he was threading a needle. Not only that, he managed to beat out one red light after another (although in a few instances this was a questionable call). And if for a good part of the ride my eyes were scrunched shut, my heart was around my ankles, and there was a slight problem with my breathing, well, it was worth it to pull up in front of Shawna Riley's apartment house in a mere fifteen minutes.

I figured the girl framed in the doorway to be about eighteen—I later found out she was a couple of months shy of her twenty-sixth birthday. Small and fragile-looking, with fair skin, enormous blue eyes, and thick, dark lashes, she immediately brought to mind a porcelain doll.

She eyed me somewhat incredulously. *Here we go again!* I warned myself, bristling.

"Ms. Shapiro?"

"Yes, but I hope you'll call me Desiree."

She nodded. "I will." And now two parallel lines materialized between her eyes, and her kewpie-doll lips puckered for an instant. "I have to tell you that you're not at all what I expected."

No, you don't—have to tell me, that is. You've made it very apparent. I said this in a decidedly icy tone—only not aloud.

"I suppose I go to too many movies," Shawna confessed with a self-conscious little titter. "But I thought I'd be seeing Kathleen Turner on my doorstep. Not really *her,* of course"—another titter—"but a reasonable facsimile, anyway." Then suddenly aware that she'd kept me standing outside in the hall for this not overly complimentary appraisal, she flung the door open wide. "Oh, please come in. Sometimes my manners aren't what they should be."

She led me into a good-sized living room strikingly decorated in deep wine, green, and pink, with white accents. The elegant Queen Anne-style furnishings looked well made and costly—particularly the lacquered credenza between the windows and the graceful mahogany desk in the corner. But whether any of the pieces were the real thing or just expensive reproductions, I hadn't a clue.

I sank into the plush green sofa, with Shawna opting for the green-and-pale-pink-striped chair at right angles to it.

I'd intended to begin with my always-welcome—although almost never truthful—promise to be brief. But Shawna preempted my opening spiel. "You want to know what I can tell you concerning that shooting incident with John, right?"

"Right. Can you think of *anyone* who might have wanted to harm him? A person with a grudge of some sort, for example. Or possibly someone he had an argument with—no matter how trivial."

She shook her head. "Scott—that's my brother—
and I have very little contact with John. We're only
in his company four or five times a year at most, when
all of us get together at my uncle Victor's."

"Well, it was worth a try," I told her with a rueful
little smile. "About your uncle, though . . . I imagine
you must have been pretty surprised at the terms of
his will."

"Yes and no. It made sense that Edward would be
his principal heir. Uncle Victor raised him, you know.
At first, though, I did find it weird that he would set
up an order of succession like that, particularly since
it was so unlikely he'd outlive any of us. But look
what's happened in just the last couple of weeks."

"You don't appear to be very disturbed by the fact
that in all probability you won't be sharing in the estate. Or anyhow, not to any great extent."

"I'm not," Shawna maintained, the soft voice taking
on a new firmness. "Listen, my dad died a few years
ago, and he was an extremely successful attorney who
was still more successful in the stock market. He left
almost everything to my mother, and Scott and I are
Mother's sole heirs."

I didn't know quite what to say to a girl who was
talking about inheriting from an apparently still-
breathing parent. So I dragged out the always depend-
able, "I see."

"Unfortunately," she went on, "I don't believe we'll
have that long to wait, either. My mother is in very
poor health—emphysema, along with a bad heart. Not
that I can even *think* about losing Mother." *No, not
much,* I interjected silently. "In fact, I've just upset
myself terribly by even bringing it up." And she wiped
an imaginary tear from her left eye.

Well, I learned a long time ago that having plenty
of money doesn't stop too many people from wanting
to get their hands on even more money. But I pre-

vailed upon myself to refrain from making any comment to this effect.

I suppose I should also tell you that in view of how sympathetic she was with regard to my aunt Grace's unfortunate digestive problem, I'd been rather favorably disposed toward Shawna Riley from the outset. But with her practically dancing on her mother's grave just now—and with poor Mom not even in it yet—my opinion of her had altered considerably.

I chose my next words carefully. "It appears evident that you have no motive for disposing of John, Ms. Riley. But just for my records, I'd appreciate your filling me in on where you were at eleven-thirty the night he was shot at. That was this past Monday."

The girl's gorgeous blue eyes were fixed unblinkingly on my face, and for a moment I visualized David Hearn's also-gorgeous blue eyes. I wondered idly how many other members of the family had been similarly blessed. But then I reminded myself that Shawna and David weren't even related.

"As you yourself just said," she retorted, "I have no reason to want John out of the way. So what I was doing that evening is immaterial, isn't it?"

"Are you saying that you prefer not to divulge your whereabouts?"

"You misunderstood me. I have no problem telling you where I was. I just resent being regarded as a murder suspect, that's all."

"I never meant to imply that you were, honestly. I thought I'd made that clear."

She kept me waiting for a few seconds before responding, and I'm certain this was intended to cause me to squirm a little. "All right. I was here—sleeping. Weekdays I'm in bed by eleven, if not before, since I have to start getting ready for work at six."

It was painful for me to even contemplate beginning my day then. Listen, I was still throwing bouquets at myself for waking up at eight that morning. (Keep in mind that it *was* a Saturday.) *But six o'clock? And on a regular basis?* If I were in that situation (God forbid!), it wouldn't take long before the only way you could induce me to leave my bed at that hour would be to set it on fire. "I hope it's a good job," I remarked.

"I hope so, too, but it'll take a while to find out. My best friend owns an employment agency upstate, and I recently became a partner."

"Well, much good luck." I pulled myself up a little straighter now in a vain attempt to strengthen my backbone. "Umm, I also have to talk to you about something else," I forced myself to say. "Where were you . . . uh . . . the night your cousin Edward was killed? That was at eight o'clock on—"

"I know when it was, and I already spoke to the police about that," Shawna snapped. "I was at Scott's from six-thirty until almost ten. He made dinner for me that evening. A belated celebration of my new business venture."

"Is he a good cook—your brother?" I asked conversationally, trying to put her in a more amiable mood. Which, I was aware, was a definite must if there was any chance of her tolerating my presence for even a few minutes longer.

"Wonderful—the best." She said it adamantly.

"I think that men, as a rule, are better cooks than women, don't you agree? I myself love to mess around in the kitchen, but I can't say the results leave my friends begging for seconds that often." (This was a big, fat lie. To be honest, I prepare a mean meal.)

"I'm sure you're more at home over a hot stove than I am. I've been trying for years to learn how to scramble an egg," Shawna informed me, chuckling at her little joke.

"What did your brother serve for this celebratory dinner, anyway?" I inquired lightly.

"Let me think." But it took only a couple of seconds for her to recall the fare. "I remember. The appetizer was stuffed clams oreganato. Following this, we had cream of wild mushroom soup. And after that, a humongous salad. Next came the most wonderful veal dish—I'm not sure just what it's called. Oh, yes, Scott served noodles with the veal. And then for dessert we had one of his specialties—crème brûlée. My brother does an absolutely sensational crème brûlée. And—"

Laughing, I held up my hand. "Stop! You're making me salivate."

Shawna smiled at this, which led me to assume that it might not be a bad time to slip in another question or two. "Did anyone happen to call you at your brother's that night?"

"The phone didn't even ring," she responded irritably.

"I'm sorry, but I had to ask. Uh, I'm curious about something else, too."

"What's that?"

"Do you know why you and Scott—and not David Hearn—are in line to inherit after John?"

"I suppose it's because we've kept in more frequent contact with my uncle over the years—David practically *divorced* him once he went off to college. And who do you think sprang for that ingrate's education in the first place? It was Uncle Victor, of course." She paused for a moment before adding thoughtfully, "Actually, if he put a member of that family in his will, I'd have expected it to be David's mother Charlotte, who's his niece. The truth is, though, the woman's an *enabler*. Her husband's an inveterate gambler, and she just stands by while he proceeds to get rid of every penny he makes. Not that he makes that much. He sells computers, and from what I understand, he's not too great a salesman. Anyway, I don't think my uncle wanted to give Clark—David's father—access to anything more he could piss away. I presume that's why David's in the will instead of Charlotte, although why Uncle Victor felt it necessary to include any one of those three escapes me."

All of which, Shawna's little barbs aside, pretty well confirmed what David himself had told me.

I figured it would be best to leave after this, before the conversation had the opportunity to turn sour again. We were already at the door when Shawna said in her sweetest, most gentle tone, "Don't worry—about your client, I mean. Scott and I both feel certain that the shooter was some juvenile hood out for a little target practice."

"I hope you're right."

She put her hand reassuringly on my arm. "I'd be willing to bet that it never happens again."

Chapter 8

Going down in the elevator, I pondered Shawna's parting words.

Was this positive spin prompted by a reversion to her earlier, more sympathetic self? Or was she hoping to persuade me to shift the focus of my investigation away from her—and possibly her twin, as well?

I was still reflecting on her motive when the car came to a stop on the tenth floor, and a middle-aged man entered. He was singularly unattractive. Short and squat (I know, but we're not talking about *me* now; we're talking about *him*), he had a wide, flat nose, watery brown eyes, and a forehead that reached all the way back to midway down his scalp, where it ended in a semicircular two-inch fringe of grayish brown fuzz.

"Turned out to be a nice day, after all," my fellow passenger commented, choosing to stand almost shoulder to shoulder with me in the large, otherwise empty elevator. Still, he seemed harmless enough, so I favored him with a faint smile in response. "I hope you don't think I'm being forward, but you're a very beautiful girl."

Well, what do you say to that, Kathleen Turner? My new beige cotton dress with the coordinating tweed jacket must work a lot harder for me than I gave it credit for. Anyway, I was stunned—but flattered. I don't know which pleased me more, the "beautiful" or the "girl." If either of those descriptives had ever been used in relation to me before, it was when I was too young to appreciate it. "Thank you," I murmured.

"You've got sensational hair, you know, and I happen to love natural redheads." *Okay, so the guy wasn't exactly a connoisseur.* I didn't even have time to get out another "thank you" before he confided that he was a lonely bachelor.

Mercifully, just then the elevator stopped at the ground floor, and I hurried out into the lobby, my admirer trotting along beside me. "If you're free for dinner this evening, I'd be pleased if you would join me at Aureole. It's a very fine restaurant," he cajoled.

"Yes, it is, but I already have plans." I pushed open the outer door and saw John Lander pacing up and down in front of the building. "Oh, there's my fiancé now."

"You might have mentioned a fiancé earlier. You definitely led me to believe you were available." And with this, my ex-admirer strode away in a huff.

"A friend of yours?" John asked when I joined him. Although he produced a grin when he inclined his head in the direction of the retreating Romeo, I instantly recognized that this was not the same composed, almost detached man I'd met just the day before. Unless, that is, my imagination was on the loose again. Which does occasionally occur.

"I don't know if you'd call him a friend. We shared the elevator."

"Where would you like to go so we can talk? Are you hungry?"

"Not really. But I wouldn't mind a soda."

"We could stop off someplace in this area," John proposed, "or we could drive over to your home turf—my car's parked only a few blocks away."

"As long as you managed to find a space, let's do it around here."

Neither of us was that familiar with the neighborhood, so we began to walk, and for once, I actually enjoyed traveling via my two feet. The rain that had been forecast earlier must have carried out its threat sometime during my visit with Shawna, because the pavement was wet. But the late-afternoon sun was out now, and the air smelled fresh and clean and springlike.

It must have been about five minutes later that we came upon a small coffee shop on Fifty-third and Sixth. John and I both peered through the window.

"What do you think?" he asked.

"Perfect," I told him.

The inside of the place was cheerful and immaculate, with yellow-and-white-checked cotton tablecloths covered in clear plastic and real cloth napkins. Once we were seated, John prevailed upon me to have some food with my Coke. Which didn't take all that much prevailing, particularly in view of the pleasant surroundings. We both decided on a cheeseburger and french fries.

Now, as I may have mentioned, I prefer waiting until after my meal before going into any big discussions. But this time I didn't really have that option. John evidently had something pressing on his mind. Moreover, I was very anxious to hear it.

As soon as we gave the waitress our order, he began. And there was a somberness in his voice. "When I tried reaching you intially, there was one thing I wanted to discuss with you. In the meantime, though, something else has happened. And now there are two matters we ought to go over."

Uh-oh.

"Hey, don't look so worried. I'm sure things'll work out." He leaned over and patted my hand. "But anyhow, to start with, I'm convinced Trudie's right about the police suspecting me of murdering Edward. Only maybe it's not merely because I have the most obvious motive."

"What don't I know?"

The explanation was delivered with unmistakable reluctance. "I have this lapel pin—or at least I did have. My Air Force wings. I was wearing it on that day the family gathered at Uncle Victor's. But weeks later, when I went to put on that same jacket at home, the pin was gone. I was sure I hadn't removed it so I called my uncle the next morning, and he said he'd have the household staff look around for it. It never turned up, though. I was upset, of course, but just because of the sentiment involved. In the light of what's transpired since then, however, I've arrived at this peculiar—or maybe I should say *sinister*—theory." And now he added sheepishly, "When you hear it, you'll probably decide that I should be committed."

John was looking at me for reassurance, and although I was totally in the dark as to what was involved here, how could I not encourage him? "I seriously doubt that."

"It didn't occur to me right away—not until this past week. And believe me, it's hard for me to accept that this might be the case. The truth is, it's really the kind of notion I'd have expected Trudie to come up with. Since she hasn't, it's most likely because the idea doesn't have any validity."

"Uh, maybe you should just lay things out for me."

He flushed. "I *have* been a little obscure, haven't I? All right. Suppose that I did lose the pin at Uncle Victor's and one of the others picked it up. Or, it's even possible someone took it off my jacket. You see, we wound up spending a good part of that afternoon out of doors. So early on I hung the jacket in the closet, where anyone could have gotten at it. I—"

Our burgers arrived at this juncture, and John

waited until the waitress walked away before resuming.

"I want you to understand that none of this so much as entered my mind until after someone took a shot at me. The NYPD's reaction to that, though—well, this is when it became clear that I was the star suspect in my cousin's murder. And then on Wednesday, I think it was, I got this gut feeling that perhaps it wasn't just my having so much to gain by Edward's death that had earned me such an exalted position. Anyhow, I imagine you can figure out where I'm going with this, can't you?"

"More or less," I lied. "But why don't you tell me about it from your point of view?"

"I believe that someone may have planted my wings at the scene to implicate me in Edward's murder." His forehead pleated up. "*But who? I keep asking myself: Scott? Shawna? David?* These are all decent people we're talking about. The problem, however, is that no matter how much I want to and how hard I try, I can't seem to shake the notion that I've been set up. Which is probably the main reason I called you in on this originally." And here John's eyes locked into mine. "Do you think I'm being paranoid about that pin, Desiree?"

"No, I definitely do not." What I was, in fact, thinking was *How can you be so slow-witted?* Only I wasn't referring to my client. After all, the minute I heard about the missing wings an alarm should have gone off in my head. Particularly since I was aware of the police's reluctance to accept that John Lander had been only inches away from becoming the late John Lander.

"The night you were shot at," I said, "I gather there weren't any witnesses."

"None." *How much simpler it was to put a question to John today—when he could actually be the one to answer it.* "I didn't spot another soul on the street," he expanded. "There was certainly no one close enough to notice what transpired. We have a doorman in our building, but just before you get to the walkway that leads to the entrance, there are these high hedges. And the thing is, I hadn't yet reached the walkway, so even if the doorman was standing with his nose pressed right up against the glass door, he wouldn't have been able to see anything."

"Your cousin's killer had evidently launched phase two," I mused.

"Phase two?"

"Look, in spite of his or her efforts, the police haven't been that quick to arrest you, although if the pin *was* found at Edward's, you've no doubt been identified as the owner by now. Incidentally, they haven't questioned *you* about it—have they?" John shook his head. "Anyhow, the fact that you haven't been taken into custody apparently made our murderer impatient enough to try to dispose of you in another way. What I mean is, whoever we're dealing with was worried that you might not go down for Edward's murder—thereby, of course, losing out on the inheritance. So he elected to ensure that you forfeited it by not being around to collect."

"Uh, speaking of my not being around, that was the other matter I thought I should mention to you. But please, not a word to Trudie, okay? Not about anything we've discussed today."

"You don't have to be concerned about that," I answered, my mouth going dry in anticipation of what might follow.

"That attempt on my life wasn't a onetime thing, Desiree. I had another close call when I went out to lunch this afternoon—around twelve-thirty, it must have been. I was crossing the street in front of my office when out of the corner of my eye I saw this speeding car. It seemed to come from nowhere—and it was heading straight at me."

"Oh, my God," I murmured.

"If I hadn't reacted in just a split second and jumped out of the way, I'd have been roadkill by now."

I was shaken. So much so that I even laid down my burger—and it was really tasty, too. It took me a few moments to compose myself. "Listen, John," I finally managed, "I may not be the person you should have working for you on this. What I'm getting at is that it might be advisable for you to bring in an investigator who is able to provide you with protection. I can give you a few names. The truth is, I probably should have recommended this to you yesterday."

"It wouldn't have done you any good. I wouldn't even have considered it. I need someone capable of unraveling this mess, and that's you, Desiree."

"I'm gratified by your confidence. But how can we be positive, either of us, that I'll succeed? And if I do—when? And in the meantime, something terrible could happen."

"I will not get myself a bodyguard—period. I can't live like that. So let's change the subject."

What a foolish, stubborn man! Well, it was obvious that I wasn't going to budge him, so with a great deal of reluctance, I backed off. "I don't suppose you saw who was driving the car? Or that you got the license plate number?" I inquired, after which I picked up the cheeseburger again and allowed myself a couple of quick bites.

John shook his head. "It was all so fast."

"What about the make of the car? The color?"

"I couldn't tell you the make—I don't have much of an interest in automobiles. To me, they're just a means of getting you where you want to go. All I know is that it was large, perhaps a Chrysler. I'm not even certain of the color, but I believe it was black. Listen, I should probably have more sense than to admit this, but once that car was safely past me, I didn't so much as glance in its direction. I just stood there for a while, quivering." John smiled weakly. "I must sound like an awful wimp to you."

"You absolutely do not. I probably would have fainted." I said it jokingly, and John chuckled. But I'm sure you're familiar with that old adage about many a true word's being said in jest. The fact is, I *have* been known to pass out after surviving a frightening experience. There was one time, however, when my yellow streak actually turned out to be a plus. In that instance, who was on hand to minister to me as I lay there, out cold, in the lobby of this apartment building, but an attractive young doctor. And once I verified that he was unattached—practically the first thing I did when I opened my eyes was to check his ring finger—it was only a question of time before I bullied Dr. Mike Lynton and my niece Ellen Kravitz, both of them kicking and screaming, into agreeing to one of those dreaded blind dates. So, really, it's thanks to my cowardice that I'll be attending a wedding at the Plaza in December.

But, anyhow, you can see that I have personal knowledge of wimpishness.

"I hope there was a witness this time," I told John.

"Apparently not. A couple of people were on the street then, and once I was able to pull myself together I questioned whoever was still around, but it appears that nobody saw a thing. As I told you, it all happened in a flash."

"Who do you know that has a large, dark car?"

"No one I can think of. Shawna doesn't drive, Scott has a red Jaguar, and David's car is beige and small-ish—I have no idea of the make."

"Whoever tried to run you over today could have gotten ahold of that vehicle just for the occasion," I offered. "And this includes Shawna. Maybe she can drive after all."

"I suppose. Still, I must admit that I can't imagine any of those three behind that wheel."

"But unless you're able to come up with an alternative," I countered reasonably, "I have to conclude that your would-be assassin was either David Hearn or one of the twins. So *can* you? Think of anyone else with reason to harm you, I mean."

"I've been wracking my brain about that for days. And the answer is no, I can't. As I told you on Friday, I don't usually elicit that strong a response in people—positive *or* negative." He smiled fleetingly. "Still, I can't be certain I don't have an enemy I'm not aware of."

"I'll keep that in mind," I assured him as I pushed away my plate—empty now except for a few globs of leftover catsup. "For the time being, though, I intend concentrating on Uncle Victor's potential heirs."

John nodded his acceptance—grudgingly, it seemed to me. "Oh, would you care for something else, Desiree?" he inquired then, noticing my naked plate.

"I'd love some coffee."

He signaled the waitress, who soon reappeared with two steaming mugs.

For the most part, we drank in silence, our conversation limited to a few totally insignificant exchanges.

A short while later John insisted on driving me home, although he lived practically on the opposite end of Manhattan.

"You will take care of yourself, won't you?" I asked as I was about to get out of the car.

"Of course."

In all conscience, I had to give it one more try. "I wish you'd change your mind about switching to another PI agency. At least for the present, you could use someone who'd guard you on an almost round-the-clock basis."

"Not according to the police," John retorted, his voice thick with sarcasm. "Just talk to Fielding—he's one of the detectives involved in the investigation. He'll tell you that I—"

"Wait a minute. Did you say *Fielding*?"

"Yes, I did. Do you know him?"

"Is that *Sergeant* Fielding? Sergeant *Tim* Fielding?"

"That's right."

"Then the answer's yes, I know him."

"Well, is this good—his being on the case?" John asked anxiously.

"Let's just say that it isn't bad."

But inside, I was smiling broadly.

Chapter 9

I was just getting out of my clothes when the phone rang.

With one foot still in my panty hose, I couldn't make it to the bedroom extension in time to prevent the recorded message on the answering machine from kicking in.

I picked up the receiver, forced to listen to the entire spiel. "Hello, this is Desiree . . ." it began. I cringed. The voice sounded depressingly like Minnie Mouse—no doubt as the result of some glitch in the instrument, I always tell myself. But faulty equipment or not, when confronted with something like that, it's not easy to maintain your self-image as a Lauren Bacall sound-alike.

"Guess what dapper gentleman is in from Florida, Dez?" my across-the-hall-neighbor Harriet Gould chirped when we were finally able to converse. "He wasn't due here until next month, but well, he decided to surprise us. Isn't that nice?" With Harriet a serious candidate for the world's lousiest actress, her cheery manner couldn't have fooled a two-year-old. However, her eighty-plus father-in-law Pop (AKA Gus, AKA "the ball-buster")—who was obviously within hearing range—is not what you'd call the discerning type.

"Crap," I muttered, my hands suddenly damp.

"I knew you'd be pleased," said the bogus Mary Sunshine.

"Oh, no, you don't, Harriet. I have no intention of being in the company of that impossible man—ever again."

"Pop's fine, thank you. Oh, he looks wonderful. Listen, we're going out for Chinese food tonight, and we'd love it if you could join us. Pop's s-o-o anxious to see you. I told him when you had to miss his last couple of visits how sorry you were about it. But still, he's gotten it into his head that you might be avoiding him. Naturally, I let him know he was just being silly."

"You can talk all you want to," I informed her sweetly. "It won't do you a bit of good."

"Well, of course. I assured him that you were legitimately tied up and that you'd *never* have hurt his feelings intentionally."

"Hurt *what* feelings!" I screeched. I mean, on a sensitivity scale of one to ten, Pop Gould rated a minus five.

"About tonight, though, Pop—"

I cut her off. "Just say that I'm sorry but that I have a prior commitment. Anyhow, I've already eaten. And by the way, what about Steve?" I inquired, my tone one of mock concern for Harriet's husband. "I just wouldn't feel right depriving him of the chance to share in his father's first evening back in town."

"Steve's at a convention in Philadelphia until late tomorrow afternoon. As a matter of fact, he has no idea yet that his dad flew in today. Hold on a second, Dez, will you?" Then to her father-in-law: "I hate to bother you, Pop, but I have this terrible headache. Would you mind getting a couple of aspirins out of the medicine cabinet for me? Oh, and a glass of water, too."

I couldn't hear Pop's response, but Harriet followed it with, "Desiree has an appointment, but I'll try to persuade her to reschedule it. What's that? No, the aspirin really can't wait. Honestly."

There was a brief silence as Pop evidently made his

exit. And when Harriet spoke again it was in a whisper, and she was in her wheedling mode. "Please, Desiree. Do this for me, and I'll be in your debt forever."

"Ask me to pull out all my fingernails or dye my hair purple, and I just might do it for you. But *this*?"

"I know, I know. If you don't come with us, though—and I realize I'm being selfish—I'll have to be alone with him. In *public*. Do you want that on your conscience?" she demanded with a nervous titter. "Besides, in spite of what you think, Pop *does* have feelings, and since he walked in that door before he's talked about nothing but you. It's been 'Desiree this' and 'Desiree that.' I—" She broke off. "Thanks so much, Pop. No, I'm still not certain Dez can make it. We—"

But Pop wrested the receiver from her grasp. "So, Desiree, how you been?" said this thin little voice.

"Fine, thanks. And Harriet tells me you're doing great."

"Not bad for a fellow in his seventies."

You wish, I countered in my head.

"Listen, you afraid maybe I got leprosy or somethin'? Or maybe you're just such a busy individual that when a friend comes all the way up from Florida, you can't even take a few steps across the hall to say hello."

"Well," I sputtered, "I don't remember why I . . . that is, I don't remember the exact reasons I wasn't able to get together on your last few trips, but it was probab— It was definitely unavoidable."

"Okay, what's past is past. But you could change your appointment tonight, if you wanted. It's not written in stone that you gotta be somewheres else. True?" This was punctuated with a few HEH-HEHs, after which Pop added plaintively, "You wanna break an old man's heart?"

"You're right," I answered resignedly. "My appointment isn't written in stone."

"Good." And as he handed the phone back to Harriet: "She's coming with us!" He sounded so gleeful that my conscience surfaced and gave me hell for having taken my original stand.

"Thanks, Dez," Harriet said in a tone that managed to convey both gratitude and relief.

"Hey, what are friends for?"

They rang my bell a half hour later. There hadn't been enough time for a much-needed shower—not at the rate of speed I move, anyway. But I did have a chance to fix my makeup and run a comb through my wig—*and* remind myself how infuriating Pop can be.

Take that incident some years back when the three of us went to this Lower East Side deli. The waiter, a crusty old man who was close to being a contemporary of Pop's, had the misfortune of informing him that the restaurant was out of mushroom and barley soup. Well, Pop did not handle this news particularly well. He carried on—and on—about how they never seem to have the aforementioned item when he's there. He even intimated that the place might be setting it aside for their preferred customers. Finally, the exasperated waiter suggested—facetiously—that Pop come to the kitchen with him and see for himself that there was no mushroom and barley soup left.

Now, Pop, not being into facetious, took the startled fellow at his word. And the two shuffled off toward the kitchen, the waiter leading the way and Pop continually stepping on his heels. Every few seconds the waiter would turn around to glare at him and mumble under his breath—something X-rated, I'm sure. The only plus was that Harriet and I, both of us totally mortified by then, were unable to make out what it was.

Upon returning from his inspection tour, Pop reported that apparently they *were* out of the coveted soup. But did this little fact embarrass him into behaving himself? In a pig's eye! Not too much later he was grousing about the pastrami's tasting like perfume. And after that it was the strudel that offended him. I won't even go into what the old dear had to say about *that.* It's enough to inform you that at this point there was a firm request that we absent ourselves from the premises.

At any rate, while I was having second thoughts about again agreeing to break bread—or, in this case, fortune cookies—with Harriet's delightful in-law, the doorbell rang.

A tanned and smiling Pop was standing on the threshold, gray felt hat in hand, with Harriet lagging a short space behind him, looking guilty. *And well she might,* I thought.

As always, the little man—he was five-three on his tiptoes—was impeccably dressed, tonight in light-weight gray wool pants, a gray-and-white tweed sport jacket, and a red tie with charcoal-and-white polka dots. His black shoes, I noticed, were so highly polished that in a pinch they could double as a mirror.

Pop and I stood there appraising each other for a second or two. Then he nodded sagely. "All in all, you're lookin' very fine, Desiree. You maybe got a little fatter since I last seen you, though."

"Pop!" Harriet exclaimed, her face suddenly redder than my wig.

Pop turned to her, shaking his head sadly. "You don't understand, Harriet. This is A-okay with me. Who wants a woman she should have these skinny little ribs poking out all over her like a chicken?"

"Uh, would you like to come in for a drink?" For some reason I felt obligated to extend the invitation. (But where-oh-where was a little hemlock when you really needed it?)

"No thanks, Dez," Harriet put in quickly. "We have reservations, and we're in danger of being late as it is."

Going down in the elevator, Pop elbowed Harriet aside in order to stand next to me. "My Frances, may she rest in peace, was no lightweight, either," he told me. "She was zaftig, like you. You know what zaftig means?"

"Yes, I know what it means." I may be a (nonpracticing) Catholic, but remember, I *was* married to Ed Shapiro, my wonderful late husband who died five tooshort years into the marriage. Besides, you pick up your share of Yiddish expressions just living in New York.

Anyhow, Pop was insisting, "Zaftig is a compliment. Honest." And Harriet was glowering at him. "All right, maybe I shouldn'ta used the word 'fat' before, but I meant it in a *good* way. Okay?" He poked me in the side.

"Okay," I muttered.

"See? Desiree isn't mad at me," he advised his daughter-in-law, "so you don't have to give me no lectures later."

Her only response was a deep sigh. But I'd have bet anything she was clenching her teeth.

The Oriental Palace was a nice, quiet little restaurant. Not exactly elegant, but softly lit and attractively decorated. What's more, the food was unusually good without being exorbitantly priced. And in spite of that earlier hamburger, I found I was now hungry enough to enjoy it. But then *somebody* managed to ruin my appetite. Which is a pretty tough thing to do.

This *somebody* wasted no time in critiquing the meal. The egg rolls, he sniffed, were greasy. The spareribs, he grumbled, were fatty. And the dim sum were so heavy that they "already are sitting there like lead in the bottom of my stomach." Nor did he restrict his complaining to Harriet and me. It wasn't long before he called over our waiter, who, planting himself alongside Pop's chair, didn't utter so much as a sylla-

ble during the cantankerous little man's entire dia-
tribe. In fact, the waiter—the small gold bar on his
shirt said "JIM"—was actually beaming. I figured he
either (a) had a very limited understanding of English
or—and this is where I came out—(b) wanted us to
think he had a very limited understanding of English.

At any rate, when the second course arrived, I
steeled myself for more of the same. Happily, though,
we got through it with a minimal amount of bitching,
Pop making only mild mention of the wonton soup's
being on the watery side.

But then came the entrees we were sharing.

As soon as we were served the shrimp with black
bean sauce, Pop frowned at his plate and demanded
that Jim explain why there weren't any beans—"no
American beans, anyways"—in the bean sauce. The
perpetual grin still in place, Jim hunched his shoulders
and signaled to the hostess, who, aware that at least
a half dozen pairs of eyes were staring in our direction,
promptly offered to substitute another selection.

"No, it's all right, girlie," Pop informed her graciously. "Only you shouldn't name it black *bean* sauce
if it don't contain real beans."

Pop helped himself to the sweet and pungent
chicken next, and—miraculously—the dish passed
muster.

It was when he was tackling the moo shoo pork,
however—which Harriet and/or I should have known
better than to order—that the man went into high
gear.

Rejecting with a cavalier wave of the hand his
daughter-in-law's offer to fill his pancakes for him, he
proceeded to tear the first one to shreds. This was
probably the only time anyone had succeeded in making a worse mess of that little chore than I did, some
of Pop's filling even squirting off his plate. I think the
embarrassment with regard to his ineptness was what
led him to confine himself to three or four mumbled

"damn"'s and a single, barely audible "oh, hell" as he proceeded to mutilate the thing. But after pancake number two met a fate similar to its predecessor's, a frustrated Pop had had enough. "They call these *pancakes*?" he whined loudly. "Tissue paper's what they should call them!" He glanced around, then addressed the entire room. "You wanta be smart? Don't order nothing comes with pancakes."

We slunk away before dessert. But at this restaurant, at least, we left of our own volition.

When we got off the elevator, Harriet made a dash for her apartment. She was to confess later that Pop had pleaded with her to allow him a couple of minutes alone with me. (An explanation that provoked an almost overwhelming desire in me to break both her legs.)

"We had a lota fun tonight, didn't we, Desiree?" Pop remarked, as we stood in front of my door with me fumbling around in my suitcase-sized handbag for my keys. I was having a slight problem locating them among the bag's other contents, which along with the expected wallet and makeup kit presently included a can of hairspray, a bottle of Poland Spring water (someone had left it in my office), a bottle of cough syrup (a holdover from last month's cold), a bottle of Extra-Strength Tylenol, a stapler (it's a long story), a pliers (don't even ask), a flashlight, a cell phone (a recent acquisition), a metal tape measure, two notebooks, three or four pens—and I can't recall what else.

Looking up, I eked out a smile. "Yes, we did."

"I'm gonna be in town until next Saturday," he told me meaningfully.

I pretended I didn't understand what he was getting at. "I'm sure you'll enjoy yourself, too." I got the impression he was about to say more, so I hurriedly threw in, "You must be really anxious to see Steve."

He considered this for a moment. "Yeah, I suppose so."

"And you have a new great-grandchild you haven't even met yet," I pointed out before going back to my fumbling.

"Harriet's gonna take me over there tomorrow. I pray the kid should only be smarter than his father—my grandson, that dope. But anyways, I'll be free later on—in the evening. Maybe you'd like to go to that deli on the Lower East Side we ate in once. But only the two of us this time, okay? We had a lota fun at that place, too, 'member?"

Words failed me—almost. Again interrupting the search for my keys, I gave the man my complete attention. "Yes, I remember. But listen, Pop, I recently became involved in a very time-consuming investigation, and I'm too bogged down with work to accept any more dinner invitations for quite a while. Umm, thanks for asking, though."

"If you don't desire to go back to the deli, we could go somewheres different," he cajoled. "All you gotta do is name it. And I don't want you should be concerned. You could even pay for yourself so's you wouldn't feel obligated in any way—if you take my meaning. Unless," he added slyly, "you *want* to be obligated."

Why, that cheeky little bugger! I could hardly believe what I was hearing. How did I get so lucky, anyway? I mean, first there was the Don Juan of the elevators, and then this randy geriatric here. And all in one day, too! "Uh, that's very thoughtful of you, Pop, but I'm afraid I don't have the luxury of a social life right now."

"Well, I'll give you a call anyways. You never can tell what'll be." And with this, he leaned over to kiss me. Fortunately, my reflexes are in much better shape than my body parts. Just in time I turned my head, and the kiss landed harmlessly on my cheek.

Pop chuckled. "Okay, okay. But what was it that O'Reilly lady said?"

"O'Reilly lady?"

"I'm surprised at you! You never heard of Scarlett O'Reilly?" He wagged a finger in my face. " 'Tomorrow's another day.' *That's* what she said."

Chapter 10

Safely on the other side of the door now, I leaned heavily against it, giving in to the strain this evening with Pop had produced. Not even the fact that the doorknob was boring into my lower back could induce me to move.

I tried telling myself I should take some satisfaction from having done a good deed tonight—two of them, actually. I'd helped out a friend and made an old man happy. Then I recalled that familiar saying about no good deed going unpunished. From here on in—until Pop left for Florida, at any rate—the answering machine would have to screen every one of my calls.

On reflection, however, I had to concede that this was really no big deal—and doubtless the price that all of us sex symbols had to pay.

Well, I could say one thing for Pop: He'd managed to chase everything else from my thoughts.

But later, after I'd finally unglued myself from that door and gone to bed, John Lander put in an appearance—figuratively speaking, naturally—refusing to let me sleep.

I liked John. I really did. Of course, I make an effort to like all my clients, and for the most part, I succeed. The way I see it, when you're favorably disposed toward someone, you tend to try a little harder for them, whether you're aware of it or not. In John's case, though, I know I'd have had those same positive feelings if I hadn't been working for him.

The man was intelligent, pleasant, low-keyed. And what impressed me most, he was fair-minded—although, to my way of thinking, foolishly so. Take his reluctance to accept that someone in line for Uncle Victor's fortune could be the perpetrator. He even berated himself for entertaining the *possibility* that one of these "decent" people wanted him dead. (I, however, had no such guilt pangs about making this assumption. I mean, it certainly didn't appear that anyone else stood to gain from the demise of both John *and* Edward.)

Still, at present my admiration for my client was almost equaled by my anger toward him. How could he refuse to consider a bodyguard—especially now, when there'd been not one, but two attempts on his life? I'd been worried about the man from the beginning. But it was nothing like the fear that gripped me at this moment.

Eventually I elected to evict John Lander from my head—a must if I had any hope of getting some sleep. But he refused to budge. My concern for John kept me throwing myself all over that bed for hours, at turns pounding the pillow and then burying my face in it. At last, when the morning light was already creeping in under the shade, he wandered away, allowing me to drop off—and head straight into a nightmare.

The day was lovely—sunshiny and warm, but with a nice, cool breeze. John and Trudie were walking together in what I took to be a meadow. He was wearing dark pants and a crisp white shirt, unbuttoned to the middle of his chest. She had on a white peasant blouse and a long, billowy skirt in a lively red print, the skirt cinched by a wide black patent belt that emphasized the tiniest of waists. In my dream Trudie was younger, more carefree than the real thing. And John had a new energy, a lightheartedness about him. The two traipsed hand in hand through the tall grass, laughing. Every so often they'd stop to admire a flower or a tree or to gaze adoringly at each other.

Suddenly it began to pour. The deluge was so heavy that the pair was unable to see much more than an inch in front of them. But now Trudie pointed to her left. Somehow she had managed to make out a house in the distance.

Soaked with rain, their clothing plastered against their bodies, the couple dashed madly in the direction of the shelter. Only to discover that there wasn't any shelter. Instead, they had reached the edge of a cliff. Blinded by the downpour, however, they hurried on. I watched in horror as, hands still entwined, they plummeted into space—and onto the jagged rocks below.

But when I looked more closely at the woman lying motionless beside John Lander, it wasn't Trudie's face I saw. It was my own.

I was clammy and disoriented when I awoke. I pinched my left forearm to establish that I was alive. Then I glanced at the clock: eleven-ten. Well, I was rising later than I'd intended to, but I was not about to apologize for it. Don't forget it was barely daylight when I'd gotten up yesterday (okay, so I'm taking a little poetic license here), and I hadn't closed my eyes this morning until well after Dracula did. Plus, in between there'd been all sorts of significant and/or unnerving matters to deal with. And listen, I hadn't exactly had a picnic in Dreamland, either.

I washed up hurriedly, then tried Scott Riley's home number without even taking the time for a sip or two of coffee.

"Scott Riley speaking," said a very precise voice in a register not much lower than his sister's. *What was it with this family's vocal cords?* I wondered, momentarily throwing David Hearn into the mix, too. Then I remembered. Sooner or later, I thought in irritation, I was bound to absorb the simple fact that we were dealing with two different gene pools here.

I opened with, "My name is Desiree Shapiro, and I'm a—"

"I know who you are," Scott interrupted. "I presume you're telephoning to set up an appointment. When would you care to do this?"

I was surprised at his lack of resistance to the idea. "Well, I'd appreciate it if we could get together as soon as possible."

"It happens that I can meet with you at any time today, including this evening. A lady friend had to cancel our date only an hour ago—she's going out of town on business this afternoon, and she won't be returning until Tuesday."

We proceeded to make our arrangements, settling on five o'clock at Scott's West Eighty-fourth Street apartment. *But why,* I asked myself in passing, *had he found it necessary to explain his availability like that?*

As soon as the conversation was over, I dialed the Twelfth Precinct.

I was very anxious to reconnect with Tim Fielding. It had been quite a while since we'd last been in touch, and I was looking forward to seeing my old friend again. And who was I to complain if our little reunion would also afford me an opportunity to determine just what it was the police had on my client? Not that I expected Tim to be that forthcoming, you understand. Not at first, anyway. But it was my intention to pump him for all he was worth.

It was a letdown to be informed that Sergeant Fielding was off for the day. But then, with a mental shrug, I bounced right back. "Well, he has himself a little reprieve, that's all," I confided to the dead receiver in my hand.

*   *   *

Over breakfast I finally had a chance to ponder my chilling dream. What could it possibly mean: that I wanted to be in Trudie's place, married to John?

No. While I liked John—I've already told you that—I didn't *like* him, like him, as Ellen would say. The fact is, he wasn't my type in the least, since I almost invariably fall for those skinny, sawed-off little twerps who look as if they're in desperate need of a bit of nourishment and a lot of TLC. (I don't know. Ed and I never had any children, so maybe it's a nurturing thing with me.)

Okay. So what else could it mean? Did I fear that John was going to come to a terrible end and that in the process I'd go down, too?

If this was the case, why was Trudie the one who went off the cliff with him?

Oh, hell. I gave up. They say that dreams are seldom what they seem, anyway. Besides, who did I think I was—Mrs. Freud?

Chapter 11

The living room of Scott Riley's sprawling five-room apartment was a paradigm of masculinity: dark wood walls, taupe leather chairs, cream leather sofas (there were two of these), redbrick fireplace, and a handsome mahogany bar stocked with spirits of every variety.

The setting was in sharp contrast to the man himself, a male version of the girl I'd met yesterday. What was attractive in her, however, was far less so in him. Both were short and small-boned, but whereas she looked delicate, he looked frail. The pale coloring that was such an asset to Shawna, in Scott was an almost sickly-looking pallor. Even his blue eyes were a watered-down version of his twin's.

"Make yourself comfortable, won't you?" he invited, waving his hand expansively to indicate the large selection of seating accommodations available. He had a precise—actually, prissy—manner of speaking. And his immaculate attire, which featured a maroon-silk ascot tucked inside his crisp, white shirt, appeared to reflect a determined striving for cosmopolitan.

"Can I get you something to drink, Ms. Shapiro?" he inquired, as I headed for the nearest sofa.

"I'd love a Coke, if you have one. And, please, call me Desiree, Mr. Riley."

"Certainly, I have one. And I'll be happy to call you Desiree, if you wish. Excuse me while I fetch our drinks." I noticed he hadn't suggested I use *his* given name. But, as I recalled, his sister hadn't made that offer, either.

"Ice?" he inquired from behind the bar.

"That would be great."

A couple of minutes later he was back with a Coke for me and red wine for himself.

Handing me the tumbler of soda, he settled into one of the club chairs across from the sofa. "An exceedingly complex 1996 Cabernet Sauvignon," he enlightened me, passing the wineglass under his nose. "Superbly balanced. After finishing the first bottle, I was unable to resist the impulse to purchase an entire case."

At this point the Coke was about an inch shy of my lips. Scott reached over and stayed my hand. "To success in your investigation, Desiree," he said, clinking glasses.

"Why . . . uh, thank you." I was taken aback. I couldn't remember any suspect's ever doing something like that before. And Scott had to realize that's what he was—a suspect, I mean.

"A revelation," he pronounced, after sampling the wine. "May I pour some for you?"

"Thank you, but I'm supposed to be working now, and it doesn't take much more than the sniff of a cork to impede my thought processes."

"As you prefer," Scott murmured, sounding slightly miffed. Suddenly, he jumped to his feet. "Oh, my heavens, I almost forgot. Be back in a jiff." And he dashed from the room.

He reappeared toting a large tray from which he removed two small platters, setting them on the brass-trimmed wood table between us. These were followed by a bunch of cocktail napkins and a couple of elegant porcelain hors d'oeuvres plates. "I don't know *where* my head is today. Do help yourself."

On one platter was a variety of cheese wedges surrounded by crackers, cherries, and grapes. The other held a crock of pâté, accompanied by artfully arranged toast rounds and cornichons.

I sampled the pâté first. It was nothing short of divine. And I told Scott so.

His chest seemed to puff out about six inches when he said that he'd made it himself.

Then, as I was topping a cracker with this creamy white cheese—St. André, Scott apprised me—I began my questioning. "I was advised that you're one of the heirs to your uncle's estate."

Scott paused in the act of spreading some pâté on a toast round to respond. "Only a very minor one—unless something should happen to John before Uncle Victor dies. That's why you're here, correct? You want me to tell you where I was the night somebody attempted to do in your client."

"Uh, yes. I'd appreciate it."

"I was right where I am now. I had a cold for a good part of last week, thanks to a terribly inconsiderate lady friend who was far too demonstrative when you take into account how infectious she was. At any rate, I was staying in as much as I could to rest it up. I even worked out of the apartment for a couple of days—which, given that I'm an architect, presented no problem."

"Did you happen to see or hear from anyone who can confirm you were at home that evening?"

"Earlier, yes. But not at eleven-thirty, which is the hour in question, as I understand it. Listen, Desiree, I don't want to tell you how to conduct your business. But if I were you, I would give serious thought to the possibility that the culprit was some teenage hoodlum out to amuse himself by taking potshots at decent, taxpaying citizens. That sort of outrage occurs all too frequently these days."

"Your sister had pretty much the same thing to say

about the incident, and I'm certainly keeping that possibility in mind."

"Good."

"Still, with Edward's having been murdered just two weeks before that, well, it does seem a bit of a coincidence."

"However, coincidences do occur. That's why they invented a word for it."

I grinned. "I've never heard the premise defended like that."

Scott grinned back at me. "I'll deem that a compliment, if I may. Now, as for the night Cousin Edward was murdered, I had prepared dinner for my sister that Tuesday, and we were together the entire evening. She arrived at six-thirty, and she didn't leave for home until ten, perhaps a few minutes earlier. But I would assume Shawna's already told you this."

"Yes, and by the way, she said the meal was absolutely delicious. I'm trying to remember exactly what you served, though."

"You're checking to see if we have our stories straight, isn't that it?" Scott challenged, looking smug. "But all right, I'll help you out. We started with clams oreganato . . ." He went on to confirm the menu Shawna had laid out for me on Saturday, even supplying the name of the dish that had eluded her: Veal Prince Orloff. "Satisfied?" he inquired, after concluding with the crème brûlée.

"Satisfied. I have another question for you though. Where were you at around twelve-thirty yesterday afternoon?"

"I was at home, preparing another of my matchless feasts; I had dinner guests last night."

"Would there, by any chance, be anyone who could confirm that you were in the apartment then?"

"Not a soul. I received a couple of phone calls, but it was when I was in the midst of preparing the *pâte*

à choux for my *croquembouche,* and I could not be
disturbed—timing is crucial. Therefore I let the machine pick up." He was looking at me eagerly now.
"Why do you ask?"

Well, I had no intention of revealing that John had
had another narrow escape, so I mumbled, "I'm sorry,
but I can't discuss that." And then so that the refusal
might be slightly more acceptable to my pouting host,
I added, "Not just yet, anyhow."

Scott made a sound that was very much like a har-
rumph, and I quickly moved on. "Would you mind
answering something else for me?"

He shrugged before responding. "Go on."

"What was your opinion of your cousin Edward?"

"He was all right, I suppose. But both Edward and
John are quite a lot older than we are—Shawna and
I. So we've never had much of a relationship with
either of them."

"Would you have any idea who might have wanted
to harm Edward?"

"Not the slightest."

"Umm, how about John? How do you feel about
him?"

"He seems to be a decent enough chap, as well."

Did he say "chap"? I suppressed a smile. "What
about enemies? Has John ruffled any feathers that you
know of?"

"No. And if you don't mind my saying this, you
don't appear to be giving much weight to my street-
crime theory."

"I assure you, I'm not disregarding it. But when a
man who is shortly due to come into a bundle is murdered, you have to at least recognize that there might
have been a financial motive for what happened. And
when soon after this an attempt is made on the life
of the person who's next in line to inherit, well, I'd
be extremely negligent if I didn't investigate the likelihood of a tie-in."

Scott dug in his heels. "I still believe it was some young punk who shot at your client."

"I'm not disputing you. In that event, though, who shot Edward?"

"This I couldn't say. As I've been trying to impress upon you, I really didn't know very much about the man, but—" Breaking off abruptly, Scott tilted his head to one side. For a few seconds he sat there silently, frowning. And when he addressed me again, he spoke slowly, his eyes focused on some point over my left shoulder. "If, however, I'm mistaken about that attack on John having been a random act, then . . ." His voice trailed off, and he blinked a few times.

"Then—what?"

"Then it's probable that the shooting *is* connected to Edward's death. And in that case . . ." He shook his head as if having difficulty accepting the thought.

"In that case—?" I prompted.

"It would have to pertain to Uncle Victor's will, with the 'perpetrator,' as you people call it, almost certainly David Hearn."

"Why David?"

"Obviously, I would know if it were I, and it wasn't. I can vouch for Shawna, as well—positively. And I assure you I'd be just as convinced of this if she hadn't been with me at the time Edward was killed. She's simply not that sort of individual."

"But *three more people* would have to die in order for David to inherit." The words were out before I'd really considered them. And, to my embarrassment, the inference was pretty clear: On the other hand, just one person—my client—stood between the Riley twins and all that prosperity. "Of course," I added in a belated—and fairly transparent—burst of diplomacy, "who's to say David didn't regard the rewards as worth the effort?"

I could have sung all the verses of *The Star-Spangled Banner*—including the ones hardly anyone's even heard of—and polished off the performance with a little tap dance (if I knew how to tap-dance, that is) in the silence that followed. At last Scott took a deep breath, let it out, and said, "I had no intention of telling you this, but the truth is, it would only be necessary for David to dispose of John in order to get his hands on a good portion of Uncle Victor's assets."

"What are you talking about?"

"Shawna and David—they're involved."

"Do you mean *romantically*?"

"I imagine you could term it that," Scott retorted snidely.

Remembering Shawna's comments about David Hearn—and his about her, as well—I had a real problem accepting that there could be anything between the two of them. "Are you certain? Your sister seemed almost disdainful of David."

"I would surmise that this was designed to muddy the waters a bit. They appear determined to keep their unfortunate affair a deep, dark secret. Shawna never even told *me* about the relationship. And we've always shared *everything*."

"How did you find out, then?"

"I did something I'm not too proud of."

"I haven't come here to judge you. Honestly."

Scott hesitated a few moments before going on. "This dates back several months, Desiree, when I encountered my next-door neighbor at the food market one day. 'I saw your sister at the theater the other night,' she informed me. 'She was with a very handsome fellow, too.'

"Well, Shawna hadn't breathed a word to me about going to the theater *nor*—and this was really *so* unlike her—about having some new man in her life. Of course, I phoned her that same evening and casually mentioned what Althea Birney had had to say. Shawna insisted that Althea had mistaken her for someone else. I didn't find that explanation terribly satisfactory, however. You must appreciate, Desiree, that the two women have more than a nodding acquaintance. The Birneys—Althea and Clayton—have been frequent guests at my little cocktail parties, and I don't think my sister has missed even one of those.

"Naturally, I was puzzled as to the reason for Shawna's denial and, yes, hurt that she hadn't seen fit to confide in me. But I elected to put the matter out of my mind. Perhaps Althea *was* mistaken, I told myself. Then several weeks ago, on a Saturday afternoon, I stopped at Shawna's. And while I was at the apartment she received a telephone call. Instantly, she became terribly flustered. She told me she'd be taking the call in the bedroom and asked that I hang up the receiver when she picked up."

It was evident that Scott was more reluctant than ever to continue, and his voice dropped to a near whisper. "I only pretended to comply, however; I listened to that entire conversation. It was David Hearn on the other end of the line, and from what was said, I was able to ascertain that he and Shawna had been seeing each other for some time and that it was serious." He seemed to be fighting back tears when he added, "I can only pray that Shawna will eventually come to recognize how unworthy he is of her.

"At any rate, I hope you believe me, Desiree, when I tell you that I'd never before stooped to a thing like that. Not even once. But this was my *sister,* and well, I cherish the woman. I had to do what was required to assure myself that she wasn't in any sort of difficulty. You can understand that, can't you?"

"Yes, I can."

"Of course, I haven't let on that I know about her and David because I dare not tell her *how* I know. I'm very much afraid that she'd never forgive me."

"Why do you think Shawna tried to keep you in the dark about the romance?"

"I presume that originally it was because I've always

disliked David Hearn—even when we were children. Shawna wasn't too fond of him, either, if the truth be told. But I suppose it's hormones *uber alles*." With this, Scott actually turned a very becoming shade of pink. "I have no doubt, though, that she would have talked to me about it eventually if it hadn't been for Edward's murder and now this business with John. I would venture to say these things are what made Shawna wary of trusting even her own brother with her secret."

"What do Edward and John have to do with it?"

"It's quite likely that David is in dire need of funds." And then, looking much too self-satisfied to suit me: "Apparently we have a case of like father, like son. You do know that the senior Hearn is a degenerate gambler, don't you? Well, that day on the telephone David told Shawna that someone with a name like Righty or Lefty or some such wasn't willing to wait much longer for what *he*—David—owed the fellow. And I gathered he wasn't speaking about any paltry sum, either. To show you how besotted she is, my sister *pleaded* to give David the money he needed—which I assume she planned to badger our mother for. But Mr. Sir Lancelot wouldn't hear of it. Then Shawna asked if he was going to speak to Uncle Victor about his situation, but David refused even to consider going to my uncle about any gambling debts. Shawna was very upset; she wanted to know if lover boy had any other way of getting that kind of capital, and he replied that he'd better *find* a way, that he didn't dare not cover the bet. He spoke about his intention of tapping some wealthy friend of his for a loan. And perhaps he did inveigle that poor chap into handing over at least some of the cash he had to pay to those nasty little playmates of his. Obviously, there was no way I could find out."

"Maybe I missed something. But I'm still having trouble doping out why the shootings would contribute to Shawna and David's decision to keep the love affair under wraps."

"Don't you *see?* No? Well, I'll explain. Edward has been killed, and if John were to meet a similar fate before Uncle Victor dies, Shawna and I would inherit. Now, say Shawna and David marry, God forbid—although at present this seems to be what they have in mind—David Hearn would then share in Shawna's portion of Uncle Victor's fortune. And incidentally, believe me when I tell you that a mere *fraction* of my uncle's assets is enough to entice someone lacking moral fiber into behaving in a . . . let's call it an *unfortunate* manner. Particularly one of David Hearn's station."

"Station"? Why, you little snob, you! But aloud, all I said was "Oh?" accompanying this with one of my most lethal looks.

Either impervious to or unaware of my reaction, Scott went on. "At any rate, if David is still up to his ears in debt, and if it should come out that he's now a step closer to a great deal of money, I presume that the police would regard him as a very attractive suspect. And even if he *has* managed to straighten out his finances, David's fondness for gambling is, in itself, a flashing red light."

Still fuming at Scott's use of the phrase "one of David Hearn's station," I inquired spitefully, "And you really feel that David would be satisfied with having access to only Shawna's half of the estate?"

Scott turned slightly green now, a color that was not nearly as flattering to him as the earlier pink. "I haven't really given that any thought, but I don't imagine he'd have any recourse. Shawna would never allow anything to happen to me."

I refrained from countering with something like, "Maybe it would be out of her control." Which not only would have been very not nice but, I could see, was totally unnecessary, my host's complexion putting a lie to the assurance of his words.

Only seconds after this, however, he brightened. "Say, has it ever occurred to you that it was your client who killed Edward and that he only *pretended* to be attacked in order to divert suspicion from himself?" Obviously my host was no longer able to tolerate the idea that if David Hearn was, in fact, the perp, it could put him—Scott—at considerable risk. So now he was grabbing on to someone else—someone who, from his point of view, was a less ominous villain.

"No, it has not," I answered firmly.

"John has a pretty fair motive, too, you know. Have you met Trudie—his wife?"

"Yes."

"Then you have to concede that there is absolutely no possibility he is experiencing any joy in living with that harridan."

"I'm not intimate enough with the state of their marriage to make any such assumption. Besides, if John isn't happy with Trudie, there's always divorce. He doesn't need his uncle's money for that."

I was reaching for the pâté one last time when Scott hit me with, "Ahh, but you're mistaken there. You see, Trudie is the one in the family with the moola. John—and more's the pity, too—has never been able to earn much of a living. I assume that's why Trudie set him up in his own real estate company a few years ago, which, so I've been told, cannot be characterized a success by even the most lenient of standards. Furthermore, she continues to finance this failing venture of his."

Scott looked at me intently now, his eyes fastened on mine. "Without that inheritance, Desiree, the poor chap has a Hobson's choice: He can either remain with that wretched woman forever or he can wind up on the street.

"Chilling, isn't it?" he concluded with a sardonic smile.

Chapter 12

Before I left the apartment, Scott had extracted my solemn word not to let on to a soul how I'd learned about the affair between his sister and David Hearn. Actually, though, I couldn't see any purpose in divulging this information to anyone anyway.

The Shawna/David relationship aside, however, Scott Riley had certainly given me a lot to chew over. In fact, on the ride home I was hardly able to make a dent in it all. But what I wasn't able to cover in the cab I reviewed during dinner, contemplated with my coffee, and ruminated on in bed.

Just consider the various theories the man had put forth.

There was his suggestion that it had been teenage punks who'd shot at my client. But now, going over this in my mind, I wondered if he'd ever believed— *seriously* believed, that is—any such thing. Look, if Scott hadn't been responsible for the events of the last couple of weeks—and, of course, presupposing he was convinced that his sister's hands were equally clean— then it stood to reason he would regard David Hearn as the logical perpetrator. But, the trouble was, this could mean that Scott's own life might be in jeopardy.

Well, maybe the man just wasn't ready to come to terms with that possibility. So choosing not to acknowledge any connection between the attacks on his two cousins, he'd banished the idea of David's guilt to the back of his mind. At the same time, he'd conjured up that random act business to provide himself with an explanation for someone's taking aim at John.

On the other hand, though, today's mention of underage thrill-seekers might only have been the jumping-off point. It was not unlikely that Scott had planned all along to work his way up to an attempt to implicate David Hearn in the crimes.

But if that *was* the case, I put to myself, why, after finally naming David, had the fellow suddenly shifted focus and served up my client to me as a suspect? Perhaps, I reflected, this about-face was another manifestation of Scott's shrinking from the personal danger his David theory could entail. (I'd even speculated about that at the time, remember?) Apparently overcome with fear, he'd supplied himself and—as a byproduct, really—yours truly with an alternative perp.

At this moment, however, something else occurred to me.

What if it had suddenly dawned on Scott that Shawna might have been her lover's accomplice? This would almost certainly have prompted him to move away from David and point the finger elsewhere. Listen, if there was one thing I'd have been practically willing to swear to, it was that Scott was every bit as devoted to his twin as he professed to be.

And just what did I think of the notion that John had murdered his cousin Edward and that his own near-fatal encounters, therefore, were pure fiction? Well, in the first place, from what I knew of my client's character, I found it pretty hard to take this seriously. Even going on the supposition that he was absolutely miserable with Trudie—and no outsider could really attest to something that personal—I just wasn't able to picture a man like John resorting to murder in order to become independent of his wife's largesse. But okay, let's say I'd totally misjudged him. And let's say, too, that he was desperate to terminate the marriage without—as that little snot Scott Riley had put it—ending up on the street. Then the obvious question was: Why kill *Edward*? After all, according to Scott, Trudie was a wealthy woman. And it seemed to me there was every likelihood that John was her heir. (I made a mental note to verify these things.) So what I'm getting at is, why not murder *her*? Maybe his spouse's demise wouldn't have been quite as advantageous to him money-wise as his cousin's, but this way John would have gained his financial freedom *and* extricated himself from an unhappy union in the process. What's more, he wouldn't have had to wait all these years to get out from under.

Sorry, Scott. I can't say whether David did the deed; I'm only confident that John didn't.

Now, so far I'd tabled the possibility that Scott himself might be the assailant. But it was time to consider this and, almost simultaneously, to take a look at Shawna, as well.

Neither had an alibi for the night somebody took that shot at John. Nor could Scott account for his whereabouts yesterday afternoon, when John had again come close to winding up a statistic. Furthermore, there was only the twins' word that they'd had dinner together at Scott's on the evening of Edward's death. Of course, it was conceivable that they'd lied in an innocent, if misguided, attempt to shield each other from coming under suspicion. But it was also conceivable that the two of them had conspired to rid themselves of the front-runners for Uncle Victor's fortune. (Assuming, that is, Shawna hadn't teamed up with David Hearn on this project.) As to the pair's reciting the same menu—puleeze. What was to prevent them from agreeing on those dishes beforehand? To be honest, I can still feel my face getting hot whenever I recall that I'd actually been silly enough to ask about that. I mean, how pathetic!

It was early morning when I got around to concentrating on Scott as a person. And I had to admit that there was a lot about the man that puzzled me.

Naturally, there were a few things I knew for certain, along with others I was fairly sure of.

As I told you before, I had little doubt as to the depth of his feelings for his sister. I could also state unequivocally that Scott Riley was intelligent. And that he was a snob—this wasn't even open for argument. Plus, he had very sophisticated tastes and, evidently, the wherewithal to indulge them. So I could assume that Scott was at least moderately successful in his profession. Either that, or the fellow had access to another source of capital that could support his kind of lifestyle. Which got me to thinking about how at odds his apartment was with his persona.

The furnishings in that place practically screamed, "Property of a man with a high level of testosterone!" Yet here was about as prissy an individual as I'd ever encountered—effeminate, almost. Why would someone like that surround himself with such masculine trappings? And, in fact, why make it a point to throw in those out-of-left-field references to a "lady friend"?

Was Scott gay—and attempting to disprove it? Or was he straight—and trying to establish it?

I pulled myself up short. I'd been spinning my wheels for no reason except that a busybody is a busybody is a busybody. After all, what did the man's sexual orientation have to do with anything?

And now I glanced at the lighted digits on my bedside clock: 3:14, for heaven's sake!

It was at this point that I abandoned any further conjecture about Scott Riley's manhood in exchange for a few hours' sleep.

Chapter 13

It wasn't easy to coax myself out of bed on Monday. And it had very little to do with my being awake most of the night before. The fact is, I had my annual gynecologist's visit at 9 A.M., something I wasn't looking forward to in the least. And not merely because of Dr. Cantor's probing finger, either.

It was really the whole setup in that office of hers. Just listen to the drill, for heaven's sake.

First you have to be prepared to spend as long as an hour in the crowded waiting room. Which can be so packed that everyone is forced to jockey for seats. But then when you're finally ushered into the examining room, things get a whole lot worse.

You're commanded to remove every stitch of clothing and put on this flimsy paper gown—"the opening to the front." Now you can anticipate another endless stay. And, believe me, once you set foot in the examining room, you actually look back with nostalgia to that waiting room wait.

The only furniture in here (besides the mandatory examining table and stool, of course) is a single, hard wooden chair, with dimensions that don't accommodate much more than half of a good-sized posterior—something I can definitely lay claim to. There isn't even one of Dr. Cantor's six-month-old-plus magazines to occupy you, either. Worst of all, however, is that in this near-naked state, you're blasted unmercifully by an air conditioner that has to be at least 14,000 BTUs—and in a space that's no more than eight-by-ten, tops. (For some reason that I've never been able to fathom, they even have that damn thing operating in the dead of winter.)

At any rate, getting back to this particular morning . . .

Before leaving the apartment, I'd taken a couple of steps to ensure that my incarceration in the dreaded examining room was going to be slightly more tolerable today. In addition to a sweater—which in the past helped a little but not nearly enough—I'd shoved a pair of calf-length wool socks in my bag. And I remembered to bring along a brand-new paperback, too.

You can't imagine my shock when after fifty minutes in the waiting room, Tina, Dr. Cantor's office assistant, marched me into the examining room—and it was like an oven! I mean, it was so hot you could toast marshmallows in the place.

"This air conditioner just went on the blink," Tina explained. "Umm, Dr. Cantor should be in shortly, though," she threw out before fleeing.

Well, it didn't take more than a few seconds to convince me that I now knew what hell was like. I figured if I read—until I passed out, that is—maybe I'd focus on something other than the temperature. But when I got out my paperback, I discovered that I'd grabbed the wrong book—this was the one I'd finished last week!

So for the next quarter hour I just sat there and stewed. In every way a person can stew.

By this time you may be asking why I hadn't found myself another gynecologist. A fair question. And the answer is, I honestly don't know. I never seemed to get around to it. Besides, according to my experience—along with everything I've heard—Dr. Cantor is a very capable physician. What's more, she's a pleasant human being, another quality I value in a doctor. Still, I make an annual vow that

I'll talk to her about this ridiculous system of hers. But thanks to that bright yellow streak down my back, the only one I wind up lecturing is myself—for chickening out yet again.

Today, however, I had reached the end of my rope. In a little while (I hoped) Dr. Cantor would be hearing how inconsiderate it was to have her patients hanging around interminably before getting to see her. I mean, didn't it ever occur to her that the rest of us had *lives*? That we had things to do and places to be? And don't think she wouldn't be getting an earful with regard to these appalling waiting conditions, as well.

At any rate, I had my speech pretty much down pat when there was a soft knock on the door, following which Dr. Cantor, a plucky smile on her face, hobbled into the room. On crutches!

Well, that ended that. After all, how could I lace into a woman who wasn't even able to stand on her own two feet?

It was close to eleven when I walked into Gilbert and Sullivan, the law firm that leases me my office space.

Now, most people laugh when they hear that name, and I can hardly blame them. I did a fair amount of tee-heeing myself initially. But there's absolutely nothing funny about being on the receiving end of one of the sweetest deals in Manhattan.

Of course, my office *is* tiny. But then, the rent is, too. Plus, without paying an extra cent, I get to share the services of the best secretary in New York. And if that's not enough, Elliot Gilbert and Pat Sullivan are two exceptionally nice guys who throw cases my way whenever they can.

Jackie, the aforementioned best secretary in New York, acknowledged my entrance with a frown. "I thought you were being held hostage," she cracked.

"I told you I'd be pretty late, remember? My gynecologist appointments take forever."

"Yeah. Only it seems you're there longer every year. But never mind. Is everything okay?"

"Dr. Cantor says I'm fine. Did I get any calls?"

"Not a one." Then, almost as an afterthought, she added, "Say, want to have lunch later? There's this new restaurant that opened only about three blocks from here—Chinese. It's supposed to be terrific."

"I'd better not. I've got quite a bit of work to catch up on; I'll grab something at my desk in an hour or so." I didn't feel it necessary to mention that I'd had Chinese food the day before yesterday. Or that the last new neighborhood restaurant Jackie had promoted had gifted her with a dandy case of food poisoning.

"My, my, you *are* a busy lady, aren't you?" Jackie's voice was thick with sarcasm.

I suppose you've already gathered that when I spoke about her being such an excellent secretary, I wasn't factoring in the woman's disposition. Frankly, there have been any number of instances when I've been sorely tempted to bring my foot in direct contact with Jackie's derriere. But while she can be just plain impossible, she's also an extremely loyal and caring friend. And I like her a lot—particularly when she's not driving me up a wall. Reminding myself of this, I bit back the sharp retort that had been about to exit my mouth, going with an attempt to placate her instead. "If I didn't have all these notes to—"

"Never mind," she grumbled, turning to her computer and starting to type. "Lately it's been one excuse after another."

"Listen, I'm genuinely sorry I can't make it. Let's get together later in the week, okay?"

Jackie's eyes remained fixed on the computer screen. It usually takes a while to get back in her good graces—the amount of time depending on the severity of the infraction. "We'll see," she pronounced.

She was certainly having one of her testier days, I

decided as I made my way down the hall. The thing is, though, when Jackie gets in a snit it's normally because I've actually *done* something she frowns upon. Which, granted, can encompass a wide variety of sins—everything from neglecting to apprise her of my whereabouts to forgetting a dental appointment to taking up with a man she doesn't approve of. But I couldn't recall her ever acting that touchy about my not being able to have lunch. I wouldn't have been at all surprised if it was something else that was troubling her. Most likely a spat with Derwin, her tightfisted, years-older significant other. Well, they'd work it out. They always did.

As soon as I was settled in my minuscule office (my *affordable* minuscule office, that is) I phoned the Twelfth Precinct. My old pal Sergeant Fielding wasn't in just then, and I was advised to try again around four.

Trudie Lander was next on my list. She seemed slightly taken aback to hear from me but agreed to a meeting readily enough. We set it up for Wednesday at two-thirty at a coffee shop not far from her Greenwich Village apartment.

After this I attempted to get in touch with David Hearn at the Manhattan DA's office. A very pleasant woman informed me that he was in court and wasn't expected back today.

At this point I couldn't come up with another reason to postpone dealing with the major project that lay in wait for me. Resignedly, I picked up the Lander file, switched on the computer, and began transcribing my notes of the past few days.

Now, being that I'm the slowest typist I know, this was a pretty intimidating task. And I have a couple of habits that stretched out the chore even further. You see, instead of waiting to study the material until it's typed, which makes sense, I have a tendency to pore over the information as I go along, which doesn't—make sense, I mean.

Anyhow, I had been at that computer for almost two hours when I finally acknowledged how pathetically little I'd accomplished. At this rate I'd be typing these same notes from my cramped little room in the retirement home.

There was only one thing to do. As frequently becomes necessary, I willed myself to keep my mind totally blank. Which wasn't as difficult as it should have been. And while I'm not claiming that I zipped right along after that, I did make noticeable progress.

At four-fifteen I broke away from my labors and phoned Tim Fielding again.

"Fielding," the familiar voice barked.

"This is your favorite girl detective."

A moment's pause. "Holy crap! And don't flatter yourself, Shapiro. You haven't been a girl since before women got the right to vote."

Same old Fielding! I should probably explain that my friendship with this man goes way back. In fact, he had been a good buddy of my husband Ed's— they'd once worked out of the same precinct. (I did mention that Ed had been a member of the force before becoming a PI, didn't I? At least, I think I did.) At any rate, I'm very fond of Tim, and I'm certain the feeling is mutual. It's just that it's become a habit with us, for some reason, to take pains not to show it. So we hide behind these innocuous little smart-ass jabs. And since Fielding had thrown down the gauntlet . . .

"It's always so nice to talk to you, Tim," I murmured, sounding like my tongue had been soaked in honey. "Tell me, are you still a sergeant?"

"That's right," he answered guardedly. "Why?"

"You know, I almost expected to hear that you'd

already made captain. By all that's holy, you should have risen to the level of your incompetence by now."

He chuckled. "You're getting better at this, Shapiro, although your delivery could still use a little work. But anyway, I have this premonition that any second you're going to tell me why I have the pleasure of hearing from you after almost a year."

"A year? Has it been that long?"

"You bet your tush, it has. And I think you're well aware of it, too. So? Out with it."

"Umm, I understand you're heading up the Sharp case."

"Please, Desiree, say that the widow didn't call you in on that one."

"She didn't."

"Praise be to God," Fielding mumbled.

"I was hired by John Lander to investigate the attempts on his life."

"Damn!" he exclaimed. And after a few seconds of recovery time: "Some attempts! I can't imagine Lander's persuading you to swallow that garbage; I'd have thought you were smarter than that. And incidentally, it's *attempt*. Singular."

"No, there have now been two of them. Plural. Somebody tried to run over John on Saturday."

"Yeah, sure they did. And I'm Peter Cottontail."

"Listen," I informed Tim firmly, "we really have to talk. Whenever it's convenient for you, of course."

"That'd be a year from next January. Seriously, Shapiro, I'm bogged down these days. Murder seems to be getting more and more popular around here. Besides, you don't want to talk to me. You want *me* to talk to *you*. And there's nothing I can give you right now."

"That's not true; I do have information that would interest you. Why don't I stop by first thing tomorrow morning—I just need a few minutes, I swear—and we can go over things while we're having our coffee and donuts? My treat, naturally."

Fielding considered this briefly before muttering his consent. "All right. Not that I believe for a second that you have anything worthwhile for me, but I suppose I might as well get you off my back. Tomorrow's no good, though. Make it Wednesday at eight-thirty. And about the donuts, be sure you bring the kind with—"

"Yeah, yeah. I know. Chocolate icing and walnut sprinkles. You got it. And thanks, Tim. Uh, by the way, I probably should be committed for this, but I'm looking forward to seeing you again."

The conversation ended with a parting grunt from Tim.

As we clicked off, I found myself smiling broadly. After which, with a real sense of accomplishment, I went back to my typing.

Chapter 14

By the time I got home from work, I was starved. I'd had a BLT at my desk around one, but it was a *skinny* BLT. The thing is, though, I was way past due for another visit to D'Agostino's. Fortunately, rummaging around in the freezer paid off. Hidden under a package of stale hamburger rolls was a container of leftover marinara sauce with mushrooms. So I cooked up a little spaghetti to go with it and prepared a great big salad. Later I discovered that there was also a respectable portion of Häagen-Dazs macadamia brittle to accompany my coffee—a relief under any circumstances but especially when you take into account my talent in the coffee-making department.

At seven o'clock I tried David Hearn at his apartment. I was a bit surprised to find him in, and it crossed my mind that Shawna might be with him.

"This is Desiree Shapiro," I said, "and I—"

"How are you, Mrs. Steinberg?" David joked.

Well, normally the "Mrs. Steinberg" thing would have gotten a chuckle out of me. Even if I had to force it for the sake of politeness. But at present I was hardly interested in pleasing this person that I'd begun referring to in my head as "David the Deceitful." My attitude, I'm sure, stemming from the fact that I'd found him so likable when we met. And it wasn't merely that I felt betrayed. Looking back, I believe that what I really held against David Hearn

was the fact that he verified my own piss-poor ability
to assess people.

You'd think, though—wouldn't you?—that by now
I'd be used to having my judgment refuted. Well, apparently not. But recognizing that it was pretty much
mandatory to conceal my hostility if there was any
chance of persuading the guy to see me, I managed
to muster up a fairly neutral tone. "I'd appreciate it
if we could get together again."

"You're kidding, aren't you?" The voice seemed
even higher to me than it had during our initial conversation. Which undoubtedly had more to do with
my mind-set than with David's vocal cords.

"No, I'm not. Something's come up, and I think we
should discuss it."

"I've already told—"

"It would be to your benefit."

He didn't respond immediately, and when he did,
he was obviously wary. "Is anything wrong?"

"There are a couple of matters we ought to clear
up, that's all—and as soon as possible."

David's "All right" was grudging. "But not tonight.
I was just walking out when you phoned. How about
after work tomorrow?"

"Fine."

"I could be at your apartment around six, unless
you think it would be better to do it in your office.
Where is it located, by the way?"

I gave him the address.

"That would be more convenient for me—if it's not
a problem for you."

"It's no problem at all," I assured him.

"Well, see you tomorrow then." He sounded about
as enthusiastic as if he'd agreed to go to a hanging—
his own, I'm talking about.

It was maybe five minutes after we hung up that
I reminded myself that, for one reason or another,

practically all suspects lie to you. But very few of them are guilty of murder.

And in spite of my displeasure with him, I realized that I was hoping David Hearn wasn't one of the few.

About a quarter of an hour later, as I was getting a pencil out of my desk drawer, the phone rang. Automatically, I began to reach for it, pulling my hand back just in time. *Pop Gould!* I just knew it.

He'd left a message on my machine yesterday, while I was at Scott's. "So, Desiree, when are we gonna have dinner?" the thin little voice had inquired. "Yeah, yeah, I know you're a busy individual. But you gotta eat, don'tcha? A person could get sick not taking in no food. You call me back—okay?—and let me know when you wanna make it."

Understandably, I hadn't returned the call.

Pop, however, didn't appear to be holding this breach of etiquette against me. Because, sure enough, here he was again.

"You prob'ly didn't get my message on Sunday— even Harriet says so. Listen, what would be so terrible if you had dinner with me this once more before I leave for Florida? Your work—whatever kind you got—will wait for you, believe me. You'll find that out for yourself when you get to be my age—which is in the seventies." I couldn't help smiling at that one. "We could go anywheres you say. Anywheres," he repeated plaintively. "And . . . umm . . . Desiree?"— I heard a sharp intake of breath now—"I'll even pay."

I want you to know that after listening to that recording, there was a moment when I actually considered spending a little time with Pop again—and in public, no less. I mean, to offer to pick up the tab, well, God knows why, but he had to be practically desperate for my company. And he *was* an old man. And he *wasn't* what you could call a bad person. Not really. Besides, before long he'd be off for Miami—and out of my hair for months.

Then it all came rushing back to me: his whining. His pettiness. His outrageous remarks. His even more outrageous behavior.

Have you completely lost your mind? What are you, some kind of masochist? I demanded of myself. *Why not take the easy way out, and just jump off a bridge or something?*

The generous impulse evaporated in an instant.

It was close to nine o'clock when I heard from Ellen.

"Are we on for Wednesday—I hope?"

"Wednesday?" I parroted.

"You forgot, didn't you?" she accused. "Wednesday's the day we were going to start shopping for your dress."

"Oh, Ellen, I'm afraid I won't be able to make it." (Notice there was no acknowledgment that our tentative plans had flown out of my head.) "But there's absolutely no reason for you to be concerned. We have plenty of time to look around."

Now, since Mike—her fiancé—had entered her life, my niece had become much less of a worrywart than she once was. Lately, though, with THE BIG DAY looming in front of her, the old Ellen had begun to resurface. After all, this was May, and the wedding wasn't until December, for crying out loud. Yet here she was, already getting *agita* over my gown. Still, maybe this was only natural—with me being the matron of honor, I mean.

"I don't want you to have to settle. And the longer you wait, the more likely that is," she said stubbornly.

Okay. If it would make her feel better, I'd start schlepping around to the stores early. "We'll do it soon," I told her. "Honest." And now, to move her off my attire, I quickly brought up Ellen's favorite topic: her intended. I made the mistake, however, of asking how he was doing at the hospital.

It took a good five minutes for her to relate how all his patients and every one of his coworkers at St. Gregory's *adored* Mike, offering up a whole slew of anecdotes to drive home the message. And then, her voice filled with more pride than ever, she reported that Dr. Beaver, who was sort of Mike's mentor—as well as St. Gregory's top cardiovascular surgeon—had just yesterday lavishly praised both her fiancé's technical and people skills. She appeared to have memorized the extensive comments verbatim, too, which she was delighted to share with me.

I was in the process of nodding off when Ellen finally ran out of Mike material. She switched over to the Lander investigation without so much as a pause. "What's been happening with your new client?"

My brain must have left on vacation, because, foolishly, I started to fill her in. When I got to the part about John's latest close call, she interrupted with a shriek, "I *told* you!"

"What did you tell me?"

"How dangerous this case was."

Well, as you know, I'm not above employing a little white lie now and then if it's to accomplish something worthwhile—like putting a loved one's mind at ease, for instance. So as I had when Ellen and I talked about that first attempt to do away with my client, I presented her with a more palatable version of this latest incident, too. "Listen, Ellen, John could have been mistaken about the driver's aiming for him. Maybe whoever was behind the wheel simply lost control of the car."

I might as well not have spoken.

"You've got to be *extremely* careful, Aunt Dez. Promise me."

Oh, we're starting that again. I pounded my forehead a few times before obliging. "I promise."

"All right, then. And incidentally, you don't really believe that—about John's being mistaken—do you?" Ellen demanded.

"I certainly consider it a possibility."

"If that's so," she countered, "I should be the private investigator in the family, not you."

Well, so much for trying to spare her.

The phone was barely back in its cradle when John called.

"The police were just here—that Sergeant Fielding and his partner. They had a search warrant. The two of them tore apart everything that wasn't nailed down—and some of the things that were. But don't ask me what they were looking for—they weren't exactly communicative. Listen, you don't . . . you don't think this means they're about to arrest me, do you?"

"No, it doesn't necessarily mean that at all. I'm meeting with Sergeant Fielding on Wednesday, though, and I'll see what I can find out." And now, sounding exactly like an Ellen clone, I said, "In the meantime, swear to me you're looking out for yourself."

"Believe me, since Saturday I'm practically on red alert."

I could only hope this was the truth—and that his vigilance would be enough.

Chapter 15

The "Hi, Dez," with which Jackie welcomed me on Tuesday morning was subdued, almost shy, in fact. "I love that dress," she said of this two-piece blue linen I'd worn to the office at least half a dozen times—and for which she had never before professed any particular affection.

Now, when Jackie has to stretch like that to deliver a compliment, it's her version of burying the hatchet. So it was safe to assume we were friends once more.

A short while later, back in my cubbyhole, I was just beginning to transcribe the remainder of my notes when I heard a subdued little cough.

"Umm, do you think you could spare me a couple of minutes?" Jackie inquired tentatively on getting my attention. She was hovering in the doorway.

"Sure." Turning back to my computer, I clicked on the screen saver, then swiveled in her direction. She was still hovering in the doorway.

"Listen, I could stop by again if this isn't convenient."

Was this really Jackie? *My* Jackie? "Don't be silly. Come in and sit down, for heaven's sake."

"Thanks." She took the few steps required to reach the single available seat. "I'm sorry," she murmured as soon as she deposited herself in it. "The way I acted yesterday? Well, it had nothing to do with you."

And in a whisper: "Nothing at all." Following which she covered her eyes and burst into tears.

Jumping up, I rushed over and knelt beside her chair. "What is it, Jackie?"

She shook her head in response.

I placed my hand on her arm and gave it a squeeze, mostly because I didn't know what else to do. I'm absolutely pathetic when it comes to that sort of thing.

In a minute or so the sobs were reduced to snuffles. I continued to crouch there in acute discomfort (but after all, my good friend was in crisis), as Jackie dug into her skirt pocket and, extracting a handful of tissues, pressed them into service. "I apologize, Dez," she murmured, managing a small, wan smile. "I didn't mean to drown you. I thought I was all cried out by now."

"Please, Jackie. Tell me what's wrong."

"It's about—Derwin." She ran her fingers through her short blondish-brown hair, and her lower lip trembled ever so slightly. "I think we may be finished."

Oh, God! Of course, over the years Jackie and Derwin had had their little spats (some of them not really so little), but never had any of them shaken her up like this. "What's happened?" I forced myself to ask.

"Before I go into that, I think it might be wise for you to try standing up."

Good idea. But easier said than done. I mean, hoisting myself to my feet was no walk in the park, even with Jackie lending assistance. During this brief but laborious struggle, it crossed my mind that maybe I should enroll in an exercise class one of these days. But once I was settled in my chair again, I concluded that there was no need to overreact. After all, how often did I find myself in that position anyway?

"He's seeing someone else," Jackie began, grabbing a handful of skirt fabric and twisting it as she spoke.

"You're certain of this?"

She nodded.

"How do you know?"

"Last Thursday we met for lunch. I got to the restaurant ten minutes early, but Derwin was already
seated at the table when I arrived. He didn't see me
walk in because he was facing the front entrance, and
I came in through the side door—I'd taken a shortcut
through the bar. Anyhow, I crept up behind him, and
I was just about to put my hands over his eyes when
I realized he was talking on his cell phone. He—"

"Derwin has a cell phone?" It just popped out. I
mean, you have no idea how out of character it is for
Adam and Eve's most tightfisted descendant to spring
for something so . . . so *nonessential.*

Jackie frowned. But whether her irritation stemmed
from my interrupting her narrative or whether she
(correctly, I suppose) interpreted my outburst to imply
some criticism of Derwin, I wasn't certain.

"I'm really sorry, Jackie," I put in hastily. "That
kind of surprised me, though. I didn't realize Derwin
was into any of that tech-y stuff."

"One of his nieces gave him the phone for his birthday," she informed me brusquely. "But as I started to
tell you, I stood there waiting for him to finish the
conversation. I heard him say, 'Fine. I'll see you tomorrow, Gale.' And then this Gale must have made
some comment because Derwin said, 'I'm looking forward to it, too, Gale.' Evidently the woman threw in
a couple of more words, because after that he chuckled—it was that insipid sort of chuckle men use when
they're trying to impress some little chippy."

I knew exactly what she meant.

"They think it makes them sound sexy. It makes
them sound idiotic, if you ask me," Jackie huffed.

"Have you considered that this Gale could be an
old friend?—a platonic friend, I'm talking about."

"I think Derwin would have mentioned that to me.
He probably would have said something like, 'You'll
never guess who I just spoke to.' But forget that he

didn't. Forget his actual words to the woman even. His voice was strange. I don't know, kind of secretive—I really can't explain it. Also, the entire time he was on the phone he was staring at that front door—keeping an eye out for me, I'm sure."

"What was his reaction when you confronted him—or didn't you?"

"No, I didn't. As soon as he hung up I retraced my steps and went back out through the bar. Then I reentered the restaurant through the front door. The truth is, the thing that was uppermost in my mind that afternoon was concealing from Derwin that I'd overheard the conversation. I was just so afraid of precipitating anything—can you believe it?"

"How did he behave toward you during lunch—any differently?"

"Not really. But that meal was sheer hell for me. I had to act as if there was nothing wrong—either that or have it out with him. Which I wasn't up to dealing with. I assure you, though, that if it wasn't for two-and-a-half good-sized glasses of merlot, I never could have managed to keep up the pretense."

"Listen, Jackie, it's quite possible you misinterpreted what you heard and that there's an acceptable explanation for it."

"I have more to tell you."

"Oh." What else could I say? I mean, so far things were not good, and I had no doubt they were about to get worse.

"On Saturday—this past Saturday—Derwin was over at the apartment. We'd made plans to spend the day together earlier in the week, and while I wasn't looking forward to having him there, I didn't want to cancel, either. I think I may have been hoping he'd say something about that phone call—something that would convince me I was mistaken in my suspicions. The subject never came up.

"At any rate, around one o'clock I went out to the

store to pick up some groceries. But almost immediately I remembered that I'd left my wallet in my other bag, and, of course, I had to go back for it. Well, Derwin was in the living room when I came in, and apparently he hadn't heard me, because he was dialing the phone. The instant he saw me he hung up—and turned beet red. If ever guilt was written on a man's face, Desiree, this was it. Anyhow, he had this piece of paper in his lap, and he quickly shoved it into his wallet."

There was something in the way Jackie related this last bit of information that led me to believe I had not heard the end of that piece of paper.

"And?" I prompted.

Shifting in her chair, Jackie stopped wringing the bejesus out of her skirt now. "And when Derwin was in the shower that night, I took the paper out of his wallet." It was obvious I was expected to disapprove of such a sneaky maneuver, since she wasted no time in defending it. "I was so upset by then that I *had* to do it. Don't you understand?"

"The thing I don't understand is how you were able to contain yourself all those hours."

She flashed me a grateful smile. "I copied down what was written on it." And reaching into her skirt pocket—the one without the tissue supply—Jackie handed me a slip of paper. "Gale," it said. And right below this was a Manhattan phone number.

"Have you tried the number?" I asked.

"Not yet; I'm afraid to. I want to know what's going on, but I don't—if you take my meaning. Do you think I *should* call?"

"I think you should let me see what I can find out."

Jackie's face mirrored her relief. "You have no idea how much I wanted you to make that offer. I'd like you to hold off for a while, though, if you don't mind. I'm not too sure I'm prepared yet for whatever it is you could learn. Okay?"

"Of course. Just say when."

"I will." Getting to her feet, Jackie thanked me—ad infinitum—after which she left the office. She must have made it at least halfway down the hall, too. But seconds later I looked up to see her in the doorway.

"When," she said.

Chapter 16

I stared down at the paper in front of me for a long while, reluctant to dial the number that could expose the truth.

Did I really think there might be an explanation for those phone calls of Derwin's?—other than the obvious one, I mean.

Let's just say I wasn't optimistic.

Still, there was a chance—although, granted, a tiny one—that the man *wasn't* playing house with some floozy. (I regarded anyone with the gall to steal Jackie's sweetie as an out-and-out floozy.)

At any rate, after frittering away another few minutes, I willed myself to act. I had to get to the bottom of this. No matter what.

My fingers were crossed when I lifted the receiver.

A woman—a mature woman, judging by the voice—answered the telephone and announced that this was Naturally Yours something-or-other. The recitation was so quick that I didn't catch it all.

"Umm, is Gale there?"

She sounded rather perturbed with this familiarity. "*Dr.* Wright won't be in until later today."

How do you like that! It was a real stretch, attempting to imagine that cheapskate landing himself a doctor. And even if she wasn't a *doctor* doctor— which I was willing to bet she wasn't—well, anyway, my poor Jackie.

"When would you suggest I try to reach her?"

"Around three."

"I'll—"

"Wait a second. Who did you say you wanted to talk to?"

"Dr. Gale Wright." This telephone person certainly didn't have much of an attention span, did she?

"Dr. Wright is a *he*."

"*Gale* Wright?"

"Listen," the woman snapped—she managed to bite back the "stupid," which you could tell took some doing—"didn't you ever watch that old Lucille Ball series where the boss was played by Gale Gordon? I'm referring to the *actor* Gale Gordon."

I made the admission timidly. "Uh, yes, now that you mention it, it . . . uh . . . sounds familiar." Well, this information opened up a second disturbing possibility. Derwin could be bisexual. Or maybe not even bi. Maybe he decided that at this stage of his life it was time he followed his true leanings. My poor, *poor* Jackie!

And then it occurred to me: Perhaps Derwin had been speaking to Dr. Wright on some medical matter. "By the way, what exactly is the name of your company? I want to write it down in my address book."

"Naturally Yours Hair Replacements," I was apprised in a tone that gave me frostbite.

I'll be damned! And also hallelujah! "There's something else I—"

"One moment," the woman said curtly. "I have another call."

It was obvious this lady regarded me as a very large pain in the lower part of her anatomy. And I was a little suspicious that she might accidentally cut me off—on purpose, of course. I actually felt a little guilty when she got back on the line.

"What more did you want to know, madam?"

"Umm, I don't suppose my friend Derwin Snyder would happen to be there now."

"There is no Derwin Snyder employed here."

"Oh, you misunderstand me. Mr. Snyder is a customer—he's the one who recommended Dr. Wright to me. The reason I'm asking is that I've been trying to contact Mr. Snyder for the past two days, and it's quite important. I hate to bother you, but I'd really appreciate it if you could check and see if he has an appointment today."

The telephone person clicked off without a word, and again I had no idea whether she'd hung up or merely put me on hold. But she made a fast return. "Mr. Snyder's appointment isn't until later in the week. And just for your information, at Naturally Yours we do not refer to our clients as customers."

And now there was no doubt what the click signified.

I had to stop myself from running out to Jackie and screaming the wonderful news. But, after all, these *were* professional offices. I settled for buzzing her.

"Jackie?"

"You've found out already," she anticipated, her attitude anything but upbeat.

"Yup. And it's cause to celebrate!"

"I'll be there in two seconds." She was, too. Or pretty close to it, anyhow.

She strode in, beaming. "Tell me," she demanded, leaning so far across my desk that we were almost rubbing noses.

"Sit down, why don't you?"

"I can't. I'm too keyed up."

"This Gale that you practically had Derwin running off to the South Seas with? It so happens she's a he. A Dr. Gale Wright. And, no, Derwin was not attempting to seduce the man—in spite of that 'funny' voice and those insincere little chuckles you thought you heard."

"Gale Wright," Jackie mused, her forehead pleated in concentration. "Gale Wright. I know that name . . . Of course!" The forehead smoothed out. "Gale used to be Derwin's next-door neighbor. He has some kind of hair-replacement facility." Her face was barely large enough to accommodate the grin that followed.

"Naturally Yours Hair Replacements. That's the place your much-maligned guy's been calling. He evidently wants to surprise you with a new, improved Derwin."

Jackie straightened up now, although her palms remained flat on the desktop. "I can hardly believe it. That must mean he's getting a transplant."

"Could be. Although they may also do hairpieces there." This seemed far more likely, considering Derwin's—I'll be kind for once and call it "frugal"—nature. I mean, while a good hairpiece isn't cheap, it's certainly a lot less costly than a surgical procedure.

"I'd settle for one of those. A decent-looking one."

I choked back a guffaw. Derwin happens to be the proud owner of a thick silver mop—the instant he dons the world's most obvious toupee, that is. Yet in spite of this, Jackie's been known to brag about his great head of hair. I never could figure that one out. It has to do with love or loyalty or something, I suppose.

"I'd better go back to work, Dez," she said then. "But I can't thank you enough for this. You're a whiz, do you know that?"

Modesty induced me to protest. "All I did was make a phone call."

"Never mind. You saved my sanity, that's what you did. A hug before I get out of here?"

I stood up obediently and went around the desk, and Jackie—who's a pretty fair-sized woman—threw both arms around me and squeezed. I guess she put something extra into that squeeze to demonstrate her gratitude. But anyhow, she knocked the wind out of me.

Another example of no good deed going unpunished.

Chapter 17

David showed up at my office at just after six.

Most likely reflective of today's unseasonable ninety-degree temperature, his suit jacket was slung over his shoulder. Also, his shirt was plastered against him, and the top two buttons were open, his tie peeking out of his jacket pocket. Even the broad shoulders seemed to droop. He looked tired and disheveled—and every bit as handsome as I remembered. I mean, the suit *was* navy and the shirt light blue. And, no question about it, blue was definitely David Hearn's color.

"How are you, Desiree?" he inquired after taking a seat. He was smiling, but he appeared nervous. Maybe I was projecting, though. After all, he should have been nervous.

"Just fine, David. And you?"

He continued to smile. "Curious. Has something happened that I should know about?"

"Actually, I wanted to see you regarding a couple of matters you're already familiar with. But first let me get something else out of the way. Would you mind telling me where you were on Saturday at around twelve-thirty?"

"I was home, working on a brief. But if that requires verification, I don't have any. Why do you ask, anyway? The police haven't even been around about that one."

"I'm afraid I can't say any more just yet, but I'll be able to fill you in soon. What we should discuss right now is that gambling debt you neglected to mention."

"What gambling debt?"

I sincerely hoped for his sake that David's game wasn't poker. Involuntarily—I'm sure—he had clenched his hands into fists, and this vein at his left temple was bulging.

"Look, I know you owe a substantial amount of money and that you're being pressured to pay up."

"Wrong," David shot back. "I did owe the money. Repeat: *did.* A friend lent me the cash I needed to get those people off my back. But my being in financial straits weeks ago has nothing at all to do with either Edward's death or the attack on John. And if that was your reason for summoning me here, I have to tell you that I resent it."

"I can't understand why you didn't level with me."

"Because, Desiree—and I don't want to be rude— my gambling losses aren't any of your business. As I said, they're totally unrelated to your investigation." And now the David I'd previously responded to so favorably put in a brief, transitory appearance. "Besides," he said, grinning, "why should I provide anyone with the kind of information that would make me a prime suspect? I may be my mother's dumbest son, but I'm her smartest, too."

"Umm, you also led me to believe you didn't care too much for Shawna Riley. In fact, as I recall, you had some pretty uncomplimentary things to say about her."

The mention of his lady love seemed to temporarily mute him; it was a good four or five seconds before David made his unconvincing assertion. "I have no idea what you're talking about."

"Come now. I understand the two of you have become a couple."

"That's absolutely false."

"I have statements from three people attesting that they've seen you together acting . . . extremely chummy."

"They were mistaken. Or else they lied."

Well, nothing ventured . . .

"You're being very foolish," I lectured. "How long before the police learn about you and Shawna—if they haven't found out about it already?"

"Even if we *are* seeing each other—which we're not—how does that connect to the assaults on Edward and John?"

"You can't be that naive, David, and I'd like to think you don't regard me as being that stupid. After all, who has a better motive for disposing of those two men than the person or persons next in line to inherit from Uncle Victor? Right now that would be Shawna and Scott. But if you and Shawna should marry, you'd join them at the top of the list."

"I would, wouldn't I?—*if* there were anything between Shawna and me."

I pretended he hadn't spoken. "You'd no doubt be the odds-on favorite, too, considering that you're so much in debt. I'm assuming your friend expects to be repaid."

"Yes, of course, but he insists that I hold off until my finances improve."

"I don't imagine you can depend on those homicide detectives taking this into account, though. So it's no wonder that you wanted to keep the relationship a secret. Tell me, whose idea was it originally—Shawna's?"

"We b—" David stopped cold. There was no humor in the brief laugh that followed. "Christ! I was never any good at this kind of thing—this cat-and-mouse stuff." *You can say that again!* "Anyhow," he added philosophically, "the truth was bound to come out sooner or later."

"So it was a joint decision to conceal your involvement?"

David nodded. "We both recognize that I'm in a pretty vulnerable position. Even if the police should accept that my friend isn't pressing me for the money, they might still peg me as some sort of compulsive gambler. Particularly if they're aware of my dad's track record—no pun intended, by the way—which is very likely the case. They'd be wrong, however. I haven't so much as bought a lottery ticket since I got myself into that bind."

"I'm glad to hear that. I hope it continues."

"It will. You can take my word for it. Uh, Desiree? You're not going to repeat our conversation to the authorities, are you? I'm not quite ready yet to deal with all of this on an official level."

• "Relax. I don't see any need to supply them with this information—certainly not at the present time. Naturally, there's always the chance that a situation could crop up that would compel me to tell what I know. But I don't anticipate anything like that. I should warn you, though, that the investigating detectives may already be one step ahead of me."

"Yeah, well, maybe not. Maybe I'll luck out long enough for them to catch the real killer." And then David looked at me intently. "You can appreciate now why I felt that I had to keep quiet about those things, can't you? And they honestly *don't* have anything to do with your investigation."

I had to concede that in his shoes I'd almost certainly have behaved in the same way. "I not only can appreciate it, but if I want to be fair—and, what the hell, I may as well be—I probably don't blame you."

Mumbling his thanks, David started to rise. "If there's nothing else . . ."

"I think that pretty much covers it."

He headed for the door, then spun around. "As

long as I've suddenly become swept up in this great blaze of truth, I can make a couple of admissions to you that I couldn't before, admissions that are actually exculpatory, for a change." Apparently slightly embarrassed, he grinned. "Oops, that was the attorney in me coming out. At any rate, last Monday, when someone took that shot at John, I wasn't home alone watching Letterman as I claimed. I was at Shawna's; I spent the night there. I can also provide you with an alibi for Saturday afternoon at this point—for whatever reason I need one. Shawna was at my place on Saturday—she came over at just past noon. We had something to eat at the apartment, and she spent the remainder of the day in the living room reading, while I was closeted in the bedroom with that brief."

Which alibis, of course, were every bit as reliable as the one Shawna shared with her brother.

Chapter 18

After David Hearn left the office I recognized that I was probably in a worse position now than I'd been in before—as far as narrowing the list of suspects, I'm talking about. After all, David's involvement with Shawna put him a step closer to Uncle Victor's assets, moving him up a notch to tie the twins for the role of most likely perpetrator. What's more, like them, he didn't have an alibi worth a damn for any of the crucial times.

I felt as if I were moving backwards. I mean, by now I should have been able to *eliminate* someone, for God's sake!

Before going up to the apartment, I paid a visit to my neighborhood D'Agostino's. I was tired, so I restricted my purchases to the essentials. Your definition of "essentials," however, may vary slightly from mine. For example, I have always considered appropriate for this category such foodstuffs as Sara Lee cheesecake, pistachio nuts, and, of course, Häagen-Dazs macadamia brittle. Which is not to say I didn't also pick up a number of other edibles that evening, along with paper goods and cleaning supplies.

When I got home—surprise!—a message from Pop was waiting for me. As soon as I'd established it was that impossible little man—which took all of a milli-second—I put my fingers in my ears. The purpose of this being as much to guard against a weakening in my resolve to steer clear of him as it was to muffle that whiny voice.

Anyway, once Pop was through with his pitch, I began to think seriously about supper. I was too hungry to wait for the D'Agostino order to be delivered, so I decided to throw a few things together.

There were enough ingredients around—but barely—to fix myself a salad, which I'd be having with my old standby, a refrigerator omelet. This name, courtesy of Ellen, reflecting the fact that the omelet contains practically every morsel that's in the refrigerator at the time of its conception. Tonight's choices were especially meager. The best I could come up with were some leftover ham that it's likely should have seen the inside of a garbage can days ago, a small piece of semislimy red pepper, and a chunk of extra-sharp cheddar cheese that, if eaten in its present solid state, could easily have broken a tooth or two.

Believe it or not, though, the finished product didn't taste half-bad. But the real test would be whether I woke up the next morning.

I'm pleased to report that I made it through the night. I was, therefore, able to show up at the Twelfth Precinct for my eight-thirty meeting with Tim Fielding.

I entered the arena armed with two cups of coffee and half a dozen donuts—four of them with chocolate icing and walnut sprinkles.

Tim got to his feet when I approached his desk, which was in the middle of a large, dingy room bustling with activity. He greeted me with an expression that bordered on a smile, following which he patted me lightly on the back a couple of times. "Well, well, if it isn't Desiree Shapiro. I thought maybe I should have asked you to put a rose between your teeth so I'd recognize you. But you look the same."

He looked the same, too. (Had it really been close

to a year ago?) There still didn't appear to be an ounce of extra fat on the short, muscular body. And Fielding's wiry, close-cropped salt-and-pepper hair remained more pepper than salt. I quickly placed the bag of goodies on his desk and gave him a nice, warm hug.

"Cut it out," he told me with feigned severity. "I'm a happily married man—most of the time, anyhow." Then with an exaggerated sigh: "Well, as long as you're here, you may as well sit." He indicated the wooden chair alongside his desk.

Taking the suggestion, I plunked myself down, and he followed suit. But before I had the chance to say boo, someone horned in. "Hey, Tim."

The man at the desk directly in front of Fielding's was calling out over his shoulder. "I was wondering," the fellow said as he turned toward us, "if—" On noting my presence, he stopped abruptly. "Excuse me, ma'am," he murmured.

Now, the guy was occupying Detective Walter Corcoran's chair in Detective Walter Corcoran's space. But unless my eyes and ears were simultaneously playing tricks on me, this was not Fielding's longtime partner.

"Hold it a minute, Norm," Fielding instructed, as the policeman started to swivel around in his seat again. "I'd like you to meet Desiree Shapiro, an old buddy—although old nemesis would probably be more accurate. Dez, this is my new partner, Detective Norm Melnick."

Norm got up and came over to shake my hand. He was young—not much more than thirty, I estimated—and medium-tall, with light hair and clean-cut, boyish good looks. "A pleasure to meet you, Ms. Shapiro."

No, I reassured myself, *this was most definitely not Walter Corcoran.*

"Call me Desiree. Please. And it's nice to meet you, too."

"Desiree's a PI," Fielding elaborated, "and you have to watch out for her. Someday she's liable to come here with coffee and *your* favorite kind of donut. And while she's plying you with sugar and calories, she's going to worm whatever she can out of you. And she's good at it, too. So my advice is, if she ever puts one of these on your desk"—Fielding tapped the paper bag—"beat it into the men's room and don't come out until you're sure she's gone."

"I'm partial to Krispy Kremes, the glazed kind—and without the jelly," Melnick apprised me. And laughing softly, he returned to his desk.

Well, regardless of his initially addressing me as ma'am (which, just as soon as I could check myself out in a mirror, would have me counting my wrinkles), Norm Melnick was certainly an improvement over his predecessor. And I told Tim so.

"Don't give me that." He dug into the goody bag and pulled out the Styrofoam cup with the "B" on the lid. After which he reached in again to extract a donut. "I've always known you harbored a secret crush on Walt," he teased.

"Geez, Tim, I was positive I had you fooled." I got up then and carried the bag over to Melnick. "There aren't any Krispy Kremes," I apologized, "but I'll keep your preference in mind for next time. Meanwhile, have one of these." Melnick settled for the strawberry, which was my choice, too. Being he was the *un*-Corcoran, however, I couldn't possibly begrudge it to him.

The instant I redeposited myself next to Fielding I put the burning question to him. "So tell me before curiosity does me in, what happened to Corcoran?"

"He accepted a big position in one of those private security firms—executive vice president, no less. I have his card if you're interested in getting together with him." His eyes were twinkling.

"I'd rather get together with an ax murderer," I

rejoined, before helping myself to coffee and a jelly donut.

As you've no doubt gathered, Walter Corcoran and I were friendly enemies—only without the friendly. The man really got under my skin. And apparently I was equally successful in crawling beneath his epidermis. I mean, to give you an idea, a couple of his least offensive appellations for me were "world's A-number-one pain in the ass" and "Miss Chubette," which was delivered with the appropriate sneer. I'll tell you, even the room here suddenly looked brighter now that I realized Corcoran was no longer in it.

Fielding licked some chocolate off his fingers. "Listen, I've already taken more time with you than I can spare. So why don't we get down to business, huh, Shapiro?"

"Glad to. Why do you suspect John Lander of murdering his cousin?"

"I have my reasons," he responded enigmatically.

"You've got to be aware that there are other people who also stand to benefit from Edward's death—that is, if anything should happen to my client. And somebody's already taken a couple of stabs at seeing to it John won't be breathing long enough to claim his inheritance."

"Precisely what is it that's supposed to have occurred this second time?"

I filled him in on Saturday's almost-hit-and-run.

"I don't imagine there were any witnesses to this latest incident, either."

"Well, the whole thing happened so quickly."

"Oh, I'm sure. Listen, Desiree, that guy's life is in no more danger than my aunt Tillie's." And with this declaration Fielding served himself another donut.

"Why are you so certain he made up the attacks?"

"Let's start with the critical fact that Edward Sharp stood between Lander and piles and piles of dough." He didn't pause long enough for me to voice a protest.

"Trust me, those 'attacks' are nothing more than a lame attempt to persuade us to look elsewhere for Sharp's killer."

"You can't possibly know for certain that John's lying." I was so frustrated I was almost shouting the words. "Why won't you at least *consider* that one of the other relatives in line for the money might have tried to get rid of him?"

Being at his most pigheaded just then, Fielding answered with an extremely irritating, "Because they didn't."

"I don't see how you can be so quick to discount that someone could have been bent on taking both men out of the running. I mean, once the first murder is behind you, it's not nearly as difficult to commit a second."

"No kidding. And where did you get that?"

"From Hercule Poirot."

"You and your Agatha Christie!" Fielding muttered. But for a moment a little smile played at the corners of his mouth. After which he told me soberly, "Look, don't think we just zeroed in on your client and left it at that. We questioned everyone who might have had a reason, however remote, for wanting Sharp dead. And this is in spite of our having pretty strong evidence from the very beginning that your guy was the perpetrator." He took a sip of coffee before adding, "And since then new facts have surfaced that make us more convinced than ever that John Lander did his cousin in." He folded his hands across his chest. "And that's all I intend to say."

"What's your idea of 'pretty strong evidence'?"

"You got ear trouble, Shapiro? Didn't you just hear me? The well's run dry. I'm not about to divulge any more than I already have."

Which, I didn't bother to point out, was practically zilch. But, at any rate, it seemed a pretty safe assumption that it was John's Air Force wings that had initially implicated him in Edward's death. Still, I couldn't be positive of this. It was conceivable, I supposed, that they hadn't been planted at the crime scene after all and that Fielding was referring to something quite apart from the wings. Or—and this is where the situation got tricky—it was also conceivable the killer *had* placed the pin there for the police to find, but being so small, it had simply been overlooked. In that case, of course, the last thing I wanted to do was provide my old friend with the information that would impel his return to the victim's home to search for it. I had to proceed very, very carefully now.

"Uh, this alleged evidence of yours. Would it be something of a physical nature?"

"What is this, *Twenty Questions*?" Fielding bellowed. I glanced around, expecting that everyone in the place would be staring at us. And they were. Moments later Tim was shaking his head slowly from side to side, a look akin to awe on his face. "You're some piece of work, Shapiro. Has anyone ever told you that?"

"You have. Frequently."

"Good for me. Anyway, listen very closely. You're not going to get anything more from me on the Sharp homicide. I mean zero, *nada*. And incidentally, I won't even bother to ask about the stuff you claimed *you'd* be imparting this morning."

"I've already told you about the second attack on John." I fortified myself for the retort with another bite of jelly donut.

"Yeah. And I don't know how to thank you for sharing that invaluable bit of crap."

"Umm, would you mind confirming one thing for me?"

"What?" He spat out the word.

I had just concluded that the only way of learning what Tim had on my client was to take the plunge. Or at least get my feet wet. "This . . . umm . . .

evidence you have. It's something you discovered at the scene of the crime, isn't it?"

Fielding's eyes narrowed. "Maybe."

"There's an explanation."

"Go ahead."

"I have to be sure we're speaking about the same thing."

"You want me to tell you exactly what, if anything, we turned up there before you'll commit yourself, right? Well, that ain't gonna happen." He stood then. "I hate to throw you out, Shapiro, but I'm afraid I'll have to overcome my reluctance, because that's exactly what I need to do. I've got a lot of work waiting for me."

"Give me two minutes," I pleaded, trying for my most pathetic expression. "Okay?"

Fielding sat back down. "Two minutes, that's all— and I'm not kidding. I should have 'sucker' tattooed on my butt," he grumbled.

I had no choice; I moved to the edge of the diving board. "It was a small item that you came across, an item you believe to be the property of my client. Am I correct?"

"You might be."

I jumped in the water. "Was it a pair of Air Force wings?"

"*Jee-sus!*" Fielding exploded before the grudging admission. "All right. Yes, it was."

"Well, those wings disappeared the week before Edward was shot," I explained, "when the entire family was gathered at the uncle's house." I went on to relate how they'd either fallen off or been deliberately removed from the lapel of John's jacket. "Obviously, when the killer shot Edward, he left that pin behind for you to find, don't you see?"

"That little scenario, I assume, was presented to you by your client."

"Yes. But for your enlightenment, Tim, this is a man

who hates to think ill of people; it was difficult for him even to imagine anything like that. But in light of the missing pin, along with the NYPD's attitude when he reported being shot at, he was forced to accept that someone might have done . . . well, exactly what they did."

Fielding was staring at me as if my mental faculties weren't all they should be. "You haven't so much as entertained the *possibility* that Lander could have concocted that story once he realized he might have lost the pin during the commission of the murder?"

"Absolutely not. But listen, something like this is far from conclusive anyway. Perhaps the pin wasn't even John's. I'm sure he wasn't the only one in the Air Force to earn his wings."

"The thing had his initials on it, for crying out loud!"

"Oh." It was a very quiet "oh."

"Yeah, 'oh.' And are you for real? First you go into this whole spiel about somebody's planting the incriminating item. Then when you realize that isn't cutting it, you do an instant turnaround and try to sell me on the cockamamie idea that the damn wings aren't necessarily your client's at all." He moved forward in his chair, preparatory to rising again.

I don't know why—maybe it was my way of making nice—but I leaned over and placed my hand on Fielding's arm. "If that's all you have, though . . ."

"It isn't," he said tersely. And removing the hand, he got to his feet. "We have enough so that we were able to convince a judge to issue a search warrant. And that's my last word on the subject."

Immediately thereafter he was propelling me toward the door.

Chapter 19

I wanted to strangle myself.

Before he could carry out that coerced departure, just for spite I should have reached inside that paper bag and deprived Fielding of one of the remaining chocolate-icing-with-walnut-sprinkles donuts.

No. If I really wanted to be spiteful—and I did—I should have walked off with both of those damn things.

I was ticked, *very* ticked, about Fielding's refusal to let me in on what other evidence he had against my client—besides the pin, I'm talking about. Plus, I'd intended to make some attempt to learn what he was looking for at John's apartment the other night—and whether or not he'd located it. But before I had a chance to say word one about that, my good friend had practically tossed me out into the street.

Well, I decided as I hailed the cab that would take me to the office, I should probably derive some consolation from the fact that my client was still a free man. And really, I reasoned then, did I need a better indicator than this that Fielding's search had failed to turn up what he had been hoping it would?

It wasn't long, however, before I went back to my fuming. After all, hadn't I gone to see Fielding in good faith, figuring we'd pool our information? (Yes, at that moment I actually had the chutzpah to view my pumping expedition in this light.)

Okay, have it your way, Tim, I threatened in my

head. *But just wait until I make some progress with this thing. I won't be so quick to share with you, either.*

There's nothing like having a mature, professional attitude, is there?

Jackie's greeting was unusually friendly. "Hi, Dez. How did it go?" she inquired, all smiles. "I hope you had a successful meeting with what's-his-name—Fielding."

"Not very," I groused. "He was kind enough to let me know that I had more to worry about than I figured. But the reason for this, he didn't deign to inform me."

"The bastard," Jackie muttered sympathetically. "Maybe he's only trying to get your goat, though."

"I wish I thought so—but I don't."

"All right. But if New York's Finest could manage to uncover anything that important, you will, too." I was still grinning at the way her upper lip curled as she uttered the words "New York's Finest," when she concluded with "And what's more, unlike those dunderheads, you'll put the correct interpretation on whatever it is."

Well, this was a real departure for Jackie, who's usually quite supportive of the NYPD. Even with regard to those incidents where the cops were found to have employed excessive force, she never once, to my recollection, made a blanket indictment of the entire police department; she always restricted her criticisms to the specific individuals involved. But apparently now that she considered herself in my debt, Jackie wanted to leave no doubt that she was 110 percent in my corner.

"Anyway, forget about the investigation for a couple of hours, will you?" she ordered. "I'm taking you someplace special for lunch today—and don't give me any of that garbage about not being able to spare the time away from your notes."

"Oh, Jackie. That's not necessary. I didn't really do anything yesterday, honestly. I simply dialed the phone and behaved in my normal abnormally nosy manner. You certainly don't have to reward me for acting like myself."

"Maybe not, but I want to. So stop giving me a hard time." There was a note of finality in her tone.

I realized then that I'd neglected to advise Jackie of this afternoon's meeting with Trudie Lander, an oversight that before my Derwin revelations would definitely have earned me a demerit or two. "I, uh, just remembered," I confessed. "I have a two-thirty appointment in Greenwich Village with Mrs. Lander."

"Don't worry about it," said the new and improved (if only temporarily) Jackie. "I know you've been up to your ears lately. But I suppose we should postpone lunch—we'd feel too rushed. Come to think of it, though, it's probably better that you're tied up. I'd prefer dinner, anyway, wouldn't you?" Clearly, no answer was expected, because she went right on. "If you're not free tonight, we'll do it as soon as you can make it. Have you ever been to the Union Square Cafe?" she asked, referring to a restaurant downtown that's consistently rated one of the most popular in Manhattan—often *the* most popular.

This time she waited for a response. "No, I haven't. But are you crazy? It's too expensive. If you're that set on being Lady Bountiful, there's a nice little trattoria in my neighborhood that—"

"If I wanted to eat at some nice little neighborhood trattoria, I wouldn't need you for an excuse. Listen, Dez, Derwin and I usually go to places that aren't . . . that is . . . umm . . . well, I have to admit that when it comes to money, Derwin *is* on the conservative side." (I wouldn't have phrased it quite that way. I mean Mr. Big Spender isn't too keen on patronizing any restaurant where you don't have to carry your own tray.) "What I'm saying—and, honest to God, it's the truth—" Jackie insisted, "is that I've been wanting to have dinner there for ages, and you'd be doing me a favor by supplying me with a reason for a little self-indulgence."

I'd have liked to suggest that we go Dutch, but I knew Jackie would veto that instantly. She seemed determined to pick up the tab for this. So being the considerate type, I decided to make her happy—even if in the process I had to subject myself to what promised to be a very good meal.

"So?" she demanded. "When can you make it?"

It wasn't necessary to check my social calendar in order to inform her that my availability wasn't likely to present a problem. "But I understand they're booked way in advance," I pointed out, "so I wouldn't count on our getting a reservation anytime soon."

Jackie was unperturbed. "My cousin Alma's stepdaughter works there. I'll just give her a ring, and we'll see what she can do."

The instant I made contact with my desk chair I dialed John's office.

He picked up on the second ring. "Can I get back to you in five minutes, Desiree?" I got the impression he was slightly frantic.

Actually, it was eight minutes before I heard from him. But eight was close enough.

"Sorry I couldn't talk to you before. I was on the telephone with a client, and I had someone else holding on the other line."

"No apology necessary. I could tell you were busy."

"It's only that my secretary's been out sick for a few days, and I'm handling the phones. An unfortunate situation. So far this week I've lost three calls. No doubt they were all from people looking to buy multimillion-dollar properties." The harsh, clipped sound that followed came out like "heh" and must have been intended as a laugh, albeit an ironic one.

Then John said anxiously, "You've had your meeting with Fielding?"

"Yes, early this morning," I responded in a voice that must have reflected my dejection.

"It didn't go particularly well, I gather."

"No, it didn't."

"How bad does it look?"

"It . . . uh . . . isn't really terrible."

"They found my wings, didn't they?" John put to me hesitantly.

"Unfortunately, they did."

"I suppose you told Fielding they'd been missing for more than a week prior to the murder."

"Of course."

"But he didn't believe you."

"I couldn't convince him. I'll keep on trying, though. Listen, John, I'm sorry, but I wasn't able to learn anything about that search warrant. Are you positive you have no idea what the police could have been hunting for?"

"None."

Actually, I was reasonably certain I knew the answer to this myself. In all probability they were attempting to track down the gun they believed my client had used to kill his cousin and then employed to set up a fake attempt on his own life.

I shared this theory with John, who muttered, "I've been really stupid, haven't I? Knowing how they think, I should have figured that was it."

"I have to ask you something else. Sergeant Fielding claims to have additional evidence of some sort against you. Is there anything you've been keeping from me?—it's crucial that you be honest with me."

"I can appreciate that. But I don't have a clue what he's referring to."

I had no cause to doubt the denial. And I was both relieved and disappointed by it. The "relieved" due to the fact that having a client who levels with you makes it a helluva lot easier to do your job. (The reason for the "disappointed" is, I'm certain, evident.)

"Before I forget," John brought up then, "Trudie tells me you're seeing her for coffee later. What's that about, Desiree?"

Now, this was not a subject I was particularly comfortable with. But he did deserve an explanation. So I told him as succinctly as possible that I needed information from his wife regarding her will and why I felt this could help us.

"Oh" was John's only response.

"And John? I hope you're being—"

"You don't even have to say it. I'm being careful. That *is* what's on your mind, isn't it?"

"Yes, it is."

"Trust me, you have nothing to be concerned about on that score. If anything, I'm overly cautious." And a split second later: "Well, I guess it's time I got back to earning a living."

I wasn't about to let him go yet. I was determined that the conversation end on a more encouraging note. "Look, about my visit to the precinct this morning— I've just given you the bad news so far. But there's a brighter side, too: If Fielding et al. had any really *hard* evidence against you, you'd be talking to me from behind bars right this minute."

Somehow John managed a chuckle. "I'll try to keep reminding myself of that."

Chapter 20

The first thing I thought when Trudie Lander strode confidently into the coffee shop was that she belonged on the pages of a fashion magazine.

Her makeup looked as if it had been applied by a professional. Her tawny shoulder-length hair had the kind of casual, almost careless appearance that it takes real effort to achieve. She was dressed in a cream-colored vee-neck silk blouse, with pearls that matched the blouse exactly, and crisp, beige linen pants. Now, I don't know anyone else—particularly on a day as humid as this one—whose linen slacks, after about five minutes of wear, don't end up as wrinkled as a shar-pei. But I have a feeling Trudie Lander's slacks wouldn't dare get creased.

"How are you, Ms. Shapiro?" she inquired as if by rote when she joined me at the table.

Well, although I had no illusions about her interest in the state of my health, I, nevertheless, felt obligated to answer. "I'm fine, Mrs. Lander." (I don't know; the woman just didn't seem like a *Ms.* to me.) "How are you? And I do wish you'd call me Desiree."

Her response as she was taking a seat was a perfunctory. "I'm fine, too." A moment later she announced, "I'm going to have coffee and a toasted English. And you?" She was already crooking her finger at a nearby waiter, who hustled over just as I got out, "Coffee and a toasted English sounds good to me, too."

The waiter had no sooner walked away when a balding little man with a giant-size Adam's apple approached us. I took him to be the owner of the establishment. "It's nice to see you, Ms. Lander."

"It's nice to see you, too, Raoul." From her constipated expression, however, I had little doubt that she resented the intrusion.

"Mr. Lander—he is well?"

"Yes, thank you." She practically hissed it.

"A terrible tragedy about Mr. Sharp. Please tell Mr. Lander how very sorry I am about the loss of his friend."

"I will." Trudie turned her head toward me in an obvious gesture of dismissal, following which Raoul took the hint and scurried off. And now she apparently felt the need to explain even this limited a familiarity with someone she considered not that worthy of her attention. "My husband and I have been coming here on occasion since we moved to the Village in 1991, Ms. Shapiro—it's as good a place as any when all you want is a light bite." She began to fidget with her place mat. "This is also one of the coffee shops where John and Edward used to meet for their weekly breakfasts. I did mention the breakfasts, didn't I? At any rate, they'd been getting together regularly like that for five or six years, I'd say—except for the time Edward canceled because his daughter Eugenie had given birth the night before and then a few months later when Edward's dog died. Although why a grown man—an *adult*—would carry on about that is hard for me to understand. The animal was over seventeen years old, for pity's sake. Anyway, they always ate in this neighborhood because Edward works—that is, worked—in the area, and, of course, it was convenient for John, as well."

Suddenly she was regarding me intently. "John and Edward were extremely fond of each other—John was almost inconsolable when he found out that his cousin was dead. Yet those two incompetents the police have assigned to this case think *he's* the person responsible. Evidently because they're too dense to come up with the real culprit."

Well, another day I would have leapt to Fielding's defense. But not today. "Eventually the truth will come out. I—"

Trudie cut me off with a wave of the hand. "All right. Why did you want to see me?" she demanded. "Have you found out who tried to kill my husband?"

"Not yet. But I intend to. Actually, I wanted to talk to you because I'm hoping you'll be willing to provide me with certain information. Information that could help convince the police that they've targeted the wrong man for Edward's murder."

"They suspected John right from the beginning, you know. They even believe he fabricated that report he made about being shot at." And then her face conveying total disgust, Trudie mumbled under her breath, "The morons."

"That's why I have to ask you what's really a very personal question." I waited for permission.

"Go ahead," she said tersely.

"The principal reason the police appear to be so convinced of your husband's guilt is because he's the only one who benefits directly from Edward's being out of the picture." Noting that she was about to object to this, I continued in such a rush that I stumbled over the words. "I had a long visit with Sergeant Fielding this morning. And believe me, I tried to impress upon him that they can't afford to overlook the possibility that one of the others in line for the money is set on removing any obstacles that stand between him or her and Uncle Victor's estate. But I think it might support my argument on John's behalf if I knew something about his financial situation."

"I don't want to be rude, but didn't it ever occur to you to find this out from John?"

"Well . . . uh . . . what I'm interested in specifically is your will." God, this was awkward!

"I don't understand."

"I'd like to . . . that is, it might bolster my position if I could . . . umm . . . point out that John stands to inherit a considerable amount of money from his own wife. If that's true, I mean."

"Am I following this? Are you saying that if you can establish that I'm leaving a tidy sum to John, you could make the case that he would just as soon wait around until I expire?"

I prayed hard—and in vain—for the ground to open up and swallow me. Luckily the waiter returned with our food at this moment, affording me the opportunity to collect myself a bit. Succeeding somehow in ignoring Trudie (who was expressing her impatience by drumming on the tabletop), I stalled as long as I could, nibbling on my muffin, then following this with a few sips of coffee and another nibble or two of muffin. But at last she was no longer able to contain herself. "Listen, you can stuff yourself *after* you let me in on what in hell you're talking about."

"What I'm getting at," I said with a sick smile, "is that if John were the sort of person to kill for money it would have made a lot more . . . well . . . sense for him to have eliminated you." I was so reluctant to utter the "you" that it was barely audible.

"What?" Trudie exploded. "Why more sense?"

Naturally, I couldn't tell the woman that her demise would have meant that John would no longer be dependent on her to subsidize his business, that he'd finally be out from under her thumb. (As a basis for this contention of mine I had to accept, of course, that my client was as miserable with this lady as it was assumed that he was.) But anyhow, I *did* have a perfectly acceptable explanation in mind—which seemed to have inexplicably vanished from my brain. I was sitting there floundering when Trudie took me off the hook and provided it herself.

"I presume you're referring to the fact that he could have done away with me a long time ago. However, I'm worth a total of between three and four million dollars, Ms. Shapiro, which I imagine you're aware isn't even a fraction of Uncle Victor's assets. Still," she added thoughtfully, "people have killed for less. The real problem is that my husband and I have a marvelous relationship, so even if John *were* a murderer—which I assure you he isn't—I'd be the last person in the world he'd want to harm. He—" She stopped abruptly, then shook her head. "But I'm being silly. That shouldn't give the police any pause. After all, they have no way of knowing how solid a marriage we actually have."

Between three and four million, I was thinking. *Definitely nothing to sneeze at. Especially if it went hand in hand with the termination of an intolerable union.* "Uh, your husband is your heir, I take it," I put to Trudie.

"My only heir. And if you want proof of this for our estimable police department"—she was sneering now—"I can give you the name and number of my lawyer. I'll instruct him to answer all their questions on the subject, including the amount of money involved." She was retrieving her handbag from the floor while she spoke. Seconds later I was presented with the card of a William Morse Connor, Attorney-at-Law. After which Trudie declared—and in not too friendly a manner, either—"And now it's my turn.

"It was my idea to bring you into this." (America's sweetheart here was certainly not above altering the truth a little, was she?) "And that, as I'm sure you can comprehend, places a tremendous burden on me. Since the night someone took a shot at my husband, I live in fear that there'll be another attempt on his life." *So he hadn't told her about Saturday's near miss, then.* "And no offense intended, but to be perfectly honest, I've begun to wonder if perhaps you may not be the proper person to handle this investigation. It *has* been a week since you began working for us, Ms. Shapiro"—*five days,* I wanted to shout—"and, unless I'm mistaken, you haven't made the slightest progress. So as difficult as it is for me even to broach the subject, if you don't find the guilty party soon, I'm afraid we will no longer be requiring your services."

I didn't respond. There was really nothing I could say—except that maybe I *should* be fired. Hadn't I myself told John that he would be wise to replace me with a PI firm that could also furnish him with a personal bodyguard? I was toying with the notion of presenting this same alternative to Trudie—although it was likely it had already crossed her mind—when all of a sudden she giggled. "Say," she said, placing her hand over mine in an astonishing gesture of camaraderie, "I believe I've just this minute come up with the perfect way of ensuring that John stays alive."

"What's that?"

"A dash of arsenic or some such in his uncle's Maalox. Don't you get it?" she clarified for my blank face. "Once Uncle Victor is gone, my husband automatically inherits. And after that John's death would no longer benefit any of the others. That's not as cold-blooded as it sounds, either—you have to take into account that the old man's days are numbered anyway."

Stunned, I looked at her closely, trying to determine if this was intended as a joke. There was what I can only describe as a Mona Lisa smile on Trudie's lips. But I didn't have a clue what was behind it. Had the woman merely been trying to shock? Or had she been feeling me out, hoping that for the right price I'd volunteer to tackle Uncle Victor's Maalox?

Reading my reaction now, she put in hurriedly, "For heaven's sake, Ms. Shapiro. You couldn't possibly have taken me seriously."

"No, of course not," I replied, but probably not very convincingly.

The truth is, to this day I haven't decided whether Trudie Lander's sense of humor is one of the most bizarre I've ever come across. Or if there's a side to her that's darker than even her harshest detractors could envision.

Chapter 21

The apartment was stifling when I got in, but I didn't stop to turn on the air conditioner. I went straight to the phone.

Now, rather than do what I felt I had to do just then, I'd have preferred to chew nails. Unfortunately, however, I didn't have that option. So swallowing the resentment I currently bore toward Tim Fielding, I put in a call to him.

"Fielding." He didn't say it; he growled it.

"Hi, Tim," I responded cheerily.

The reaction was not what you could call heart-warming. "No, not again!"

"I realize that you gave me a lot of time this morning, and I really do appreciate it." (I almost made myself gag with that one.) "But the thing is, I just learned something you should be aware of."

"And what would that be?"

"I can't go into it on the phone."

"Then forget it."

"This is information that's important to your investigation," I argued.

"Fine. I'm listening."

"It would be so much better if we talked in person. Suppose I buy you lunch tomorrow? Anyplace you choose."

"Tell me, Shapiro, how long have we known each other?"

"I can't say offhand. Maybe—"

"Never mind. It's been years, right? And how often have you called me with an offer like this one? In fact, if my memory isn't playing tricks on me, as recently as this morning you were supposed to enlighten me. The only thing on your devious little mind, though—and don't think I wasn't aware of it, either—was to find out what evidence we had against your client."

"That's not true. Didn't I—"

"You're the female version of the boy who cried wolf, Shapiro. And, accept it, it's not going to work anymore."

Well, it got through to me that this time Fielding wasn't about to budge. So rather than subject myself to further *agita,* I gave in. "It would make more sense to do this face-to-face," I grumbled. "But okay. What I've discovered is that John Lander's wife is worth millions, and John is her only heir. Her attorney can verify this for you." I supplied him with the phone number of William Morse Connor, which he didn't seem particularly eager to receive.

"So? What's your point?"

"Look, maybe you're not aware of this, but my client's marriage is far from idyllic. I've been informed of this by a number of people." *(Yeah, all two of them,* I reminded myself—a reminder I then proceeded to ignore.) "But it wouldn't have been practical for him to seek a divorce under the circumstances. The circumstances I'm referring to being that John has very little money of his own. His real estate business, from all reports, isn't any too successful; apparently he has to rely on his wife's generosity to keep it afloat. The consensus is—and this is among people in a position to know—that if it weren't for John's financial dependence on his wife, the Landers would have been kaput a long time ago. I'll tell you, though, it's beyond me how he manages to stay with that ball-buster. You've met Trudie Lander, Tim. What was your impression of her?"

"All right, so she's not exactly Miss Sweetness and Light. But where are you going with this, anyhow?"

"You believe that John shot his cousin for the inheritance, correct? But if he were willing to commit murder to improve his finances, he could have done it way back when by getting rid of his wife. Think about how *that* would have benefited him. He'd not only have become around four million dollars richer, but that awful woman would have been permanently out of his hair. Little Trudie is still alive and kicking, however. And why is this?"

"I have a feeling you're going to tell me."

"Because John Lander is not an assassin, that's why."

"It really pains me to burst your bubble, but your argument isn't worth diddly," Fielding said dryly. "In the first place, maybe the man just didn't find four million as tempting as a few hundred million."

"Four million isn't exactly small change," I retorted. "Especially when it carries the built-in bonus of freedom from Trudie."

"Listen, where do you come off deciding what that marriage is like? In spite of your less than charitable view of Mrs. Lander, you can't be certain how her *husband* feels about her. There's no way an outsider can determine a thing like that."

Well, regardless of having previously made this same assertion myself, I had no compunction about disavowing it now. "John is not happy with Trudie," I insisted. "That's common knowledge."

"I suppose the people who imparted this 'common knowledge' share a bedroom with the Landers," Fielding shot back.

"I still say there's trouble there."

Tim Fielding refused to let me have the last word on the subject. "Maybe, maybe not."

"Will you at least talk to this William Morse Connor—Mrs. Lander's lawyer?"

"Sure. What have I got to lose?"

"Thanks, Tim."

"If I were you, though," he put in, "I wouldn't count on anything coming of it."

An admonition that, not being a complete idiot, I considered definitely uncalled for.

I can't claim I was surprised by Fielding's attitude. Still, I hadn't been able to keep myself from hoping that when I presented my argument, he'd realize that I was making sense. Which goes to show that a little misplaced optimism can be a painful thing.

I was hardly in the best of moods as I got dressed for dinner at the Union Square Cafe that evening. (As you can gather, Cousin Alma's stepdaughter had come through with flying colors—unless, of course, there'd simply been a cancellation.) *Snap out of it,* I said to the woman in the mirror as I applied my mascara. *It means a lot to Jackie that you enjoy yourself tonight. So you'd better have a good time—even if it kills you.*

As it turned out, though, it didn't require anything that drastic.

The restaurant itself is a very relaxing place. Our waitress was friendly and efficient. And the food, terrific.

Jackie pulled out all the stops, too. As soon as we were seated she ordered a bottle of merlot to accompany the meal. In case you're interested—and even if you're not—I began my dinner with a delicious portobello mushroom salad with sliced Parmesan cheese. Jackie had the bean soup, which was unusually tasty. (I know this firsthand, having sampled it.) For an entrée she chose the Black Angus steak with mashed potatoes and practically twisted my arm to do the same. Well, after those two courses we both maintained we were too filled up for dessert. But an instant later we decided that this didn't mean we were too stuffed to share. We wound up digging into a banana tart with honey-vanilla ice cream. Yum.

The evening also proved to be a revelation, with Jackie confiding that she was seriously considering putting the screws to Derwin to make an honest woman of her. Although, naturally, she didn't phrase it quite that way. The angst she'd just experienced with regard to his supposed infidelity had, she stated, made her more mindful than ever of how much the man meant to her.

Almost immediately, however, Jackie started to backtrack a bit.

"Of course, marriage might put an unnecessary strain on a perfectly good relationship," she murmured as she carefully deliberated the idea. "After all, until this . . . umm . . . misperception of mine, the status quo suited me fine. Most of the time, anyhow. And maybe having Derwin around constantly could present some difficulties—mostly because I'm not always as tolerant as I should be." *She can say that again!* Then almost to herself: "He can't really help that he snores like that. Still, it drives me crazy—I can never get a good night's sleep when we're together. And he *is* pretty sloppy. One day I found four pairs of socks under his bed. *Four!* But on the other hand, I'd hate it more if he were a neatness freak. He's also terribly stubborn. Even if you prove to Derwin in black and white that he's mistaken about something, he won't own up to it. It was the newspaper that was wrong. Or the book misprinted the date of the battle. Or whatever. It drives me insane when he acts like that. I suppose I should simply 'yes, dear' him to death, but as you know, it isn't in my nature." A fleeting smile here. "And he is awfully . . . careful about money. But it's not his fault," she was quick to add.

"When Derwin was growing up, his family was very poor. More often than not, they had to worry about where their next meal would be coming from."

Jackie was silent for close to a minute now. And—for once—I wisely refrained from commenting. "Over the years I've adjusted to a lot of his other faults, though," she went on, "so it's very possible that I'll eventually become accustomed to those things, as well. That nervous habit he has of jiggling his leg whenever he's sitting down? It doesn't bother me in the least anymore. Honestly. Also, I used to be ready to scream every time Derwin whistled through his teeth, and I'm barely aware of it these days."

She sighed. "Oh, I'm just not sure. Maybe I should hold off on pressuring him for a while—I mean, until I'm satisfied that I really do want to marry him. At this moment I'm still so grateful that I haven't lost him to some baby-faced little chippy that it might not be the time for me to come to any decision. What do you think, Dez?"

Well, since my opinion had been requested . . .

"I think you're absolutely right, Jackie. Why not wait and see how you feel in a few weeks?"

Jackie nodded. "Who knows? By not delivering any ultimatum, I could even be sparing myself from rejection. After all, Derwin may have a few issues with regard to me, too. I'm certain you're not aware of it, Desiree, but I do have one or two minor little flaws of my own."

And if you're wondering, she was grinning when she said it.

Chapter 22

On Thursday morning I forced myself out of a stress-free sleep. But as soon as I opened my eyes I was having that telephone conversation with Tim Fielding again. And fretting about my client again. And worrying—again—whether I'd ever discover who had sent Edward on to his Maker and was attempting to do the same favor for John.

Then I remembered: Sara Sharp was coming home today.

This was a reason to be hopeful—and Lord knows, I needed one. Maybe there was *something* Edward's widow could tell me. But as anxious as I was to talk to the woman, I convinced myself to wait until the next day before contacting her.

I got to the office early (for me); it was barely nine-thirty.

Ten minutes later, just as I was about to—what else?—begin typing up some notes, Ellen called.

"Oh, you *are* in already." She sounded surprised.

She was spared the irritated comeback she'd no doubt have been treated to if I hadn't been in this fairly optimistic mood. (Not that her reaction wasn't merited, you understand; I just resented having to hear it.) Instead, I limited my response to an offhand, "I got here a little while ago."

"Brides by Genevieve is having another sale this week," Ellen informed me excitedly, referring to the establishment in Englewood, New Jersey, where she'd purchased her wedding gown. "I received a flyer from them yesterday, only I didn't check my mail until this morning before I left for work. I was thinking that if you were free tonight, we could drive over there and see if maybe they have something special for you. Any chance you can make it?" Her voice was almost pleading.

Well, I didn't have anything that pressing on my agenda, and as I've mentioned, I'd already made up my mind to placate Ellen and start shopping for my matron of honor dress soon. "Tonight would be fine."

"No kidding? That's great. We'll have to use your car, though. Mike took his to the hospital this morning."

"That's no prob—" Suddenly I remembered. "Uh-oh. Minnie works there on Thursday nights." My palms went instantly damp.

We'd had our problems, Minnie and I, from the second Ellen and I walked into the place. Right away the saleswoman took umbrage at the expression she *imagined* seeing on my face when she introduced herself. Her sister Genevieve hadn't always had such a fancy moniker, either, Minnie had advised me testily—Brides by Genevieve's proprietor, it seemed, was really named Gertie. Anyway, we finally got past that little bit of ridiculousness. But then, once Ellen had selected her gown—an absolutely stunning white lace, incidentally—Minnie tried to convince me that she was uniquely qualified to assist me in purchasing my own dress for the wedding. In substantiation of this she pointed out that "not exactly being another Olive Oyl myself" (actually, the woman was so enormous she made me look like a nail file), she could tell just what would flatter someone carrying around all my weight. Which is not quite the way one likes to hear oneself described. The upshot of that visit to the bridal shop was that Minnie was the very last person in the world I'd allow to outfit me for my niece's nuptials.

At any rate, Ellen was insisting that I was mistaken, that Minnie came in on Wednesday evenings and Saturdays.

"*Thursday* evenings and Saturdays."

"Why don't I check? I'll call you right back."

In two minutes Ellen was on the line again. "You were right," she admitted sheepishly. "I phoned the store, and guess who answered? Minnie. I said I just wanted to know how late she'd be working today. Until 9 P.M., she told me. I hung up before she had a chance to ask who I was."

"Well, that takes care of that. Do you have any plans for tomorrow night? If not, we can do it then."

"Mike's on duty, so I made arrangements to have dinner with Ginger, who lives in my building." (I don't recall Ellen's ever mentioning her friend Ginger without tagging on the "who lives in my building." It appears to have replaced the girl's last name.) "This is definitely more important, though," Ellen said at once.

"Of course it is, but we've still got loads of time. We'll drive out there next week—even if the sale is over by then." Not that I'd have been delirious about having to fork over full price—in fact, I consider it practically un-American to miss out on a sale. Plus, the kind of fees I command in my profession haven't exactly turned me into a Mrs. Gotrocks. Nevertheless, just about anything was preferable to a second encounter with Minnie.

"No, no. We'll drive out to Englewood tomorrow. You're so busy with that investigation of yours that if we put this off, something's liable to crop up, and who knows when you'll be able to spare the time to shop. Also, I forget exactly how long the sale's supposed to last, but it's definitely still on tomorrow." Her voice held a smile when she added, "Listen, how would it look if it got out that the aunt of full-fledged Macy's buyer Ellen Kravitz went around paying retail?''

Well, like aunt, like niece, I decided, forgetting for the moment—as I so often do—that Ellen and I aren't even blood relations. She's the daughter of my late husband's sister. But she couldn't be dearer to me if she were my own sister's daughter.

If I had a sister, that is.

Chapter 23

The phone rang at five minutes past two, right after I swallowed the last mouthful of my turkey-and-brie-with-honey-mustard sandwich. It was Harriet Gould.

"I swore to myself I wouldn't get involved in this, Dez, but well, here I am. Umm, Pop's heading back to Florida early Saturday morning."

"Goody."

"Listen, no one knows better than I do what a pain in the you-know-where my father-in-law can be. But the thing is, he's pretty depressed about not getting to see you again before he leaves. And—I can't help it—in spite of myself I feel bad for him. I mean, he may be a little bastard, but he's kind of a pathetic little bastard."

Why me, God? I was juggling a whole lot of emotions just then: resentment, annoyance, self-righteousness—and, okay, pity, with maybe a sprinkling of guilt, as well. "Damn," I grumbled. "In case you're not aware of it, last night was the first night since that Chinese restaurant fiasco that the man didn't leave a message on my machine. So I had allowed myself to hope it had finally dawned on him that I wasn't interested in continuing our passionate affair."

"You're not that lucky. Yesterday we were upstate visiting Pop's great-niece, and I persuaded him to wait until we returned to our place before calling you. We didn't get in until close to eleven, though, which is pretty much what I figured would happen, and I convinced him it was too late to try you at that hour, that he'd only succeed in making you angry."

"I appreciate it."

"I can't blame you for having had your fill of him," Harriet said charitably. "It doesn't take very long to reach that point. In fact, knowing that Pop'll be around just one more day is the only thing sustaining me right now. Still—and please don't hold it against me for butting in like this, Dez—I was wondering if you could possibly find it in that warm heart of yours to let him pay you a quick visit after you get home from work tomorrow. It would mean so much to him. You don't even have to offer him a cup of coffee. All you have to do is tolerate him for ten minutes—*ten minutes*. If he stays any longer than that, I'll come over and drag him out by the ears. I swear."

"I'm sorry, Harriet, but I promised Ellen we'd go shopping for my matron of honor gown Friday evening."

"Oh, hell. And he isn't able to make it for lunch—not that I think I could actually persuade you to do *that* again. At any rate, he has an appointment with his old doctor for a checkup at twelve-thirty."

Now, I hadn't intended to say it. And I certainly didn't want to say it. But I found myself saying it anyway. "Maybe he could stop by tonight."

"You *are* a doll. And I wish he could. But Steve's cousin in Queens invited the whole family over for dinner."

Well, I'd made the gesture. Was it my fault things didn't pan out? I can't tell you how pleased with myself—and also how relieved—I was at this juncture.

Both emotions, however, were short-lived.

"Dinner's not until eight, though." Harriet spoke slowly, turning things over in her mind. "Which means we wouldn't have to drive out there until after seven." Then sounding so goddamn chipper that I felt like punching her: "So why couldn't he drop in to see you around six-thirty?"

As it turned out, Pop never showed that evening.

I called Harriet at a quarter of seven to find out what was what.

"You mean Pop isn't with you?"

"Nope."

"Well, how do you like that?" she murmured. Following which she proceeded to inform me that some tenant in the building, a young widow her father-in-law had met up with in the lobby that afternoon, thought he was "just adorable"—*she'd learn*—and had invited him to her apartment for a drink at five. It appeared, Harriet said, wonder in her tone, that the woman hadn't tossed him out yet.

"Bless her!" I exclaimed.

"She must be crazy," Harriet suggested.

"Or deaf," I offered.

"Or stupid."

"Or a masochist."

"Or a gold digger."

"Or a really, *really* kind person."

Which sparkling repartee concluded with Harriet's wry, "Nobody could be *that* kind."

It wasn't until I was in the taxi on my way to work Friday morning that it even occurred to me that I'd been stood up. And by Pop Gould, of all people! The gall of the man!

But an instant later I was giggling out loud. Prompting the cab driver to turn around—narrowly missing a bus in the process—and give me one of those "I've picked up another nutcase" looks. I hadn't been able to contain myself, though. After all, I'd been spared what might well have turned out to be the worst ten minutes of my life, and here I was, bitching about it.

It'd serve me right, I decided, if—heaven forbid!—Pop made a return visit to New York soon.

I didn't arrive at the office until just before ten. But it was obvious I was still in favor with Jackie, because she forbore chastising me with so much as a raised eyebrow.

After a brief exchange of pleasantries I hurried back to my cubbyhole, where I wasted no time in dialing John.

He was fine, there'd been no "incidents" since we'd spoken on Wednesday, and naturally he was being cautious. I was not to worry.

"How are things going?" he asked then.

I had to admit there was nothing to report.

"Well, you'll come up with something," he responded gallantly. "I know you will."

Immediately after we hung up I was on the phone with Sara Sharp.

"Yes, this is Mrs. Sharp. You're investigating Edward's death, you say?" The voice was low and pleasant.

"That's right. I was hired by John Lander. Whoever killed your husband has also made two attempts on Mr. Lander's life."

"Are you serious?"

"Very serious."

"Oh, my God! Is he all right?"

"Fortunately, yes."

"And you believe the same person who shot Edward was responsible?"

"I'm all but certain of it."

"Oh, my God," she repeated, more softly now. An extended silence followed, the woman apparently needing some time to absorb the disturbing news. Then she said firmly, "I'm assuming the purpose of your call is to question me. But I've already spoken to the police about my husband's death, and I was no help at all, I'm afraid. As for John, I can't even imagine who might have attacked him."

"The thing is, you may be in possession of some important piece of information without even being aware of it. And that information could lead me to uncover the perpetrator. If we could just get together for a few minutes I'd—"

"I'm sorry, but I'm still pretty traumatized by the murder of my husband"—this was attested to by the catch in her throat—"and I'm really not up to going over all of that again, especially since I have nothing to tell you." She sounded as if she might be only a breath or two away from tears. Nevertheless, I made myself persist.

"Please don't think I'm insensitive to your loss, Mrs. Sharp. I'm very, very sorry about your husband. And I wouldn't pressure you like this if it wasn't my experience that people often know a lot more than they realize they do. I've seen that sort of thing dozens of times."

"Maybe you have," Sara Sharp retorted brusquely, evidently having sidestepped the tears. "But that's not true in this instance. Why don't you leave me your number, though? I'll be sure to call you if anything occurs to me. You'll have to excuse me now, Ms. Shapiro; I have a great deal to do."

I had no doubt she was about to put down the phone, so in my most commanding tone I shouted, "Wait!"

"What is it?"

"I have one last question."

"Which is—?" the exasperated woman demanded.

"How would you feel if something were to happen to Mr. Lander—and you hadn't even *tried* to prevent it?"

"But I have no idea who's trying to harm him. Honestly."

"And you're sure there isn't some tiny scrap of information you might have overlooked?"

"Yes, I am."

The pit-bull gene that must have been passed down to me from some long-expired relative, however, refused to take that yes for an answer. "Remember, Mrs. Sharp, John Lander's life is at stake."

Seconds ticked off before the response. "Well . . . I'm 99 percent sure, anyway."

And right then I knew I had her.

Chapter 24

My conversation with Sara Sharp left me feeling pretty good about things. Not only had I succeeded in persuading her to meet with me, but I was more hopeful than I had any right to be about the outcome of that meeting.

It didn't take long, however, for anxiety to set in. What if it was just as the woman claimed: that she really didn't have anything to tell me? I mean, where in heaven's name did I go from there?

I realized that if I wanted to get any work at all done before tomorrow's eleven-thirty appointment with the widow, I'd have to drag myself out of what was rapidly turning into a semidepression.

Somehow I succeeded in barring from my mind both the pending get-together and the fears I'd managed to conjure up with regard to it. Sort of, at any rate. But while I painstakingly studied my notes, my concentration wasn't what it should have been. And every few pages I fretted about what I might have missed.

At three-thirty I finally gave up and closed the folder.

I was able to reach Ellen at home, my niece having given herself a mental health day (something I should have considered, too). And we agreed that our scheduled five o'clock drive out to New Jersey should be pushed up an hour. Then after a brief visit to the ladies' room followed by the mandatory detailed explanation to Jackie, I was ready to go gown-hunting.

The shop was in a white-shingled, two-family house that looked exactly like every other white-shingled two-family house on the block. Except that this one had a sign that read "Brides by Genevieve."

I'd taken only about five or six steps into the showroom, with Ellen immediately preceding me, when I had a conniption.

The nerve! She'd told us Thursdays and Saturdays that last time, and we made our plans, Ellen and I, to accommodate her schedule. Yet here she is on a Friday, big as life. Uh-uh, bigger!

She hadn't seen us yet; her back was to the door. So I gave Ellen's arm the slightest little yank with the intention of dragging her out of there as fast as these short, underused legs could manage it.

Ellen's loudly proclaimed "Ouch!" however alerted the occupants of the room to our presence.

Minnie whirled around to face us, a smile of recognition instantly spreading over her face.

"Well, look who's here! Auntie! And Elaine, isn't it?"

"No, Ellen," my niece corrected politely.

"Yes, of course. You bought that *gorgeous* lace dress—you were a vision in it, too. See? I remember." She narrowed her eyes. "Say, has anyone ever told you that you look like Audrey Hepburn?" A blushing Ellen opened her mouth—to protest modestly, I'm sure—but Minnie barreled ahead. "Don't you think so, Auntie?"

Well, of course, I've been saying this same thing for ages, but I'm always happy to hear it verified. No matter who's doing the verifying. "She's the spitting image of her," I answered proudly.

"Well, let's not go overboard." And now my favorite saleswoman returned her focus to Ellen. "You've come in to select your headpiece this afternoon, am I right?"

"Umm, not exactly." Ellen was peering at me helplessly.

I took her off the hook. "Actually, I thought I'd check and see if you had anything for me. I'm the matron of honor. But you're pretty busy today"—I indicated the other three people there with an expansive gesture—"so I think it would be better if we stopped by another time."

Minnie laughed. Or to be more accurate, she cackled. "Uh-uh, you're not getting away that easy. It happens that I'm free as a bird at the moment. That one's waiting for her fiancé to pick her up." She tilted her head in the direction of a very pretty girl sitting at one of the small round tables that dotted the showroom. "And little Donna over there?" Minnie was jerking her thumb toward another table at which a chubby teenager was arguing loudly with a visibly perturbed but more circumspect older woman—most likely her mother. "She's being helped by my sister Francesca."

Suddenly Minnie sidled closer to me, leaving no more than a claustrophobic six inches between us. Automatically, I backed away. Minnie was undeterred. Leaning over and bending way down to reach the vicinity of my ear, she put a cupped hand to the side of her mouth. There was a hint of malice in her eyes when she whispered, "You wanna guess my sister Francesca's real name? It's Fannie."

"Listen, I have sort of a headache, so maybe—"

"We've got aspirin and Tylenol. What's your poison?"

"I think it would make more sense if we did this another day."

"Look, why don't you sit down and relax for a few

minutes? In the meantime I'll show you a couple of gowns—only a couple—and if you don't like either of them, you can cut out. Fair enough?"

"I'd rather—"

"Come. Take a load off."

I found myself dutifully following the woman, Ellen close behind me. Wuss that I am, I didn't know what else to do.

Well, this provided me with the perfect view of Minnie's rear. A treat I'd gladly have forgone.

Now, while I admit that I myself have more than adequate natural padding, I do avoid the kind of clothes that make me appear to measure practically the same across as I do up and down. So I couldn't help shaking my head over Minnie's choice of apparel.

She'd encased hips the width of your average New York City kitchen in an outfit that not only called attention to her girth, but practically screamed it. As on our last visit here, she wore a muumuu, but this one actually managed to outdo that other nifty little number—something I wouldn't have thought possible. I mean, the flowers on the thing were positively huge and in the most vivid shades imaginable. But it wasn't just the dress that was so outlandish. You had to factor in the profusion of bangle bracelets that covered both arms almost to the elbows. Not to mention the scuffed gold sandals, which were further enhanced by purple toenail polish (the polish, by the way, matching not only our girl's fingernails but her lipstick, too). And, oh yes, perched precariously atop Minnie's sparse yellow curls was a rhinestone butterfly.

Ellen and I had just settled in our chairs when a tall, slender woman emerged from the back of the house. She had short auburn hair and nice, even features. And she was impeccably turned out. The black silk pants and long-sleeved black silk shirt fit as if they were made for her. (Very possibly because they were.) Draped over the newcomer's arms were three dresses, which she was carrying across the room to the now noncombative young Donna and companion.

This couldn't be Francesca, Minnie's sister—could it? I asked myself.

Nah, I promptly answered myself.

Minnie, who was standing over us, aimed a purple-painted thumb at the object of my deliberations. "Francesca, formerly known as Fannie," she said tartly.

Well, how do you like that! I was still marveling at the fact that these two had been born of the same parents, when Minnie announced, "Pink."

"I beg your pardon?"

"Pink is your color."

"I don't want to limit myself like that."

"You leave everything to me. I've got thirty years of experience to tell me what's right for my customers. I'm not only talking about color, either. What I want you to keep in mind is that someone of your weight has to be extracareful about the lines of a garment, as well." (I really appreciated these words of caution, coming as they did from a giant lump parading around in a neon-hued muumuu.) "You seem offended, Auntie, and you shouldn't be. I'm not casting any aspersions. I'm a fat lady, too, remember?" And she punctuated this with one of her extremely irritating cackles.

Well, I think you can see what I meant about Minnie. Being in her immediate vicinity had the same effect on me as listening to someone scrape his fingernails on a blackboard. And if I heard that "Auntie" one more time, I might be seriously tempted to take out a contract on the woman.

"So what's it going to be—long or short?" she demanded.

"Long." Ellen was the one to respond, probably because she noticed that I was busily engaged in gnashing my teeth.

Minnie nodded her approval. "Good." She turned to me. "It won't make you look as dumpy. Be back in a jiff."

The instant Minnie was out of earshot Ellen said softly, "I hope you're not paying any attention to that stupid cow." And placing her hand gently on my arm, she favored me with a tentative smile. "You're not the least bit dumpy-looking, honest to God."

"Don't worry, Ellen. That didn't bother me." (Not precisely true.) "*Minnie* is what bothers me. How would you feel about our picking up and getting the hell out of here?"

"If you want to," Ellen reluctantly agreed. "They have such lovely things, though, so if you could possibly manage to put up with her . . ."

I thought for a moment. "You're right, I suppose. After all, we're already here. I'll just have to try my best to tune her out."

Seconds later Minnie returned. Her "couple of gowns" adding up to four.

"You're gonna love this. It's my favorite," she told me, holding up the first of her selections. Pale pink chiffon, the dress had a low, round neck, long sleeves—and bugle beads strewn over virtually every inch of it. I'm not claiming it was ugly or anything. But it was a little too *too* for me, if you know what I mean. I said as much to Minnie who, I was pleased to note, took it personally.

"You're kidding, aren't you?"

"No."

"Trust me, it'll look sensational on you. A friend of my sister Gertie's—that's Genevieve to you—wore a gown exactly like this to her son's wedding last month, and it was the hit of the affair. I can let you have it for half price, too."

"Incidentally, where is she—your sister Genevieve?"

"Home with the flu all this week. And you're lucky

she is. Otherwise, I wouldn't be here to take care of you. I'm sure I told you this—I guess you forgot—but normally I only work Thursday nights and Saturdays. Anyway, Gertie's a string bean like your niece. She really hasn't got a clue about what's becoming to girls built like you and me. But never mind. Just slip into this as a favor to me. I promise you'll thank me for making you do it."

"Listen, Minnie, I have no intention of getting into a gown I don't even like." I half hoisted myself out of the seat. I'd had enough.

"Okay, Auntie, okay. Keep your panties on. Far be it from me to force a customer into anything."

The second dress, to my astonishment, was pale yellow. An ankle-length, modified A-line, it had a vee neck and graceful butterfly sleeves. The only ornamentation was a double row of seed pearls outlining the bottom of the sleeves.

"I just brought this out to prove to you that pink is your color," Minnie informed me as I fingered the delicate silk fabric.

"I love it," I declared.

"Really?" She hastily stuck the gown under my chin. Then, her finger to her cheek, she pretended to check out the effect. "I'm not ashamed to say I was wrong. It happens that this particular shade of yellow is very nice with your skin tones. Shall we try it on?"

"*We* certainly shall," I responded, unable to resist interjecting a bit of sarcasm, which Minnie either wasn't aware of or chose to ignore.

At any rate, I'm delighted to report that the dress fit beautifully—or at least it would after a couple of minor alterations. Even lacking those, however, Ellen oohed and aahed all over the place. To say nothing of you-know-who.

"It's *divine* on you," Minnie gushed, as I stood on the platform, admiring myself in the mirror while a seamstress took in a little material here and let out some more over there. "It's true that I originally had pink in mind. But I get these hunches sometimes. And—I don't know—something told me this was the dress for you."

Chapter 25

You wouldn't exactly call her pretty. Nice-looking would be a better way to describe her—although at present Sara Sharp's appearance clearly reflected the impact of her recent loss.

The large brown eyes were red-rimmed and swollen, and there was a tightness at the corners of her mouth that very likely hadn't been there before. Her fashionable, blunt-cut blond hair was in desperate need of a touch-up, revealing a good inch of dark roots. What's more, the faded, outsize green sweater and baggy tan slacks did nothing at all to enhance the widow's round, womanly figure.

"Can I get you something to drink?" she inquired politely as I gingerly lowered myself onto a delicate damask Louis Somebody-or-other chair. "Coffee? A Pepsi, maybe?"

"I'd love a cup of coffee," I said—which wasn't even partially true—"that is, if you intend to join me."

"I'm trying to cut down on my caffeine intake. But I'll be happy to put up a pot for you. It'll only take a few minutes."

Now, I've found that it can be helpful to do your questioning over refreshments of some kind. It seems to produce a more companionable atmosphere, frequently leading people to speak more freely. But if Sara wasn't going to partake, there was no point in my sacrificing myself. "Thanks anyway, but on second thought, I think I'll pass. I should really cut down, too."

"Then you may as well ask away." She settled into the brown velvet sofa, one leg tucked under her.

"Umm, I realize this must be very difficult for you, but do you think you could tell me about the evening your husband was . . . that your husband died?"

The response was delivered in a flat, almost monosyllabic tone. "There's very little to tell. I was at my Tuesday evening pottery-making class—at a place called Going to Pot down on Varick Street. I came home to find Edward on the kitchen floor." With this, Sara put her hands in her lap and began to alternately intertwine and release her fingers. "He was dead."

"I understand you phoned him that night at a little after seven."

"Yes, I was just about to go into the studio, but then I decided to give him a call on my cell phone and remind him about the tuna casserole I'd prepared."

"You arrived back here at what time?"

"It was close to eleven. The course is from seven to nine," she clarified, "but I went for a bite afterward. I had a book with me—I always do when I know I'm going to be alone at a restaurant. Anyhow, I was reading over coffee, and I became so absorbed in my novel that I wasn't aware of how late it had gotten."

"Did you normally stop off for something to eat after class?"

"Always. I never seemed to have time for supper beforehand—I almost invariably wound up staying at the office until well after six. I work at an ad agency, or at least I used to. I took a six-week leave of absence, but I'm not even sure I want to go back."

"What happened after you found your husband mur—after you found him?"

"I screamed, and I kept on screaming." The voice was agitated now, and Sara had begun to manipulate

her fingers at an accelerated pace. "Two of my neigh-
bors came rushing over, thank goodness. I'm afraid I
wasn't up to much of anything; I was in shock. They're
the ones who called the police. They also got in touch
with my sister—the one who lives here in town."

As if on cue, a considerably younger, taller, and
more vibrant version of Sara Sharp entered the living
room from somewhere else in the apartment.

Sara made the brief introductions. "And speaking
of that, this is my sister—Jane Beck. Jane, this is
Ms. Shapiro."

I shook the outstretched hand, then glanced from
one woman to the other. "I hope you'll both call me
Desiree."

"All right. And please call me Jane."

"And I'm Sara," the widow put in. "Look, if it's all
right with you, I'd feel more at ease if Jane joined us."

Before I had time to respond, however, this was a
fait accompli, with Jane already plopping down on the
sofa alongside her sibling. Nevertheless, just to be polite, I mumbled, "That's fine"—only with zero sincerity. I mean, you can never predict how a third party
will affect the dynamics of an interrogation.

"I was about to ask if there's anyone you can think
of who might have wanted to do away with your husband," I said, proceeding with the questioning. (After
all, what options did I have?)

Sara shook her head vigorously. "Edward was a
sweet, gentle man."

"There's no one who had a grudge against him—
no matter how trifling it may have seemed?"

"If I had any inkling of who took my husband's life,
Desiree," she retorted, glowering at me, "wouldn't I
have shared my suspicions with the police?"

"Yes, of course. And I'm sorry for pressuring you
like this. It's only that I'm so intent on uncovering the
killer that I got a little carried away."

"Anyhow, didn't you tell me on the phone that you felt Edward and John were attacked by the same person?"

"That's right. And I strongly believe the reason to be Uncle Victor's fortune. Nevertheless, I can't allow myself to overlook the possibility that the two men might have had a common enemy. In the absence of evidence to the contrary, though, let's go under the assumption—at least for the present—that the motivation does center around the will.

"Well, with Edward gone, it's John who comes into all that money. And since *his* life is in jeopardy now, the perpetrator would have to be one of the other potential beneficiaries, someone who's determined to get his or her hands on that inheritance, no matter what."

"John seems to have reluctantly arrived at the same conclusion," Sara said softly.

"I gather you've spoken to him."

"I called him yesterday—right after I telephoned Uncle Victor. Uncle complained about not having heard from John in a few days, and I figured I should pass that along." Abruptly, Sara stopped playing with her fingers (you can't imagine how distracting this had been), placing her palms flat on the sofa, one on either side of her. "But mostly, once you mentioned those murder attempts, I wanted to reassure myself that John was okay."

"I was told that your uncle hadn't been informed of Edward's death," I brought up at this point. "Have you managed to continue keeping this from him?" It's funny. I was asking out of concern for the old man, but until that moment I can't say I'd given much thought at all to the family patriarch. As a person, that is. It was almost—and this must sound awful—as if I'd been regarding him as already deceased.

"Yes, although it hasn't been easy. But the doctors

felt it was best, and we—the family, that is—certainly concurred. The story Victor was given was that Edward had to go out of town on an extended business trip."

After this no one said anything for a few seconds. Then Sara burst out with, "My poor Edward! Who could have done that to him?" And covering her face with her hands, she began to sob.

Jane threw a protective arm around her sister's shoulders and held her close, while I shifted uncomfortably in my chair and glanced idly around the room. (I've said it before; you can safely bet your firstborn on my being totally useless in a situation of this sort.)

It seemed like forever—although it was probably not more than a minute or two—before Sara's hands came down. Apologizing sheepishly, she patted her wet, reddened eyes with a tissue. But it was apparent she was still shaken, so I figured I'd confine myself to small talk for a bit. "Did you make that lovely green bowl?" I asked, seizing on an item I'd noticed on one of the end tables a few moments earlier.

Sara chuckled. "Good God, no. I'm not *that* talented."

"Not true," Jane contradicted. "Sara's always been very artistic."

"Only compared to you and Dana," the widow responded offhandedly.

"Stop being so modest. I remember when you—"

Sara turned completely around now, so that the faces of the two women were only inches apart. "And *you* stop being so patronizing," she said shrilly.

The chastised Jane reddened. Ditto Sara, who appeared to be as startled by her outburst as I was. "I'm so sorry, Janie," she murmured. "I can't imagine what got into me."

It was obviously an awkward moment for them both. Which meant that it might be a good time to get back to what I'd come here for. "You mentioned your husband's business before, Sara. What was it he did?"

"He owns—owned—an antique shop in Greenwich Village."

"So then it wouldn't have been that unusual for him to travel."

"Actually, his manager was the one who normally did the traveling, especially if there was flying involved—Edward wasn't too keen on flying. But anyhow, Uncle Victor was told that Jay—he's the store manager—was ill, so Edward had to make this buying trip to Italy himself. Of course, things are never that simple. Uncle Victor was angry when he didn't receive even a single telephone call from my husband. Mrs. Clarke—Uncle's housekeeper—did her best to pacify him. She claimed that Edward had phoned numerous times, but always when Uncle Victor was sleeping, and that Edward had insisted he not be disturbed. From what I understand, poor Mrs. Clarke got plenty of heat from Uncle for not waking him regardless. And he was none too pleased with his favorite nephew, either."

"He felt Edward should have tried harder to reach him," Jane interjected.

Sara nodded. "When I spoke to Uncle Victor from Richmond last week, though, I pretended I'd just had a conversation with my husband and that he mentioned how he always seemed to call Uncle at the most inappropriate hours. I insisted Edward was very upset about their not connecting yet. I also put in that he was taking a lot of day trips now but that he'd try Uncle Victor again as soon as he had a chance. Then I said that in the meantime he'd made me promise that I wouldn't forget to send his love. Uncle Victor seemed pleased by that. In fact, when I telephoned him yesterday, there were no more complaints. He just wanted to know how Edward was doing and when he was expected home."

"How is your uncle's health at this point?"

"All right. Or anyway, as all right as it *can* be, considering that he's terminally ill. Strange," Sara observed sadly, "it's Uncle Victor who's been given the death sentence. Yet here he is, still managing to hang on, while one of his heirs is already gone, and the other seems to be in danger of, God forbid, meeting the same fate." And now she dabbed at her eyes, which were beginning to look suspiciously moist again.

Anxious to head off any further tears, I hastily posed another question. "Just when was it you went to Richmond?"

"Almost three weeks ago. Right after Edward's funeral. My sister Dana insisted I fly back there with her, and to tell you the truth, I really wasn't up to doing any coping yet, so I welcomed the invitation. Besides, my daughter doesn't live too far from Richmond—she's in Maryland—and she promised that she and her four-year-old twins would join me at Dana's for a few days. I couldn't pass up the opportunity to spend some time with my grandchildren."

"That was probably wise of you—getting away for a while."

"I had to. Thank heaven for my family. Janie is even staying in the apartment with me temporarily to help me handle all the things that have to be dealt with at a time like this." Reaching down, Sara patted the other woman's knee. "She's taken a couple of weeks off from work to do it, too."

"Actually, it gives me an excuse to play hooky from that boring, underpaying job," Jane kidded.

"What can you tell me about my client, Sara?" I inquired then. "Uncle Victor's will aside, do you have any idea who might have had reason to murder *him*?"

The widow appeared to flinch before answering carefully, "I'm not that familiar with John's personal life. But it's hard for me even to imagine that anyone would want to do away with him. As you've probably discovered for yourself by now, John's . . . well . . . he's a good person."

"I can see someone wanting to get rid of that wife of his, though," Jane piped up. "Probably a lot of someones."

"Trudie isn't that bad, Janie," her sister responded.

"That's your story," the other insisted.

"Listen, I can't say that I'm crazy about her—and we've certainly never bonded—but it isn't as if she's public enemy number one." Jane looked as though she was about to take exception to this, but Sara out-hustled her. "Do I get to ask *you* a question now, Desiree?"

"Of course."

"John claims that the police suspect him of murdering Edward, that they don't believe he was attacked himself. Is he right?"

"Unfortunately, yes."

"I *know* John Lander. He isn't capable of a thing like that. Besides, he and my husband were more than cousins; they were friends."

"I was the one who had to break the terrible news to people," Jane informed me. "I phoned John at his office around eleven the next morning to tell him about Edward, and I had the impression he was not only shocked, but really, *really* upset. He doesn't strike me as being that good an actor, either."

"The two men enjoyed each other's company a great deal, Desiree," Sara embellished.

"I heard that you and your husband even went on vacations with the Landers."

"Only once, a couple of years ago."

"It didn't go that well?"

Sara hesitated almost imperceptibly. (However, not so imperceptibly that I failed to notice.) "It was fine. But last year Trudie was set on the Caribbean, and Edward and I preferred Cape Cod."

"Why anyone would want to be in that Trudie's

company is beyond me," Jane sniped. "And that goes double for your client, Desiree. How can the man stay married to somebody like her? She never gives him a chance to open his mouth, for Christ's sake! You know something? I've been at gatherings with those two exactly twice. But it didn't take me nearly that long—about five minutes, actually—to conclude that Trudie Lander is a bitch. With a capital 'B.' "

Sara smiled indulgently at her sibling before remarking lightly, "At any rate, you can't complain about having to worm an opinion out of Jane, can you, Desiree?"

Well, as innocuous as that statement was, it prompted Jane to take offense this time. Which, when you think about it, is understandable. Giving Sara a hand with whatever practical matters needed to be addressed was the easy part. I mean, just consider the tension involved in helping a loved one cope with their grief. "At least I'm no phony," the younger woman shot back.

"Are you implying that I *am*?" Sara challenged.

"Don't be silly. I—"

"Because I'm no such thing. That's something I shouldn't have to tell *you*, Jane, of all people."

"You don't, honestly. What I said had nothing to do with you. I just meant that I believe in telling it like it is."

"All right." Somewhat placated, Sara managed a half smile. Then, looking her sister full in the face, she murmured thoughtfully, "Speaking generally, though, I do wish you could learn to be a little more charitable, Janie. Sometimes things happen to people that can affect them for the rest of their days."

I pounced. "Something traumatic happened to Trudie?"

Sara turned as red as a ketchup bottle—I'm referring to a full ketchup bottle, of course. "I wasn't talking about Trudie; I thought I'd made that clear.

Although it is conceivable, you know, that her . . .
well . . . abrasive nature is the result, at least partially,
of some adversity she's had in her life."

Naturally, no busybody worthy of that term would
let her off so easily. "I hope you're aware that I'm not
jut asking out of idle curiosity; I'm trying to prevent a
second homicide." This was, at least, not a *total* lie. I
mean, regardless of how much she protested, I had no
doubt that when Sara delivered her little lecture to
Jane she did have Trudie in mind—which, I told myself, *could* turn out to be relevant.

"But this has no bearing on your investigation."

"Probably not. But my client's safety may depend
on my making absolutely certain of that."

Sara frowned. "I don't—"

"For heaven's sake, Sara, tell her," Jane broke in.
(And, to think, I'd resented her presence!) "I'm sure
Desiree's not going to go around blabbing about it—
whatever it is."

"All right." The sigh emanated from her toes. "But
you have to give me your word that this won't be
repeated. Trudie would be devastated if it should get
back to her that anyone found out."

"Her secret is safe with me, as long as there's no
tie-in with the case."

"There isn't," Sara maintained. And she pressed her
fingers into service again—those on her right hand,
anyhow—running them nervously through her hair.
Then, her voice not quite steady, she muttered, "But
at any rate, here it is. . . .

"A long time ago—when Trudie was barely thirteen
years old—her uncle raped her." She seemed to be
gauging my reaction. "An experience like that, well,
you can see how it might have caused permanent psy-
chological damage, can't you?"

"Yes," I responded meekly, feeling guilty at that
instant for ever having had a single unkind thought
about Trudie Lander.

"He had warned Trudie not to tell her parents." Sara went on. "He claimed they wouldn't believe her, that he'd be able to convince them she fabricated the whole thing. But Trudie went straight to her father anyway, and he beat the uncle so badly that the bastard—his own brother, by the way—wound up in the hospital."

"Please tell me the uncle ended up in jail."

"I wish I could. But for her sake, Trudie's parents decided not to press charges against him."

"Where is he now?"

"Dead. For over twenty years, I believe."

The chilling revelation concluded, Sara leaned back against the sofa cushions. But she was apparently unable to resist an I-told-you-so. "See? Didn't I say that what had occurred with Trudie was totally unrelated to the attacks on Edward and John?"

"I guess you're right. Unless I just haven't made the connection."

When I said good-bye to Sara Sharp and her sister that afternoon, I was more than a little disheartened. Waiting in the hall for the elevator, I recalled how hopeful I'd been yesterday about this meeting. Initially, that is. But then almost at once I'd had to acknowledge that Edward's widow might fail to shed any light on the crimes. And faced with that possibility, I had put a theoretical question to myself: *Where did I go from there?*

I'd had no answer.

Unhappily, that question was no longer theoretical. And still I had no answer.

Chapter 26

I was home by two.

Now, I hadn't had anything to eat since breakfast. Which, because I'd overslept, had consisted of only a puny little corn muffin (I swear, it was about the size of a quarter) and a cup of coffee. Yet—and I'm still marveling over this—lunch never even occurred to me. An indication, if there ever was one, of my frame of mind.

Hold on, I finally told myself, *maybe there* had *been a clue of some kind today.* Praying that I'd been too obtuse to appreciate its significance—and hoping for a sudden infusion of smarts—I sat down at my nine-year-old Mac and began transcribing my notes.

I was at it for almost two hours, trying not to study the words but doing it anyway. If there was something of significance to be found on those pages, though, it was eluding me.

When I shut down the computer I was more disheartened than ever.

I had no idea how to proceed at this point.

Of course, I could check out Sara's alibi for the night her husband was killed. But what reason could she have for lying about her whereabouts? I certainly didn't suspect her of doing away with the man. After all, with Edward gone, so were his widow's hopes of coming into all those millions. Nevertheless, I supposed I *should* verify that she'd been at her pottery-making class as she claimed.

It was three-forty-five when I looked up the number of Going to Pot in the telephone directory. A recorded message informed me that they'd be closing at five today.

And now I suddenly realized how hungry I was. Apparently, once I was able to plan my next move—and never mind that I didn't actually expect anything to come of it—I could focus on more mundane things. Like a stomach that was starting to give me what-for. So right before leaving the apartment, I slathered some peanut butter on a slice of Jewish rye and ate it standing up.

I didn't want to be late for school.

Going to Pot was a storefront studio way, *way* downtown. And with the Saturday traffic extraheavy this afternoon, it took close to a full hour to get there.

When the taxi deposited me at the address, a tiny white-haired woman was already locking the door to the premises.

She turned her head, and I saw that she was surprisingly young and pretty. "Do you work here?" I asked. (Not exactly a perceptive question considering that she was holding the keys to the place.)

The woman smiled. "I suppose you could call it that. I'm the owner, as well as the sole full-time instructor—Lucinda Frankel."

"My name is Desiree Shapiro. I'm a detective," (okay, so I left out the "private"), "and I'm looking into the death of the husband of one of your students."

I held my breath in anticipation of the possibility she might ask to see my shield. She didn't.

"You mean the husband of one of my *former* students," Lucinda said. "Understandably, Sara didn't continue with us after the murder. I assume you *are* talking about Sara Sharp." I decided it was okay to resume breathing. "But a couple of detectives were here about that weeks ago."

Oh, crap! However, I nodded knowingly. "Sgt. Fielding and Detective Melnick."

"Could be. I'm not very good at names. The younger one was fairly nice-looking, though."

"Detective Melnick," I supplied automatically.

"It's possible," the proprietor conceded, reddening. Then before I could get out anything more she added, "Listen, I'm in kind of a hurry right now. And I've already told those other detectives all I know."

"I'm aware of that. But there's been some mix-up— a clerical thing—and we just want to be certain we have all the facts straight." (I mean, what else could I say?)

"I have to get home on time tonight: it's my daughter's first formal."

I felt that I should acknowledge this disclosure in some way, but I had no idea as to the appropriate response. I settled on an insipid, "Oh, how nice."

I guess it was all right, though, because Lucinda grinned proudly.

"I only have one or two matters to clarify," I pressed. "And it won't take more than a minute or so." She seemed to hesitate, so I tagged on, "It could be very important."

"We-ll . . . All right, but you'll have to make it brief."

It was plain that she had no intention of opening the door to the studio again. We were going to do this right here—on the sidewalk. I glanced around me. It was still light outside. The weather was warm, but not oppressively so. And the passersby of the moment looked reasonably respectable. (I chose to ignore the drunk sprawled in the doorway across the street. And anyway, he was passed out.) "Umm, Sara Sharp. She was at school the night her husband was murdered?"

"Oddly enough she was here for the whole two hours."

"What do you mean, 'oddly enough'?"

"Sara rarely stayed until the class was over, which is at nine. Normally she was out of the place by eight, eight-fifteen."

"Did she ever give a reason for cutting out like that?"

"It seems to me she may have said something the first time she did it—which, as I recall, was the same night the course began—something about some personal business she had to attend to. But I wouldn't swear to it. It's possible I have her mixed up with another student." Lucinda tittered ruefully. "Not that I have so many of them that I have an excuse for being confused."

"But you *are* sure that it was on the evening her husband died that Sara remained until nine?"

"Look, I always check the obituaries," the woman admitted sheepishly. "So when I read about her husband's death in the *New York Times* I thought it was kind of ironic that this was the one instance where Sara actually hung in until the bitter end. Although it wouldn't have made any difference if she *had* taken off early. She never left before eight o'clock, and I understand that's around the time Mr. Sharp was shot."

Lucinda shifted her weight from one foot to the other, a good indication that she was getting antsy, so I was slightly taken aback when she continued. "Besides, I can pretty much swear that Sara wasn't going straight home all those nights. She was meeting someone. And at the risk of sounding like a gossip—but, after all, this *is* a murder investigation and I suppose I shouldn't hold back—I'm quite sure the man wasn't her husband."

"What makes you feel that way?"

"Because shortly before eight on the evening of the shooting Sara received a call on her cell phone. I was on my way to check out how another member of the class was progressing on the potter's wheel, and I had to pass Sara to get to her. Sara had her back to me, so she didn't see me approaching. Anyhow, the caller was evidently canceling their appointment, because I heard Sara ask, 'Are you sure you can't make it to-night?' Then she said in this kind of adoring tone women don't ordinarily waste on their husbands, 'All right, I understand. I'll talk to you tomorrow, so-and-so.' "

" 'So-and-so?' You mean Sara mentioned a name?" I was tingling with excitement.

"I believe she did. But, unfortunately, I didn't catch it. I was pretty much out of hearing range by then." Lucinda was doing that foot-to-foot thing again. The only difference was that at this point she looked at her watch, as well—a pretty reliable sign that my time was about up.

"Did you tell the police—er, the officers you spoke to before—any of this?"

"They seemed to be interested only in whether or not Sara was in class that night and how long she remained. The rest of it—about her usually leaving early—that never came up. I would have volunteered the information, honestly," Lucinda added apologetically, "but—I don't know—it just didn't occur to me then. Do you think it's relevant?"

"I'm not sure yet; it could be, though. So thanks for bringing it to my—to our—attention."

"I hope it helps." And distributing her weight evenly then, Lucinda announced, "Well, Detective, I'm afraid there isn't anything more I can tell you."

And now there was no doubt at all. I was dismissed.

Chapter 27

As soon as the taxi dropped me off, I bumped into Harriet—literally—who was leaving the building at the exact moment I was entering it.

We stood on the sidewalk and chatted for a little while. Steve was out of town on business again, she told me, so she figured it would be a good day to hit the department stores. She'd spent the afternoon shuttling from Bloomingdale's to Saks to Lord & Taylor, *desperately* looking for a pale blue sweater to go with her new navy slacks. But the stores had *absolutely nothing.* "I called your apartment around twelve"— her tone was slightly accusatory here—"because I was hoping to persuade you to accompany me, but there wasn't any answer."

I'd been spared!

Now, if you had ever experienced the pleasure of shopping with my friend Harriet, you'd be able to appreciate that reaction. You have to understand; this woman is the Queen of Undecided. I mean, I've seen her vacillate for over ten minutes trying to choose between two shades of panty hose, for God's sake! I made a valiant effort to sound disappointed. "I'm sorry I wasn't able to make it, but I had to see someone with regard to this case I'm involved in."

"That's okay," Harriet responded magnanimously. "And anyway, I'll most likely be going to Macy's one night during the week. Maybe you can come with me then." I was right in the middle of a shudder when she made another suggestion. "Say, I was just on my way to the deli for some takeout. And the truth is, I don't feel the least bit like deli, only I hate to eat out alone. But if you haven't had anything yourself yet, we could grab a bite together. Wherever you like." I hesitated for a second or two, so she put in quickly, "Unless you've made other plans, of course."

"The thing is—"

"If you want to change first or anything, I don't mind going back upstairs to wait. I'm in no big hurry."

Well, in light of what I'd learned at the pottery school (or in front of it, if you want to be technical), I had a lot of thinking ahead of me tonight. "I wish I could, but I've got a kind of work crisis." And then because she appeared to be slightly crestfallen, I added, "But if Steve will still be away tomorrow evening, why don't I fix dinner for the two of us here?"

"I accept," Harriet responded instantly. "Steve won't be home until Tuesday."

I ate a ten-minute supper—a bowl of Manhattan clam chowder, courtesy of Progresso, and a ham sandwich. After which I cleared away the dishes and sat down at the kitchen table again with a cup of coffee. Just coffee. I wouldn't let myself take the time to swallow so much as a spoonful of dessert. I was *that* anxious to assess the impact of Lucinda Frankel's revelation on the investigation.

Did the fact that Sara had been having an affair change the entire picture?

Very possibly, I decided. While it was conceivable that the woman's lover had done away with her husband, this wouldn't account for the attacks on my client.

For the first time I had to acknowledge that I might actually be dealing with two different perpetrators.

Let's assume the mystery man—for reasons of his

own—*had* shot Edward. A consequence of his act, while doubtless inadvertent, was to bring Uncle Victor's remaining potential heirs that much closer to acquiring a fortune. Certainly this could have prompted one of them—Shawna or Scott or David—to attempt to become closer still by removing the remaining obstacle to all of that beautiful money: John Lander.

And what were the chances that it was Sara's inamorato who'd murdered her husband? Well, in view of my long-standing problem with coincidence, I considered them pretty damn good. I mean, it was a lot easier for me to accept the man's being a killer than to swallow that he was suddenly—and legitimately—unable to see her on the very night Edward met his end.

At this point in my introspection I contemplated Sara's involvement in the crime. If the boyfriend *did* kill Edward, was she also culpable? Had the two of them conspired in his death? Not too likely, I concluded. After all, it appeared that she'd been intending to meet her beau as usual until she received his phone call.

I wondered then about how Sara herself regarded the cancellation of that rendezvous. Presupposing she was innocent, wouldn't this, in retrospect, give her cause to suspect that the guy had planned to be too busy eliminating her spouse to keep their appointment?

Sara's demeanor today had led me to believe that she was genuinely grief-stricken. Perhaps Edward's death had left her saddled with some heavy guilt feelings about having cheated on him. Or it could be that she was experiencing *two* losses—that of her husband and of the person she might very probably be blaming for his murder. Or maybe Sara Sharp just had a talent for feigning anguish.

There was another thing that puzzled me. Since it was hardly the best-kept secret in town, I couldn't help but think that the "other man" was aware that Edward had been about to come into a windfall. So if this *was* the case—and still going on the assumption that our Mr. X was the perpetrator—why didn't he wait until his intended victim had inherited before taking any action? I mean, almost certainly poor Edward's wife was his beneficiary—or the major one, at any rate—and would then have become an extremely well-to-do widow. And after all, we were only talking a matter of months here, following which Mr. X— whoever the hell he might be—would have had the opportunity to reap some financial rewards for his efforts.

I could only speculate that he'd been out to prevent the woman from coming into that money. Why? Who knows. Maybe he didn't want her to have the independence this sort of wealth could bring. Maybe he was filthy rich himself. Maybe he was some kind of eccentric. Maybe he . . .

Damn! Why hadn't Lucinda overheard the guy's name!

Having driven myself crazy with all of these "maybes" and "could bes" and "perhaps," I realized I was overdue for a little TLC break.

I spent the next half hour up to my neck in warm, fragrant bubbles. It was so relaxing, so pleasant that I might have been there until morning if the phone hadn't rung.

I jumped out of the tub, grabbing a towel as I scurried out of the bathroom. Nevertheless, I managed to leave a small river to mark my route to the kitchen telephone. And wouldn't you know it? By the time I picked up, the caller was gone. Worse yet, he (she?) hadn't even had the courtesy to leave a message.

Anyhow, at least I'd been pried away from all of those seductive, mind-numbing bubbles.

Minutes later I was dried off and back at the kitchen table, rereading my notes on this afternoon's meeting with Sara Sharp. Only this time with her secret lover in mind.

Again, no luck.

I like to think that the reason I was unable to spot what was right there, staring me in the face, was because I was so tired by then.

Which explanation definitely beat the alternative.

Chapter 28

My very first thought when I awoke on Sunday morning was that I'd have to arrange to see Sara again as soon as possible.

"I don't understand the purpose of another meeting," she said petulantly when I phoned her at ten-thirty. "I was under the impression we'd already gone over everything."

"Something's come up," I insisted, "and I really need your input." Then when she didn't answer at once: "It could be the key to finding out who killed your husband."

She finally agreed, sounding dubious. "I suppose I should make myself available if you believe it's that important. I can't do it today, though. Is tomorrow all right?"

Of course, I'd have preferred hearing "Come right over," but I settled for what I could get. Which was eleven-thirty on Monday.

Well, since the appointment with Sara wasn't going to make it necessary to withdraw my invitation to Harriet, I proceeded to devote some thought to our dinner that evening.

Now, when I'm feeding company, I usually give myself a pretty decent head start on the preparations. But in this instance I'd been so preoccupied with that new development in the investigation that I hadn't even shopped. So although I'd planned a fairly simple meal, I was still feeling a little pressured.

Hastily throwing on some clothes, I wound up making a hole the approximate size of the state of Delaware in my panty hose—and right near the ankle, too. I decided to ignore it. I also elected to shut my eyes to the fact that my hair looked as if I'd just stuck my finger in an electric socket. Plus, I was halfway out the door when I realized—and I can't imagine how it happened—that I'd neglected to put on makeup. I rushed back inside, did a slapdash job of remedying the oversight, and, saying a small, silent prayer that I wouldn't run into anyone I knew, headed for the elevator.

Well, better I should have taken the stairs. Because there he was: the short, skinny, slightly balding tenant who had recently moved in on the sixth floor. My heart plunged down to my kneecaps. (Can I help it if I have weird taste in men?) He smiled broadly at me—most likely because I was such a sight—and I saw that his teeth were slightly bucked. (Could it get any better than that? I mean, he was practically perfection!) I barely managed to stretch my lips in a return greeting before switching my gaze to the floor. Which was *definitely* because I was such a sight.

On the way to the supermarket I suddenly recalled my mother's long-ago admonishment about always leaving the house in clean underwear in the event you were hit by a truck. Well, how come she'd never mentioned what precautions to take in case you ran into a cute guy in the elevator? You know, like making your hair presentable, and cleaning up those globs of mascara under your eyes, and instantly changing your holey panty hose—that is, unless the holes didn't show.

But almost immediately, I turned philosophical. Maybe I should be thankful that I did look so singu-

larly unattractive this morning. Since Ed's death, my
experiences with regard to members of the opposite
sex could bring tears to your eyes. I wouldn't have
been surprised to learn that some Higher Power had
intervened to spare me from another disaster. And
after all, it wasn't as though I were the kind of woman
who considers it essential to have a man in her life.

Still, it would be nice if one of these days I could
find someone—the right someone—to scrub my back
and zip up my zippers. . . .

I was finished in D'Agostino's in fifteen minutes—
probably a personal record—and from there, I made
a brief stop at the greengrocer's.

When I got home I worked on the starters first:
zucchini-Parmesan puffs and a chilled salmon mousse.
Then I fixed a humongous salad. Following which I
prepared the wild rice with mushrooms and onions. I
even got in a little measuring and mincing for our
entrée: orange chicken with almonds. Fortunately, I
didn't have to be concerned about dessert. I had some
very nice cheesecake squares in the freezer.

Harriet arrived at seven with a bottle of Pinot
Grigio. As we drank the wine and nibbled on the hors
d'oeuvres I mentioned the fellow in the elevator.

"You must be talking about Nick," I was informed.

"How do you know his name?"

"We met in the laundry room last week. He wasn't
wearing a wedding ring, either." And now she was
eyeing me pityingly. "But do you really think he's
cute?"

"Yes, I do," I snapped, feeling defensive. Also irritated. Listen, much as I like him, her Steve would
make precious few hearts go pittypat.

"Well, I suppose it's fortunate we don't all have the
same taste," Harriet concluded sensibly.

A short time later I left her in order to finish up
the chicken and reheat the rice. When I returned to

the living room I was pleased to note that the hors d'oeuvres hadn't been neglected in my absence. I only hoped Harriet had left enough room for the rest of the meal.

I needn't have been concerned. She did herself proud.

At any rate, over dinner she recounted a couple of heartwarming anecdotes starring the world's most obnoxious dog—her "adorable" little Pekinese, Baby. (Whose days, I swear, are numbered; just let him piddle on my shoes one more time.) We talked about Pop for a few minutes, too. It seems he'd met a very nice divorcée at his senior citizens' club the previous Thursday. "He claims she's quite taken with him, too," his daughter-in-law advised me with a chuckle.

I couldn't afford the luxury of a chuckle myself. "I really hope things work out for them," I said fervently.

It didn't take long for Harriet to polish off everything on her plate—*twice*. And from the lingering look she fastened on the empty serving dishes, I suspect she'd have been up for thirds. She contented herself with raving about her new grandson instead.

"I just happen to have a few recent pictures of him. Would you like to see them?" She was out of her chair like a shot. Retrieving the handbag she'd left on the sofa, she pulled out a yellow envelope, which she promptly slapped in my palm.

Had she said *a few* pictures? There were at least thirty of them in there.

"Well, what do you think?" Harriet demanded when I returned the envelope. "Isn't he *gorgeous*?"

Now, that's hardly the word I'd have used. "Uh, he's quite a boy."

"Yes, isn't he? He looks a little like Steve—at least, I like to think so."

Well, as she herself had said, thank goodness we don't all have the same taste.

It wasn't until dessert that my investigation entered

the conversation. I gave Harriet a brief summary of the whole mess, finishing with tomorrow's scheduled visit with the widow. "I'm hoping I can persuade her to let me know who the man is."

"Do you really believe she'll tell you?"

"Well, it's possible—right?"

"Oh, it's definitely possible."

But she sounded very much like I had when commenting on her grandson. So I was hardly reassured.

Chapter 29

When I got to the office on Monday I suspected that Jackie had been crying.

She was on the phone at the time, and her voice was low and choked. Plus, she was clutching a couple of Kleenex, and her eyes were red. Which seemed like pretty good evidence to me.

She terminated the conversation—I think it was a personal call—as soon as she saw me. "Can we talk for a little while, Dez?"

"Of course." I was a few feet beyond her desk at this point, and I started to backtrack.

"No, no. I have a letter to finish. I'll stop by in about ten minutes, okay?"

"Sure, whenever you're through." I almost retraced my steps anyway, though, just to give her a reassuring pat on the shoulder or something. But I always feel awkward about doing things like that.

Now, unlike some other people I could name, Jackie is a very rapid typist. So she showed up at least five minutes ahead of schedule. In fact, I had barely warmed up my desk chair when she put in an appearance.

Following a brief coughing spasm in the doorway—at which time Sam Spade here realized that her symptoms were the result of a cold, not an emotional trauma—she flopped down on the seat opposite me. "You were right," she announced dispiritedly.

"I was? About what?"

"About my waiting a while before giving Derwin any ultimatum. I've decided I don't want to marry him after all."

"You arrived at that pretty quickly, didn't you?"

"You bet," Jackie answered emphatically.

"Has something happened?"

"Listen, a few weeks ago I mentioned that I'd always wanted to see *Les Miz,* and Derwin surprised me by getting tickets for Saturday night."

"Is this supposed to be a bad thing?"

"You wouldn't be asking that question if you saw where we wound up sitting. We were so high up I got an attack of vertigo."

"Well, maybe those were the only tickets available."

"No, Desiree," Jackie snapped, "they were not. And why are you defending him, anyway? You know how cheap he is."

I tried to couch my next words in the most benign terms possible. I mean, how Jackie talks about the guy is one thing. But I wouldn't blame her if she didn't take too kindly to *my* raking him over the coals. "I don't understand. Surely Derwin's . . . umm . . . his conservative approach to money didn't surprise you."

"It's not that it surprised me. It—" Another round of coughing, this one more prolonged than the first, prevented her from continuing. "That effing cough medicine," she said when she was finally able to say anything at all. The almost-epithet was so totally un-Jackielike that for a moment I thought I might have heard wrong. "It hasn't done a damn thing for me," she crabbed. "And it tastes like insecticide, too. But I started to tell you: The seats weren't the worst of it. It was beginning to rain when we left the theater, and I was wearing a new silk dress—which, if Derwin had any idea what it cost, would have sent him into cardiac arrest. I also had on an expensive pair of strappy, high-heeled sandals. So, naturally, I suggested we go home by cab."

It didn't require any crystal ball to see what was coming next.

"According to Derwin, though, it wasn't raining that hard, and anyhow, I'd be less waterlogged on a brisk walk to the subway station than I would be if we stood there for fifteen minutes or so trying to hail a taxi. Imagine! Either it didn't occur to the man that I could wait under the marquee while he did the hailing—or he was hoping it wouldn't occur to me."

"I'm sure that if you'd insisted, Derwin would have gone along."

"Don't you get it? I shouldn't *have to* insist. At any rate, the dress is now kaput. The dry cleaner actually laughed when I asked if there was any way he could salvage it. And the shoes are in only slightly better shape. I'll probably wind up throwing them away, too."

"What a shame!" I told her—and meant it. "I have to be honest with you, though. I—"

"You consider it my own fault that my clothes were ruined and that I've come down with this miserable cold, besides. You feel that if I hadn't been so stubborn, I'd have gotten Derwin to spring for a cab. Am I right?" She didn't wait for confirmation. "Like I said, you shouldn't have to *force* someone to act like a human being."

"And this convinced you not to marry him?"

"Not by itself. But it served as a giant reminder of about a thousand other incidents. And if Derwin pulls this kind of garbage now, what can I expect if we ever get married?"

Well, regardless of her present frame of mind, I knew that Jackie sincerely loved this man. (What I didn't know was why.) And I figured it might do her good to hear something of a slightly more optimistic nature.

Particularly, I decided (having just entered my rose-colored-glasses mode), since it could actually be true.

"If Derwin's having a hair transplant, though," I put to her, "or even if he's getting himself a better toupee, he could be loosening up a bit. I mean, he's had that ratty old hairpiece of his for how long? And suddenly he splurges on an expensive replacement." Jackie's protest was aborted by a couple of dry hacks, so I forged ahead. "Listen, you can't expect an overnight transformation; it takes a while to abandon the habits of a lifetime. And obviously a person is going to have a relapse once in a while."

"Ha!" said Jackie. "I was going to tell you. He came over with his new head of hair on Friday night. It's not a transplant, of course—but I didn't really expect that it would be. What it *is* is the cheapest-looking toupee you've ever seen. And I don't care how much he paid for it. That's another thing. The man has absolutely no taste. To tell you the truth, Dez, I can't imagine why I even continue to go out with him. In fact, I'm seriously considering breaking it off."

But I knew she didn't mean it. And what's more, she knew that I knew it.

The phone rang practically on the heels of Jackie's exit.

"I figured that surely you'd have something to report by now."

No "Hello." No "How have you been, Desiree?" Not even a "This is Trudie." But, of course, I had no problem identifying the caller anyway. In fact, the instant I heard that voice, I cringed.

"So?" Trudie demanded before I had a chance to collect my thoughts. "It's been close to a week since our little get-together, and I told you then that I expected results."

"I can appreciate that. Look, I've just come across

some information that I believe could have a direct impact on this case."

"All right. I'm waiting." I could picture the woman drumming on the table with her fingers now.

"I'm hoping to be able to tell you about it soon, Mrs. Lander. But since certain individuals could be adversely affected by my revealing what I've learned, first I want to be totally certain that this actually does have a connection to the crimes."

"I suggest that you explain what you're talking about, or I'll see to it that John finds someone to succeed you."

"Of course, that's your prerogative—and his. But I think you should be aware that whoever steps in at this stage would have to start almost from square one. I wouldn't be comfortable passing along what I know before I've established to my own satisfaction that it has a bearing on either the attacks on your husband or his cousin's murder."

Trudie took another tack. "Do you have any idea what this has been like for me? Every day I'm worried sick that it isn't going to be my husband at the door that night, but some policeman who's there to notify me that I won't be seeing John ever again."

There was pain in her voice. And this, coupled with what I had been told of her childhood, made me feel genuine compassion for the woman. But I couldn't let it influence me. "I'm sorry," I said softly. "I sincerely am. But please know that I'm determined to identify the person who's responsible for what's happened—and as quickly as I can."

It was a while before Trudie deigned to respond. "All right," she said at last. "You seem to be in the driver's seat at present. Consider yourself warned, however, that I have no intention of allowing this to go on much longer."

*   *   *

The conversation with Trudie left me feeling uneasy. I mean, suppose there *were* two perpetrators—as I more than half suspected. And say that I was able to identify the individual who—because of his involvement with Sara—pulled the plug on Edward. What did that have to do with the safety of my client?

I was deep in thought when Elliot Gilbert, one of the two princely gentlemen who rent me my office space, rapped gently on the open door to my cubicle.

"Can you spare a couple of minutes?" he asked in that slightly timid manner of his.

"For you? You bet."

He walked in tentatively, parking his round bottom on the very edge of the chair. "I'm kind of up against it, Desiree," he began. "A good friend of mine—another attorney—recently underwent emergency surgery, and I agreed to take over a few of his cases. The one I'm primarily concerned about right now is a hit-and-run that occurred a year ago this past January—on the tenth, to be specific. The problem is, I have very little time to prepare for trial, which is scheduled to start in less than three weeks."

"You weren't able to get a postponement?"

"I tried, but . . ." Elliot hunched his shoulders. "Look, just let me give you some of the particulars, all right?"

"Sure, go on."

"My newly acquired client, Charlie Weist, has been accused of running a red light and injuring a ninety-one-year-old man—although, thank God, not critically—and then fleeing the scene. And while the vehicle involved in the accident does belong to Charlie—apparently somebody managed to get the license plate number—Charlie swears that his niece, age seventeen, had borrowed the car that night without his permission. Which the *niece* swears is a lie."

"You've spoken to her?"

"Yes. And so did Dennis, the previous attorney.

Her story is that she had a tooth pulled that morning—which, incidentally, Dennis verified—and that she was at home sleeping off the pain.

"As for Charlie, he does have an alibi, but I'm not entirely comfortable about how it will be perceived. Charlie claims he was out with his former wife on the evening in question and that at 8:45 P.M.—when the accident occurred—they were at a bar having a couple of drinks before going on to dinner. His ex will testify to this in court. Still, the jury might not regard Clara as the most reliable witness in the world, considering that the two are planning to remarry."

"This bar they went to—I gather no one there was able to identify the couple."

"Unfortunately, no. Right after the accident Dennis showed a photo of Charlie and Clara to the waitstaff who were working at the place at that time. But nobody remembered them."

"How was the tab paid?"

"In cash. So no help there, either." Elliot regarded me earnestly. "I value your opinion, Desiree. That's why I'd appreciate it if you could meet with the former wife and give me your take on how credible a witness she'll be. I have an idea that she'll make a pretty good impression on the jury in spite of her current status with regard to the defendant. Possibly, though, that's because she's all I have." He smiled ruefully. "At any rate, I'd feel better if you verified my opinion—assuming you agree with my assessment of the woman, of course. Now, with reference to the niece, the way I see it, there's very little chance she'll admit the truth. But maybe you can come up with something else that might give us a little edge."

There was no mistaking the appeal in his eyes. "What do you think? Can you see your way clear to doing a little legwork for me?"

Well, normally when I'm immersed in a really heavy-duty investigation I try not to handle any additional business. The thing is, as much as I can use the extra money, I value my sanity more. But Elliot needed someone to check into things pretty quickly. Besides, this didn't appear to be the type of case that would take up a great deal of time. Plus, I'd turned down some other work from Elliot quite recently, and I still didn't feel too great about that. I mean, it's not easy to say no to anyone who's as nice as Elliot Gilbert is. Particularly if he also looks like a cherub.

I gave him a yes.

A decision that I still say played its part in enabling me to finally get to the bottom of who did what to whom in Uncle Victor's family.

Chapter 30

When Sara Sharp opened the door to her apartment a forced smile was fixed on her face. Either that, or she'd had a sudden attack of gas.

"Eleven-thirty on the dot, Desiree. I can't say you're not prompt."

I didn't think it necessary to reveal that I'd been walking around the block for the past ten minutes. I mean, if there's one thing that ticks me off more than people being late for an appointment, it's their showing up early.

We went into the living room, where Jane, in cutoff jeans and sans makeup, was curled up in a corner of the sofa. I made myself forgive her for expending zero effort to look so fresh-faced and adorable.

Sara's appearance, however, did not require this same generosity.

The widow's eyes were every bit as red and swollen as they'd been a couple of days earlier. The tightness around her mouth remained, too. And the dark roots were still begging for a touch-up. She was even wearing the same unflattering sweater and slacks.

"Well?" she demanded the instant we were seated.

I had trouble getting started. "Uh, what I . . . the thing is . . . umm, there's no easy way to tell you this, Sara."

Her eyes narrowed. "Then just say it," she instructed curtly.

"All right. Over the weekend I discovered that you'd been involved with another man at the time your husband died."

"That's ridiculous," Sara responded evenly. But her complexion had gone chalk white.

"I have it on the best of authority."

She turned to her sister, who was only a cushion length away from her on the sofa. "It isn't true, Janie. I swear it."

For a moment the younger woman just sat there, staring at her wide-eyed. Then very quietly she said, "I wondered why you were trying so hard to hustle me out of here today. You suspected this was the reason for Desiree's phone call, didn't you?"

"Of course not. There was no other man. What would it take to convince you of that?"

"Aren't you even curious about how I learned this?" I inquired.

Sara continued to maintain her composure. "Not really. Because it's a damn lie."

I opted to take the response as a yes. "You saw your lover on Tuesday nights, while you were supposedly at your pottery class."

"I attended that class regularly, for your information."

"Yes, you did. But every week you'd cut out around eight o'clock to meet him."

"That's totally false!" Sara protested, her agitation apparent now. "I did leave early sometimes, but it had nothing to do with any fictitious lover. On one occasion I went home before the end of the session because I had these terrible stomach pains. And a couple of other times there was a particular matter that I had to attend to." She faced her sibling again. "Edward and I were considering moving uptown, and I ran out to look at some available apartments."

"You never mentioned any plans to move," Jane told her. It sounded like an accusation.

"There wasn't anything definite." Sara frowned. "But I get the impression you don't believe me."

"I want to, honestly. You're my sister, and I love you. But I loved Edward, too—he was like a father to me. It hurts me even to *think* that you might have cheated on him."

"I didn't." And now the widow focused on me. "I'm stunned that you would come to the conclusion that I was engaging in these clandestine trysts simply because I didn't always remain at the school until nine o'clock."

"That's not the reason I'm so convinced you were having an affair, Sara. But first, let's clear up something. You're claiming that you didn't always stay until the session was over. The fact is, though, that you *never* stayed for the full two hours—not until the Tuesday your husband was murdered. And then you hung in until the end because your . . . um . . . friend contacted you during class to cancel your date. The instructor overheard the conversation."

"You're right about one thing: I did get a phone call. But it was from a girlfriend. I was supposed to have dinner with her later that evening, and she wanted to let me know that she wouldn't be able to make it."

Hoping for some assistance, I addressed myself to Jane. "The call wasn't from a woman. Ms. Frankel—she was Sara's instructor—is absolutely certain of that." (Okay, so Lucinda Frankel hadn't used the precise words "absolutely certain." But it was close enough.)

"Ms. Frankel was mistaken." Sara's jaw was jutting out about a mile now, a fairly reliable indication that she intended to stick to her guns. It crossed my mind then to fabricate a story about someone's having spotted her and her playmate together, looking cozy. Which sometimes gets people to open up—and more often does not. But Jane, bless her, made the subterfuge unnecessary.

"Ohh, Sara," she murmured, her eyes brimming with tears, "how could you do that to Edward? He adored you."

"I know he did, Janie, I know. And he was very dear to me, too. That's the truth."

"But there *was* someone else," Jane badgered. The widow didn't respond, and Jane's tone became appreciably louder. "If you couldn't be faithful, at least be honest, for God's sake!"

Sara spent the next three or four seconds contemplating her shoes. And when she fastened on her sister again, her expression was an unspoken plea. "I didn't mean for anything to happen with . . . with anyone else. I— Before I knew it, it just did." She spread her arms wide in a gesture of helplessness. "I realize you'll find this hard to understand, Janie, but I didn't stop loving Edward. Not ever."

"Of course not. That's why you were sleeping around on him."

"I'm not condoning my behavior. But it's as if . . . as if things were out of my control. You see, as much as I cared for Edward—and I cared a great deal—I never felt about him the way I did about . . ." I held my breath at this juncture, but Sara caught herself in time, biting her lip and then completing the sentence with "this other individual.

"I wish I could explain it. All I can say for certain is that what was between us was . . . well . . . overwhelming." She reached for the tissue box on the coffee table and wiped a tear from her eye. "I tried to break it off, believe me. But I couldn't do it. I'm just not as strong as you are, Janie; I never have been."

"Bull."

"Look, whatever you think of me couldn't come close to what I think of myself."

And now it was Jane who reached for a tissue. "Edward deserved better than that. And you know it."

"Yes, he did," Sara agreed in a whisper.

"Okay, who is he—this other guy?" Jane inquired sharply.

"I'm afraid I can't tell you that."

"Can't?"

"All right. I'm sorry, Jane, but I won't. There isn't any point in revealing his name."

"Are you still seeing him?"

"No."

Now, all this time I'd left it to Jane to interrogate her sibling, and she'd been doing a bang-up job of it, too. In fact, I seriously doubt if I could have persuaded Sara to admit to an affair. But there was a point that had to be made, and it didn't appear that Jane was going to make it.

"Let me ask you one thing." Both women seemed startled by the sound of my voice. It was as if they'd momentarily forgotten I was in the room. "Doesn't it strike you as strange that the only Tuesday night your lover broke a date with you was on the very evening your husband was murdered?"

"I don't see anything strange about it at all. Something had come up, and he just wasn't able to keep our appointment."

"Jesus," Jane muttered.

"He didn't kill Edward, Janie. If you knew him, you'd realize I was telling the truth."

"You honestly think that cancellation was a coincidence, Sara?" I asked.

"Of course. This man was not responsible for Edward's death. Violence isn't in his nature."

"Then why aren't you seeing him anymore?" Jane challenged.

"I'm not sure. Perhaps it's because there's a strong possibility that going on with the relationship would make me feel even guiltier than I already do. Or it could be that it's a kind of self-punishment for betraying Edward. The one thing I'm just about positive of, though, is that I'll never have peace of mind unless I can manage to forgive myself. And continuing to be with this person is not the way to accomplish that."

Her sister presented her with yet another explanation. "Or maybe you're not *really* so confident that Mr. Wonderful didn't shoot Edward."

Sara shook her head. "You're totally off base about that."

"Maybe you refuse to admit it even to yourself," the other persisted.

I jumped in here. "Are you saying, Sara, that it's never occurred to you—not even once—that the reason your gentleman friend might have been unavailable at the time Edward was murdered was because he was busy doing the murdering?"

The widow peered at me as if I were some disgusting little specimen she should be viewing under a microscope. "No, it never has," she seethed.

But I was convinced she was lying. Just as I was convinced that if I kept at this until the cows came home, I'd still get that same answer.

Chapter 31

I stopped off at Little Angie's for a slice (or three) of pizza before heading back to work.

As soon as I was secluded in my cubbyhole I got started on the legwork—or in this instance, mouth-work—for Elliot.

In spite of his feelings about the likelihood of Charlie's niece owning up to the crime, I was anxious to have a crack at her. I called the number he'd given me for the girl, hoping I could convince her to meet with me. There was no answer.

Next I phoned Clara, Charlie's ex-wife, to schedule an appointment. But she informed me that she was off on a six-day Caribbean cruise in the morning. She sounded embarrassed about it. "Months ago—this was prior to Charlie and me deciding to give our relationship another try—I promised my sister I'd take this vacation with her. And she'd be just heartbroken if I canceled."

"Could you possibly spare me a few minutes today? We'll make it wherever you say. And I'll keep it brief—you have my word on that." For good measure, I threw in, "It's important that we talk in person."

"I'm awfully sorry," Clara answered, her tone genuinely regretful, "but there's no way I can do it; I have a million and one things to take care of before the trip. I'll get in touch with you as soon as I return, though, and we'll set up something then, okay?"

"Sure." But my voice must have reflected my frustration.

After this we spoke briefly about the accident. Clara mentioned that just as she was about to leave the apartment that night for an eight-fifteen date with Charlie, a neighbor had popped in unexpectedly, causing her to show up at the bar a little late. Still, she stated emphatically, she'd arrived well before eight-forty-five—the time of the hit-and-run—and Charlie was already there, waiting for her.

I had my fingers crossed when I posed what was the natural follow-up question.

Clara thought for a moment. "You know, come to think of it, I probably did tell Emily—my neighbor— that I was spending the evening with Charlie."

The woman's tone took on a new intensity here. "Listen, Ms. Shapiro, I hope you believe me when I say that my husband—I mean my former husband— couldn't have been driving his car when it happened. He was having drinks with me. And that's the God's honest truth."

I recrossed my fingers when I dialed Emily, who fortunately (for me) was home with the flu today.

"Two Januarys ago—on the tenth? Yes, I do remember. Clara was seeing her ex that night. Although why she doesn't give that loser a ball four is beyond me. Is his lawyer aware that Charlie Weist's been in jail twice—*so far*—and that when he isn't in the pokey he's cheating on his tax returns and smacking women around?"

"I don't have any idea what his lawyer knows." Then, just to be agreeable, I added, "He sounds like quite a prize to me, though. But, I'm curious, how can you be so certain of the date?"

"My mother-in-law's birthday is the next day—January 11—and I was late buying her a present that year.

I went to Clara's because I was counting on her to come up with a suggestion for me. But she was in a hurry to go out, and she gave me the bum's rush. Of course, a couple of days after that I heard about Charlie's being in hot water for mowing down that poor old guy—probably the only time Charlie's been innocent of anything in his life." And now, maybe to satisfy my curiosity—which, in this instance, was totally lacking—Emily tagged on, "I ended up buying my mother-in-law a scarf. And she hated it."

"You wouldn't recall what time you stopped in there, by any chance?"

"Sez who? It was five after eight, give or take a minute or two. I ran over as soon as *Wheel of Fortune* went off. I don't budge from the TV until then."

I was smiling when I put down the phone. While Charlie Weist was not exactly her favorite person, Emily could—and, equally important, *would*—testify to his appointment with his former wife that evening.

Elliot's position had just gotten stronger.

I rushed around to his office to tell him so, but he had left for a client meeting.

Submerging my disappointment, I busied myself with transcribing the notes on today's visit with Sara. Although considering how that had turned out, it hardly seemed worth the effort.

Later, at home, I began to marvel at how well things had gone with this new investigation. I told myself that maybe, all of a sudden, I was on a lucky roll. And the funny part is, I even got myself to believe it.

Ellen called right after supper, and she commented on how up I sounded. "What's going on?" she demanded.

"Nothing, really. I just had a decent afternoon, for a change."

"Anything to do with your case?"

"With *one* of my cases. I'm working on something for Elliot Gilbert, too."

My niece's next words were hesitant—and predictable. "You haven't gotten involved in anything that could . . . well . . . endanger you, I hope."

"You don't have to worry about that. It's an accident matter."

"That's good." But evidently, she had second thoughts, because a moment later she piped up with "What *kind* of an accident?"

I was shaking my head and rolling my eyes when I responded. "A not serious one, that's what kind."

I actually couldn't wait to go over the Lander file that evening.

At around eight-thirty I sat down at the kitchen table with the usual cup of atrocious coffee and the manila folder marked with John's name.

I began right at the beginning—the Friday the Landers showed up at my office—rereading every word, many for the umpteenth time. Only there was one difference with this present go-around: my mind-set.

You see, that folder had become increasingly intimidating each time I opened it. And the possibility that I might now be faced with having to identify not one perpetrator, but two, hadn't contributed to my confidence.

That night, however, I was still taking bows for what was in reality a very moderate success. I mean, I wouldn't even let myself *think* that my coming up with a witness like Emily could be attributed more to luck than to brainpower. That night, too, I refused to allow myself to be burdened by my previous failure to unearth even a single lead.

I studied the file with a clear head and an optimistic attitude. And suddenly, something leapt out at me.

Just how, I wondered, *could she have known that?*

Chapter 32

Of course, what I picked up on at this moment should have hit me between the eyes the instant I'd heard it. But somehow it had sailed right over my head. And while I believe that even without my (temporarily) upbeat outlook I would have discovered the truth eventually, I'm convinced that my state of mind facilitated things.

At any rate, as impatient as I tend to be, it's rare that I have quite as much trouble restraining myself from lifting the telephone receiver as I did just then. But my watch read, "11:10." And I recognized that this might not be the ideal time to deliver my message, particularly when you considered its contents.

I expected that I'd be too agitated to sleep that night. And I was right. I didn't even close my eyes until after 6 A.M., and I was up by seven—*with no prompting from the alarm clock*. Which, in my entire life, probably hadn't happened more than once or twice before.

I was at the office at exactly nine o'clock. Jackie's jaw dropped to her chest when she saw me.

"Why are you here so early?" she asked suspiciously.

"Yesterday I learned something about the Lander investigation that's got me so wired I practically bolted out of bed this morning."

Jackie squealed. "You found out who did it!"

"Whoa. It's nothing that significant. Let's just say that I've made a little progress. Actually, I suppose, a very little."

"So you still don't know who tried to do in your client and offed that other fellow—his cousin?"

Offed?

I can't figure out why Jackie—or Ellen, either, for that matter—deems it necessary to dip into cop-speak every so often. Maybe they've OD'd on *NYPD Blue*. Or maybe it's intended as a show of solidarity with me—although I almost never use that jargon myself. Anyhow, it sounds so unnatural coming from the two of them that it's all I can do to prevent the grin I feel inside from sneaking out onto my lips.

I managed to keep a straight face, though. "The killer is still a great big question mark."

"Well, even if you haven't worked it all out yet, you will."

That's the nice thing about having good friends; they always try to say something encouraging. Whether they mean it or not.

It was ten after nine when I dialed Sara Sharp. I'd held out as long as I could.

Now, it was hard to tell whether Sara's reaction to the sound of my voice was one of annoyance, anger, or fear. But for sure it wasn't pleasure. Her response to my "This is Desiree Shapiro" was a clipped, "Listen, I thought I'd made it clear that I have no intention of giving you the name of the man."

So how's that for a non sequitur?

"I don't want the name of the man," I apprised her.

"Oh?"

"I already have it."

There was a gasp, then silence.

"Sara?"

"I'm here."

"We need to talk."

Another interval of silence. "That would probably be wise."

Less than an hour later Sara was ushering me into her living room.

She seemed to have lost weight since the last time, and there hadn't been that much of her to begin with. But considering that "the last time" was only a day earlier, the weight loss was doubtless entirely in my addled brain.

"Coffee?" she offered mechanically.

"No thanks, nothing." Taking a seat, I glanced around the room.

"My sister isn't in," Sara notified me, reacting to my wandering gaze. She sank down on the sofa. "Jane'll be gone until at least one-thirty. That's why I thought it would be best if you came by now."

Damn! Jane had spoiled me, proving herself an invaluable ally when I'd questioned the widow previously. Well, I was on my own today—like it or not. And, to be honest, I didn't really like it that much.

"All right, go ahead," Sara commanded. "Just who is it you suspect me of seeing?"

"My client. And I don't suspect; I'm positive."

She actually smiled. "You're kidding, aren't you?"

The woman was convincing; I'd give her that. Nevertheless, I was sure of my ground. "Hardly." And removing a notebook from my handbag, I opened it to the page I'd folded down. "We were speaking about Trudie, and you made the comment"—I went to a short phrase underlined in yellow—" '. . . we've certainly never bonded.' "

"That sounds familiar. But what significance is it supposed to have?"

"You'll see in a minute," I answered, peering down at the notebook again. "Later, when you were about to disclose the abuse Trudie had suffered in her childhood, you told me"—and I read from another under-lined passage—"'Trudie would be devastated if it should get back to her that anyone found out.' Do you recall this?"

"Not really, although it's possible that I said it. But I still don't have any idea what you're getting at." She was, however, plucking away at some nonexistent threads on her jeans now and looking as strained as I'd ever seen her.

"According to your own words, you and Trudie weren't close. So why would she divulge such a painful secret to you?"

Continuing the preoccupation with her jeans, Sara stared down at them as she responded, "Obviously, Trudie felt the need to unburden herself to someone, and I happened to be around at the time." She raised her eyes while continuing to pluck. "Listen, I've known people to pour their hearts out to complete strangers—individuals they meet on a plane, for example."

"That's not the same thing at all. The chances of ever seeing these strangers again are pretty slim. Which is what makes them such appealing confidants."

"Well, I don't know why Trudie decided to reveal this to me, but she did."

I shook my head. "John confided in you regarding what had happened to his wife—he must have. And I can't picture him doing that if you and he were merely casual friends. My guess would be that he spilled the beans to explain—or maybe the word is 'excuse'—why Trudie was the way she was and why he continued to remain in the marriage. Isn't that how it came about?"

"Absolutely not. Listen, I allowed you to come over today to determine whether you really do have some idea as to the person I had been going out with. Well, I'm very relieved that you don't." She leaned toward me now. "It wasn't John, Desiree."

I was beginning to waver (I told you before that she was good, didn't I?), but I couldn't afford to entertain any doubts at this point, so I promptly banished them. How to get Sara to open up, though . . .

The only thing I could think of was to employ a bluff of some sort. I mentally dusted off "old reliable"—you know, the claim that she and John had been spotted together. Like in the vicinity of the school. But at that instant an alternative intruded itself into my head, and before I had time to even consider its merits, I found myself declaring, "Tell that to Trudie."

Sara's agitated fingers abruptly stilled, and she met my eyes. "What are you saying?"

"That Trudie learned about the affair."

"Oh, please," she scoffed. But the woman didn't look anywhere near as assured as she sounded. In fact, moments later she added uncertainly, "Are you telling me that Trudie talked to you about this?"

"Yes, briefly. Listen, what do you imagine induced me to reread the notes I'd taken on my earlier visits here?"

"At the risk of sounding crass, Desiree, you're full of—" She hesitated before completing this with "baloney." Which I can swear was a last-minute substitution.

"I'm telling you the truth. If you don't believe me, though, give her a call." I hate to brag, but, well, the way I said it practically oozed sincerity.

Sara didn't respond at once, during which time I became so antsy I started to scratch a nonexistent itch on my forearm. Finally, she put to me in a small, tremulous voice, "How did she find out?"

"I haven't a clue. But she knows."

"The last thing John and I wanted was to hurt anyone," Sara murmured. "It's just that our feelings for each other were so . . . so *overwhelming*. But we did make every effort to be discreet. Apparently, though, we weren't terribly successful." She shook her head sadly. "Trudie's already been through so much, too.

"You're probably thinking that I'm a complete hypocrite," the widow added. "But I wasn't aware of the incident in Trudie's past, not until John and I were already involved. Maybe if he'd told me about it right at the start, I'd have ended things before they really got off the ground."

I must have looked skeptical.

"No, you're right," she admitted, noting my expression. "If I was willing to deceive a wonderful man like Edward, it's not likely I'd have allowed what occurred with Trudie to deter me, either—especially since I don't even care that much for the woman. Still, I felt guiltier than ever about being in a relationship with John once I heard about her horrendous ordeal. I can't explain it; in a way, it's like a sisterhood thing. Does that make sense to you?"

"I imagine it does. Rape is the sort of horror every woman can relate to. Umm, when was it this thing with you and John began, anyhow?"

"Almost two years ago. Shortly after the four of us went on vacation together."

"And the last time you saw him was—?"

"At my husband's funeral."

"But I assume you two have been in touch since then."

"Only twice. John called me on my first evening in Virginia. I asked him to please not phone again." Sara smiled wanly. "These days I intend to occupy myself with doing an awful lot of soul-searching."

"And the second time you spoke to him?"

"That was when I returned from my sister's, and you informed me of the attacks on his life. I was the one who did the calling then."

"And John's okay with this—your ending things, I mean?"

"Not exactly. But he doesn't have much choice." Sara went back to pulling at the invisible threads on her pants before asking, "Is he aware that his wife knows about us?"

"Probably not. Apparently she isn't ready to confront him yet."

"You haven't said anything to him?"

"I believe that should be left to Trudie. Wouldn't you agree?"

The widow nodded. "Don't worry. I have no intention of being the one to break the news to him."

"Good. Besides, John has enough to be concerned about at present. I'd like to see him concentrate on just staying in one piece."

Sara's "amen" came out in a whisper.

"There's something I'm curious about, though," I brought up then. "How did you come to use a pottery school as a cover for your meetings with him?"

"I needed an excuse to get out of the house, and I read an ad for Going to Pot in the *Village Voice*. Well, I'd always wanted to take a course in pottery-making, and the school is located about as far downtown as you can get—right near the Brooklyn Bridge. Which is ideal, since John takes the bridge home from work every day. Also, being so far out of the way, we figured it wasn't likely that we'd run into anyone we know."

"You, uh, would go to a motel around there?" I didn't actually have to ask this—not insofar as the investigation, I mean. But frankly, my nosy nature demanded it.

"John rented a flat near the school—over on Spring Street," Sara answered casually. I'd really expected her to take umbrage at the question, but I guess she felt that in view of all that I was already privy to, this little tidbit didn't amount to very much.

Suddenly she regarded me searchingly. "Yesterday you didn't seem to place much stock in the possibility that it could have been a coincidence that my . . . my lover called off our date on the night of the shooting. But now that you know it was John . . . well, you *must* have an idea of how hard he works and how many evening commitments he has. In fact, every week I was half-expecting that he wouldn't be able to make it." She sat up a little straighter before stating firmly, "John had nothing to do with my husband's death, Desiree."

"I agree."

Now, I can appreciate what you must be thinking. After running off at the mouth for so long about how improbable it was that this cancellation had been coincidental, I was totally reversing myself. And it wasn't merely because the man involved was my client, honestly. As Sara pointed out, John was a workaholic. So the odds were that he would have had to break some of their Tuesday evening appointments. The only surprising thing was that he hadn't done it before then. Plus, I certainly didn't share Tim Fielding's skepticism about those attempts to eliminate him. And tell me this: Why would a murderer bring in a PI to conduct an investigation of the murder? I mean, does that make sense to you? Even more important than all of this, though, I *knew* John. And I simply could not accept that he was a killer. "If Edward hadn't been shot when he was," I told Sara, "I'm quite sure it would have happened soon afterward. And for the same reason the perpetrator is out to get rid of John."

"Those are my thoughts exactly. It never even occurred to me that John could have been responsible for Edward's death."

It was funny. But something in her tone made me wonder if it was me Sara was trying to convince of this—or herself.

Chapter 33

So okay. Now that I'd knocked myself out persuading Sara to confirm the identity of her mystery lover, what did I intend doing with the information?

Get this: absolutely nothing.

The thing is, I didn't see how it could possibly have any bearing on Edward's murder, much less those two attacks on John. That being the case, I had no legitimate reason for going to my client with what I'd learned. And although I can't say I wouldn't have liked to hear something from him on the subject, occasionally even a Class A *yenta* reaches her limit. This, however, does not mean that I wasn't disappointed in John Lander.

It wasn't so much because he'd cheated on his wife, either—although not always being as "now" as I like to imagine I am, I do think that adultery . . . well, sucks. But while I couldn't condone his straying, my acquaintance with Trudie—limited though it was (fortunately)—enabled me to understand it. In a way, anyhow.

What really bothered me, though, was that John had betrayed his very good friend—who only incidentally happened to be his cousin, as well.

But, look, I'm not perfect either. Even if sometimes—like at this moment—I find it necessary to remind myself of that.

And then, for the first time, it sunk in that there

was a plus side to John's being the widow's inamorato.
At least, from my point of view. Listen, it was now
obvious to me that Edward was killed because of that
damn will—and by the same person who was attempting to take John out of the running. Which meant
that I could scratch that burdensome two-perp theory
and concentrate on unmasking a single adversary.

Back at the office again, I decided to put the Lander
investigation out of my mind for the rest of the afternoon. As soon as I'd checked on John, that is.

A woman with an extremely nasal voice answered
his phone. "Who's calling, please?" she inquired politely—and nasally—when I asked for Mr. Lander.

"Desiree Shapiro."

"Ohh, Miss Shapiro." Her tone conveyed recognition.

"You know me?"

"Well, uh, not really. I've heard of you, that's all.
Mr. Lander is at a construction site right now."

"Could you have him give me a call when he gets
a chance?"

"Certainly. I should be hearing from him in about
an hour."

And now it was time to concentrate on Elliot's
assignment.

Anxious to impart what I'd found out yesterday, I
had tried to see Elliot immediately upon returning
from Sara's—even before I headed for my little cubbyhole. In fact, right after Jackie waylaid me in order to
relate that Derwin had been feeling positively awful
about the theater incident. "You know, basically he's
a very sweet guy," she insisted.

It appeared that, happily, the current crisis had
passed.

At any rate, Elliot was tied up in court. So I had
yet to give him Friday's encouraging report. But there
was a possibility, however slight, that I could present

him with some additional positive news when he came in later. I proceeded to dial Charlie Weist's teenage niece.

Somebody fumbled with the receiver, then dropped it. Finally, a young female growled, "Mmm, ho-oo?" It took a moment for this to register as an irritated, sleep-logged version of "hello."

Bemused, I automatically glanced at my watch. It was twenty to one.

"Is this"—I glanced quickly at my notes—"Mandy?"

"Who's this?" The kid was wide-awake now—and wary.

"This *is* Mandy, isn't it?"

"So if it is?"

"My name is Desiree Shapiro, and I'm looking into an automobile accident that occurred in—"

"You with the NYPD?"

"Well, no. I've been hired by your uncle's attorney to—"

"Get lost, will ya? I don't have to talk to you. Or any of my creep uncle's fuckin' creep lawyers, neither."

And so saying, that sweet-tempered and obviously well-bred young lady slammed down the receiver.

I consoled myself with the fact that Mandy's cooperation had been a long shot anyway.

I ordered some lunch then, having given up all hope of inducing myself to walk over to the sandwich shop, which was, after all, an entire block away. Listen, it had been an emotional morning, and I was drained. Or maybe I was just being lazy. (But I prefer "drained.")

No sooner had I finished the last bite of my BLT— only without the "L"—than Elliot poked his head in the room.

"May I come in?" He was his usual cheerful self.

"You'd better. I've been dying to talk to you."

"What's happened?" he inquired, taking the same precarious edge-of-the-chair position as on his previous visit. (I swear, someday that man is going to wind up on his head.)

"I contacted Charlie's former wife yesterday. Unfortunately, however, she left for a six-day vacation this morning. She'll be getting in touch with me when she comes back so we can set up a meeting. But don't worry. She sounded perfectly fine on the phone, and I have every expectation that she'll make a good witness."

"I'm glad she struck you that way. It was my impression, too." He was smiling broadly.

"A couple of other things. I spoke to the niece, and it was as you suggested—the kid wouldn't budge. On a more promising note, though, we have further confirmation of sorts that your client was busy courting his ex at the time of the accident."

"Really?"

I told him about Emily.

"That should help," Elliot responded, flashing an even broader smile. "I have something to tell you, too. A couple of minutes ago I received a telephone call from a young man who claims—and I have no reason to doubt this—that he is the niece's boyfriend. *Former* boyfriend, I should say. Evidently the pair had a nasty argument last night, and he's rather anxious to testify at the trial. He'll be in to see me in the morning."

"What is he going to testify to?"

"He was a passenger in the hit-and-run car that night—*which* the niece was driving."

"That's terrific!"

Elliot was positively beaming. "Yes. A very fortunate break. But I'm grateful for your assistance, as well, Desiree. You've done a wonderful job."

Now, having made a return to reality since yesterday, I was aware that I hadn't done a wonderful job at all. Like Elliot, I, too, had lucked out. But I graciously accepted the thanks. I didn't think it would be polite not to.

This had been such a brief, effortless investigation, with everything falling so neatly into place, that it pretty much demanded contrast with the Lander case.

It had been almost two weeks since I'd been hired to find out who wanted John Lander dead, and as yet I hadn't made any appreciable headway.

And I was afraid.

Was my client still in danger—or had the perpetrator decided to leave it to the police to dispose of him?

And speaking of New York's Finest, things had been remarkably quiet there, too. What was Fielding up to, anyway?

I felt a sharp pang.

Please, God, I murmured aloud, *don't let my lack of progress cost John his freedom. Or worse yet, his life.*

Chapter 34

I'd had every intention of cutting out a little earlier that afternoon and paying a sorely needed visit to the beauty parlor, which is only a couple of blocks from the office. I knew there wouldn't be any problem about an appointment, because luckily—or maybe not—the place is never really that busy. To tell the truth, Emaline—my longtime hairdresser who brags that she has "golden hands"—doesn't. But I'm used to her. And besides, with Emaline my expectation level is so low that she rarely disappoints me.

At any rate, having just made myself half-crazy with thoughts of my client's possible incarceration or demise, I decided to shelve Emaline for a while. *And why hadn't John returned my call yet, anyway?*

I promptly dismissed the question from my mind. What was I carrying on about, for God's sake? It was only a couple of hours since I'd tried him.

I was about to start typing up my notes on that morning's talk with Sara when I altered my priorities. It could wait until tomorrow, since the possibility of this latest visit's providing a lead to the perpetrator I estimated to be only slightly above zero. Of course, with all the time I'd previously spent buried in the Lander folder, my chances of suddenly uncovering some vital piece of information there weren't exactly encouraging, either. *Still,* I put to myself, *it's conceiv-*

able that I've been consistently overlooking something, right?

It was a question based more on despair than optimism. For more than an hour I read diligently, finally becoming so bleary-eyed that I could barely make out the words, much less determine if they contained a clue.

I had just placed the file folder in my attaché case when I heard from John.

"Sorry it took me a while to return your call. But I've been tied up with so many back-to-back appointments this afternoon that I haven't had a free minute."

"I hope that means it's been a profitable day."

"That makes two of us," he remarked dryly. "Any particular reason you phoned me? Has something turned up?"

What I really would have liked to hit him with was "Yes. I found out about you and Sara." But I willed myself to show restraint. "Nothing yet, I'm afraid. I just wanted to touch base with you."

"I appreciate that. Uh—" Breaking off, John cleared his throat, then tried again. "Uh, Desiree, you *do* think we'll discover who's responsible for the things that have happened, don't you?" It was apparent that asking me this hadn't come easy to him.

"I'm confident that we will." (At this juncture a lie if there ever was one.)

"Have you spoken with Sergeant Fielding?" he inquired.

"Not recently. I gather you haven't had any contact with him lately, either."

"No. Should I take that as a good sign?"

"I would."

He chuckled. "All right, I will."

"John, I trust that you're still on your guard, even though there haven't been any, well, incidents for a while—thank heaven."

"You don't have to be concerned. I'm being careful. Maybe too careful."

"Why do you say that?"

"I'm beginning to suspect that I've gotten totally paranoid."

Uh-oh. "And this is because—?"

"Last night, on my way home from the office, I stopped for a bite at some little restaurant in the Village. I had to park on a fairly dark side street, and when I went back for my car after dinner, the street was just about deserted—it was past midnight by then. At any rate, I could have sworn I heard footsteps behind me and that they kept getting closer. But I turned around a few times, and there wasn't a soul in sight.

"It was probably only in my mind, Desiree. I have to admit, though, that I was really in a sweat. I was seriously considering making a dash for my Range Rover, but all of a sudden a whole group of people— at least eight of them—came pouring out of this house directly in front of me. There must have been a party of some kind. Anyhow, one of the couples was headed in the same direction I was, so if I *was* being stalked— and that's a big 'if'—this pretty much put the kibosh on it."

"Ohh, John," I wailed.

"Please. Don't worry. The more I think about it, the more convinced I am that my imagination was working overtime."

But I, on the other hand, wasn't convinced at all.

There was no question of my *not* going over the remainder of the Lander file that evening.

I stuck with it to the bitter end, too. It was ten after one when, rubbing my eyes, I finally closed the dog-eared folder. If there was anything to be learned from it, though—once again I hadn't learned it.

On Wednesday I transcribed my notes on the con-

versation with the widow, following which I read over
them carefully. I struck out there, too.

I had reached the point where I was starting to be
even more disgusted with the results of my investigation
than Trudie was. In fact, I was seriously considering firing
me myself—before my client met the same fate his cousin
had. After all, what else could I do? I seemed to have
come to a dead end. Either I was dealing with a very clever
assailant here or he/she was dealing with a really stupid
PI. But whatever the reason, it was becoming more
and more apparent to me that the case needed to be
examined by a fresh set of eyes.

As we'd arranged a couple of days earlier, after
work my neighbor Barbara Gleason and I met in front
of a theater in the neighborhood of our mutual apartment building. I'd left the selection of the movie to
Barbara, since there wasn't anything I was particularly
interested in seeing, and besides, she invariably pokes
fun at my taste. Take *Babe*. So okay, I'd had a slight
hissy fit when it didn't walk away with the "Best Picture" Oscar that year. But this *was* quite a while ago,
you know. Yet there's still a good chance that when
Barbara and I talk films, she'll manage to sneak in a
reference to "that silly talking pig you're so enamored
of." Anyhow, we wound up watching some inane Jim
Carrey picture. Barbara absolutely adores Jim Carrey—which is *so* not what you'd expect from her.

As soon as the show was over it began to rain.
Not having been forewarned by the weather mavens
(thanks a heap, WLIW), neither Barbara nor I had an
umbrella. But fortunately there's a decent restaurant
on Eighty-fifth Street that's practically around the corner from the theater. Noreen's, it's called. While not
exactly a four-star establishment, the atmosphere here
is pleasant, and the food is usually pretty tasty. Although why they insist on referring to their fare as
"Continental cuisine" escapes me. The extensive

menu is loaded with dishes like Manhattan clam chowder, Maryland crab cakes, and Texas chili. But I suppose they feel justified in the "Continental"
designation since they do offer one or two entrées
with French- and Italian-sounding names. Which I
doubt that many people have the courage to order
there.

Now, with Barbara I can never predict whether I'm
going to be having a pleasant dinner with a friend or
a lecture from a pain-in-the-butt diet guru. That night
she was a friend. This I sort of determined almost
immediately, when my choice of the Southern fried
chicken with mashed potatoes and gravy escaped without so much as a mild censure. And my initial feeling
was confirmed big-time later on when she didn't blink
an eye after I asked the waiter if I could have my
brownie topped with vanilla ice cream and hot fudge
sauce. (I could.)

Well, since she'd been equally nonjudgmental during our last outing, it occurred to me that she might
have reformed—although because I know Barbara as
well as I do, this was not an easy concept to accept.
It wasn't until she'd finished her last forkful of grilled
salmon that I learned the reason for tonight's particularly benign behavior. This past week she'd received
a Teacher of the Year award from her school, and she
was still in such a mellow mood that I'll bet she would
even have tolerated my adding whipped cream to that
dessert order.

"I really thought I'd be able to hold off and tell
you over coffee," she said with a smile so huge that
it seemed to cover most of her face, "but I couldn't
wait. It's terribly gratifying to be honored like that,
Dez. Throughout your career you do everything but
stand on your head in an effort to motivate your students—some of whom have absolutely no inclination
to learn. And let's not forget the abuse you have to
take from the parents; they can't comprehend how

you could possibly have given their little twelve-year-old gangster-in-training a 'D.' Never mind that he deserved an 'F,' but you didn't want to discourage him completely. And then, of course, you have the administration to contend with, with all of that petty politicking. I tell you, there have been times I was almost ready to chuck everything and get a job driving a bus." The picture this conjured up might have sent me into a paroxysm of laughter if I hadn't been able to exercise such iron self-control. "But now," Barbara went on, "I receive an award like this, and it makes me feel . . . *validated.* I would imagine you experience a similar type of satisfaction after wrapping up an especially difficult investigation."

"I suppose I do," I responded uncertainly.

"By the way, you had just started on a new project when we went to the ballet that night. How did that work out?"

Luckily, I'd already consumed the last morsel of chicken; otherwise, I don't think I could have managed to get it down—that's how the case had begun to affect me. "It's still up in the air. Somebody's out to kill John Lander—he's my client—and I haven't been able to figure out who that somebody could be. Actually, it's very possible I'll resign and let the Landers bring in another PI. Maybe the new guy can get a handle on things before anything dire happens to John."

"Don't tell me you're *that* discouraged. This isn't like you, Desiree."

"Look, it's been almost two weeks. And I've already interrogated everyone involved about everything I can think of, without making any real headway. I just don't know where to go with this anymore."

"I take it you're not leaning toward any particular suspect."

"No, not really. I'd like to believe that the perpetrator must have slipped up somewhere, though—most of them do—but if he or she *has* made a mistake, I haven't caught it."

"You know, sometimes these things have a tendency to percolate. What I mean is, on some level we're aware of something, but we don't recognize that we are. I'm certain it's happened to you, too. You'll drive yourself crazy attempting to come up with some piece of information that's been eluding you. And then after you finally give up and manage to put whatever it is entirely out of your mind—consciously, at any rate—*that's* when your brain suddenly appears to work at full function.

"What I'm suggesting, Desiree, is that you not withdraw from the project just yet; give yourself a few days. But stop going over every tiny detail in your head again and again—which I don't doubt is exactly what you've been doing, true?"

"Guilty."

"Give it a little rest." She reached across the table and briefly clasped my hand in a gesture of encouragement.

The conversation returned to the teaching award now, so in spite of my appetite's having eluded me minutes before, by the time the waiter took our dessert selections (Barbara's being fresh fruit salad, naturally), I was primed to enjoy that rich, gooey, incredibly yummy indulgence described earlier.

As soon as we were served I invited my good friend to enjoy a spoonful or two before I dug in. Which seemed to me only mannerly. Her "no thank you" was accompanied by a withering glare, one so potent it would have totally unnerved the uninitiated. But having been on the receiving end of her unspoken rebukes for so long (the spoken ones, too), it didn't even give me pause. Actually, I welcomed it. It was reassuring to know that the real Barbara still inhabited that skinny-as-a-stick body.

The thing is, while on occasion she does have this

tendency to be bossy and overly critical—you might even say impossible—I realize that it often stems from genuine concern. I mean, Barbara's harshest reprimands center around my food intake, the woman being calorie- and cholesterol-obsessed. Also, while it takes a while to discover this, she's a kindhearted and generous person. If you ever need a favor, you don't have to ask her twice.

When we were leaving the restaurant, Barbara prepared me. "Listen, about your investigation, don't be surprised if something occurs to you in the middle of the night."

It didn't happen that way, though. The solution to the Lander case didn't arrive in the wee hours at all.

It was to come with the salad.

Chapter 35

Guess who went up in the elevator with Barbara and me that evening.

Nick.

He looked really spiffy, too. He was sporting a well-fitting cotton tweed jacket in beige, white, and brown with beige slacks and, to complete the outfit, a white shirt and brown-and-yellow rep tie.

Immediately after confirming Harriet's information about the naked state of his third finger, left hand, I noted that he wasn't toting a briefcase. Which, being that I'm such an experienced PI, instantly communicated that he hadn't been working late at the office. *Most likely coming home from a night of debauchery,* I concluded sourly. (I was to subsequently find out that the man owned a flower shop, so a briefcase wasn't exactly a mandatory appendage.)

"Hi," he said, smiling. His glance took in the two of us.

My "hi" and Barbara's were simultaneous. But while I automatically smoothed down my hair and tried to think of something sparkling to say, Barbara was the one to begin making friendly conversation.

"You just moved in recently, didn't you?"

"A few weeks ago."

"Welcome to our building. Have you managed to settle in yet?"

He smiled. "I'm kind of pokey, I'm afraid. I still have a lot more cartons to unpack."

"It can be a pretty daunting task," I piped up. "When I moved here, it took me forever to put everything away." Not what you'd call "sparkling," but at least I managed to contribute *something*.

The exchange ended there. Barbara and I only live on the fourth floor, and although our elevator is pokey, it's not *that* pokey. As we were getting out of the car, however, Nick called after us, "The name's Nick Grainger, by the way."

I turned around. "Mine's—" But the door—which normally takes six months to creak to a close—this night slammed in my face.

"Seems to be a nice guy," Barbara remarked as we headed down the hall. "He wasn't wearing a wedding band, either."

Now, I don't know at what age little girls discover how essential it is, when in the company of an appealing member of the opposite sex, to zero in on that all-important finger. But I do suspect that once learned, this is a lesson that remains with us until the grave.

I tried to be cool. "Oh? No kidding."

"Don't give me that, Desiree Shapiro. You started blushing the instant that fellow entered the elevator."

"You're crazy," I mumbled.

"I am, huh? And there's a good chance he's available, too. You should thank me for checking out his hand for you."

We had reached our respective doors by then, so I escaped with a " 'Night, Barbara, talk to you soon" instead.

Once in my apartment I made a beeline for the bathroom mirror. The hair was slightly messy, but fortunately it wasn't dripping wet, the rain having ended during dinner. And while I hadn't done a very neat job of reapplying my lipstick, I *was* wearing a nice dress—a cap-sleeved turquoise shantung. All in all, I concluded, I looked fairly presentable. Which was a giant step up from my first encounter with Nick Grainger.

Preparing for bed that night, I had a frightening thought. Suppose I did drop out of the Lander investigation and another PI was brought in. And what if John was murdered before this new person was able to get to the bottom of things? I could never be certain that if I'd stuck with it a little longer, I wouldn't have uncovered the truth—and prevented this tragedy.

Barbara's advice—you know, about putting the case out of my mind for a time—made sense. But it turned out that I was too much of a compulsive to follow it.

The instant I sat down at my desk on Thursday morning, I was opening the all-too-familiar manila folder. Less than an hour later, however, I closed it decisively.

What was I accomplishing, anyhow? And to *really* complicate matters, thanks to last night's bedtime "what-if," I was not only apprehensive about remaining on the case but equally leery about getting off it.

Well, since I was so ambiguous about things, I determined that I'd have to devise a new course of action in the event I *should* decide to hang in a bit longer. And this, obviously, required some hard thinking.

I reached into my desk drawer for a couple of Extra-Strength Tylenol. Which I regarded as a start.

And then I went totally blank.

After ten unproductive minutes I figured it might be best to take a break and start fresh a bit later.

I began the hiatus by polishing my nails—three coats, no less. Following this I phoned my old college friend Christie Wright in Minnesota. Thank goodness we had a lot to catch up on, so we wound up chatting for the better part of an hour.

Ellen called before I had a chance to conjure up any other delaying tactics. She wanted to go over the guest list for the wedding with me. Now, with the BIG EVENT so far in the future, I might ordinarily have put her off. But today I was delighted to be of assistance. The final matter under discussion was whether the beau of "Ginger, who lives in my building," should be included among the chosen. Well, since her friend's sizzling romance was only of two weeks' duration, I suggested Ellen wait and see if the couple had any staying power before coming to a decision. And with that sage advice the conversation ended.

Right after this I visited Jackie at her desk. Her close-to-perky attitude apprised me, even before the words did, that Derwin was continuing to behave himself. We were only able to visit for a few minutes, though, because she soon got busy with the phones.

Waving good-bye to Jackie, I went out for a sandwich and some window-shopping. But I chickened out on the window-shopping part when Mother Nature let loose with what I swear was the loudest clap of thunder I'd ever heard. Needless to say, it sent me scooting back to work.

It was probably just as well, however. I mean, enough was enough. I had a job to do.

I'm not quite sure how long I sat in my office, attempting to think of something—*anything*—that would enable me to move forward with the investigation. Provided I elected to move forward, that is. I do remember that I swallowed a lot and that most of the time my head was in my hands. At any rate, I finally settled on an approach that, while hardly inspired, beat having another go at that despicable folder. (Also, it was the only thing I was able to come up with.)

My plan? To reinterview the suspects. Listen, who knows where that could lead, right? Of course, I'd have to invent a plausible reason for requesting that David and the twins see me again. And this would require some serious brain wracking. But I'd tackle that tonight.

Opening the bottom drawer of my desk, I got out my umbrella and plastic kerchief.

Right now, client or no client, rain or no rain, I was going to have my hair done.

Chapter 36

Emaline did a mediocre job on my hair. But with Emaline, mediocre is good—even to be hoped for. Of course, I can't say that I was crazy about the Shirley Temple curls, but about ten minutes of energetic brushing should uncoil them.

That, however, would wait. Right now I was hungry. There was still a little leftover marinara sauce with mushrooms in the freezer, and this over a dish of rigatoni along with a nice salad would suit me fine.

While the sauce and the water for the pasta were heating, I shredded some lettuce and halved a few cherry tomatoes. I was about to slice up a couple of radishes when suddenly—pretty much as Barbara had suggested could happen—it struck me: the realization that something was very wrong here.

Setting down the knife, I leaned against the counter for a moment to steady myself. Then, in a kind of daze, I went into the living room for my attaché case. I pulled out my notes and thumbed through them quickly until I found the corroboration I was looking for.

Shaking, I sat down on the sofa to sort things out in my mind for a bit. After which I buried my head in the pillow and cried.

It isn't easy to accept that someone you liked, someone you *trusted,* is a diabolical killer.

Especially when that someone is your own client.

Chapter 37

Now, what had come to me somewhere between the cherry tomatoes and the radishes was that John didn't react the way common sense dictates he should have reacted.

I'd better make that a little clearer.

According to Trudie, it was the custom for John and Edward to see each other every Wednesday for breakfast—she'd specified the day during our initial meeting. And there's no reason to believe that their long-standing date had been scratched for the morning after the shooting. Actually, quite the opposite. When Trudie and I had coffee in the Village last week, she'd commented on how those get-togethers had been canceled only twice: at the time Edward's daughter gave birth and again when his dog died.

Obviously, however, on that particular Wednesday Edward never made it to whatever restaurant the cousins had arranged to patronize that day.

But what does John do about this?

Strangely, nothing.

And in the face of Edward's absence, wouldn't it have been only natural for a concerned John to attempt to reach the man at home? My client, however, never phoned that apartment. And why do I say this? Because if he had, it wouldn't have been necessary for Sara's sister to contact him at work with the tragic news.

". . . I got the impression he was not only shocked, but really, *really* upset," Jane told me of her conversation with John.

Apparently, he had made no reference to his earlier appointment with Edward or to Edward's failure to show up for it—which should have provided John with a pretty good clue that *something* wasn't kosher.

There was more. Sitting in my living room now, trying to piece things together, I became aware of the fact that my client had also never mentioned that final engagement to me.

Think about it. He should have been able to offer it as a kind of substantiation that he'd had nothing to do with the murder.

"Would I have waited at that coffee shop for half an hour" (or fifteen minutes or whatever) "if I hadn't expected Edward to be there?" is how he could have phrased it. "Check with the manager, Mr. So-and-so," he might have added. "He'll tell you how long I stuck around."

Instead, having very personal knowledge that Edward was dead, *John had been a no-show himself.*

At this point it also occurred to me that John had never even apprised me of the *existence* of this long-standing practice of theirs. I imagine he must have been ready to go for Trudie's jugular when she referred to it that time in my office. After all, this might well have precipitated my making inquiries at the restaurant where he and Edward were supposed to meet that morning. I mean, I'd have been anxious to present Fielding with verification of my client's presence at the eatery—you know, as a further indication, however slight, of his innocence. Unfortunately, however, I'd been as thick as pea soup, not latching on to the significance of Trudie's information until this very minute.

At any rate, with my newfound wisdom, I could

certainly appreciate why John had kept mum about the Wednesday thing. Which is why I've always maintained that what *isn't* said often turns out to be far more revealing than what is.

Chapter 38

I could barely manage to get the food down. Of
course, my mood was definitely not aiding the digestive process. But the meal itself didn't help, either.
While I did remember to put up the rigatoni, I then
promptly forgot it existed. When I finally turned off
the flame, what lay at the bottom of the pot closely
resembled a big blob of white paste. Add to this that
most of the marinara sauce had boiled out by then.
Plus, after that devastating revelation, I'd abandoned
any further salad preparation, so I wound up picking
away at plain—and boring—lettuce and tomatoes.

Once supper was over I sniveled a lot, blotting my
eyes at frequent intervals. I'd been totally deceived,
convinced that John was a fine and decent human
being. So much so that almost immediately I had become more than a hired PI; I'd turned into a staunch
advocate. And let's not forget how much time I wasted
worrying about the man. It was a toss-up at this juncture who it was I despised more: my treacherous client
or myself for believing in him.

It took a while for the tears to turn to anger and
even longer before I made a resolution: That bastard
was going to pay for his cousin's murder—I'd make
sure of it. I only wished I knew how.

The next morning—Friday—right in the middle of
my Cheerios, I came up with the germ of an idea.

Now, it seemed fairly likely that what was holding

up John Lander's arrest was the missing murder weapon. And while I certainly couldn't pinpoint its whereabouts, I had this little inkling as to the *kind* of place John might have chosen to dispose of the gun. At any rate, it was worth checking into.

I finished breakfast, then contacted Jackie at home to let her know I probably wouldn't be coming to work. Listen, even if my apartment building had just been razed to the ground or I'd been attacked by a swarm of killer bees, I still wouldn't dare stay out without notifying Jackie.

At nine-thirty I phoned John's office, first arranging a hankie over the receiver to alter my voice.

"I'm sorry," his secretary informed me, sounding, if possible, even more nasal than she had on Tuesday, "Mr. Lander isn't in just now." (WHEW! Of course if he *had* been there, I would simply have dropped the receiver back in its cradle.) "May I take a message for him?"

"No, thank you, I'll try him later. When is he expected?"

"Not until after two o'clock. May I tell Mr. Lander who called?" she persisted.

"Uh, it's okay. I'll be in touch with him this afternoon." *As it happened, was I ever right about that!*

It had rained on and off for the past couple of days, sometimes heavily. Now, however, the sun was turned on full blast, making the city appear to positively sparkle. Actually, it was an almost perfect morning, with the temperature hovering around sixty-five and the humidity so low that it didn't even perturb my Shirley Temple curls. (No, I still hadn't managed to get rid of them completely.) Under other circumstances, it would have been a lovely day for a drive. But not today.

For most of the short ride out to Brooklyn Heights I went through the routine that always seems to go hand in hand with my discovery of a perpetrator's identity. I began by cursing myself for taking so long to spot what should have been all too obvious. And then, once I'd had my fill of the self-abuse, I did an about-face and made excuses for my myopia. Although in this present instance, I almost did have a legitimate reason for failing to see the light.

It was, I alibied, *no wonder I hadn't considered John a suspect and had therefore directed my focus everywhere but.* After all, why would a guilty person hire a PI to conduct an investigation that could wind up implicating him in a killing? It didn't make sense. Besides, apparently on some level I *did* appreciate that something was amiss with my client. I mean, how else could I explain the truth's suddenly hitting me over the head like that?

And speaking of that truth, why *hadn't* John brazened it out and shown up at the coffee shop that Wednesday?

One explanation, of course, is that he was still too shaken by the enormity of his crime to carry off the deception. It was also possible that the breakfast had flown completely out of his mind. Understandable when you take into account that this *was* his first murder—that I'm aware of, at any rate.

I was already in Brooklyn Heights when I began chewing over another sticking point.

Trudie, of course, was familiar with those once-a-week get-togethers, and very probably Sara was, too—and who knows who else? *So,* I put to myself, *what would John have told anyone who questioned him about that morning?*

I imagine he could simply have claimed that Edward had telephoned him on Tuesday to cancel. And while this would have been only the third time that had occurred in how many years?—there was really no way to dispute it.

But did I consider for a moment that this is what actually happened?

Pul-eeze! I may have been willing to accept as coincidence that John had called off his appointment with Sara on the night of her husband's murder. But I wasn't about to make the same kind of mistake with regard to the morning after.

John Lander's office was on the ground floor of one of a group of four- and five-story brownstones that took up a good portion of what looked to be a mostly residential street. Only a few minutes by car from the Brooklyn Bridge, it was, I observed with disgust, a very convenient location from which to commute to those weekly trysts of his.

"Yes?" asked a female voice when I pressed the bell.

"I'm here to see Mr. Lander," I advised the gizmo on the doorframe. "I'm Desiree—"

I was cut short by the buzzer admitting me to the building.

An attractive blonde, who appeared to be in her early twenties, sat just inside the door to the apartment, completely surrounded by a huge semicircular desk in a light brown wood laminate. A small brass-and-black sign on the desk informed me that this was Eloise Flugelman.

Ms. Flugelman was busy at the computer, and I watched in admiration as her hands flew effortlessly over the keyboard. Then when I realized that she was chatting on the phone at the same time, the receiver pressed against her shoulder, my admiration for Ms. Flugelman knew practically no bounds. She held up her index finger as a signal that she'd be with me in a minute. But the minute dragged on. And on. Standing off to one side, I began to get impatient. Particularly since after a while, being forced to listen to that nasally voice was like a punishment for my sins.

I glanced around the room, which was a pretty decent size, owing to its no doubt having served as a living room in a previous incarnation. The place was furnished sparsely, with four black leather-and-chrome chairs and a couple of chrome tables. A chrome bamboo-style magazine holder sat on the floor in one corner and a wooden coatrack occupied another. A few colorful modern prints decorated the stark white walls.

"Is Mr. Lander in?" I asked when the call was finally over.

The question seemed to trouble the girl. "I'm afraid he's out just now. Did you have an appointment?"

"Oh, no. I was in the area, so I thought I'd stop in."

She relaxed then. "Good. I was afraid I might have forgotten to write it down or something. Mr. Lander should be here about two." She checked her watch, and automatically, I did the same. It wasn't quite twelve. "Umm, I don't suppose you'd care to wait."

"I can't. Maybe you can help me, though."

The secretary smiled tentatively. "Well, I'll try."

"My name is Desiree Shapiro. I was—"

"I know who you are," she informed me, grinning. "You're a private detective. I'm the one who told John about you."

"You *did*? How did you hear abut me, anyway?"

"I'm a friend of Elvin's."

"Elvin?"

"Elvin Blaustein. You remember, the fellow who lost his boa constrictor."

"Good grief! That was years ago. How did you happen to recall my name?"

Eloise giggled. *"Desiree Shapiro?"*

She had a point.

"Elvin told me you handle a lot of cases like his— lost pets and stuff."

Handled, past tense. But I refrained from setting the record straight. "And you mentioned me to Mr. Lander?"

"Correct. It came up in conversation one day after I overheard him talking to his wife on the telephone.

I suppose you're aware that somebody took a shot at him." Embarrassed, she tittered. "That was really silly. Of course you are. Anyway, it was obvious to me that she—his wife—was really after John to call in a private detective, and I started telling him about you."

"Did you also inform him that I deal primarily with missing-pet-type projects?"

"Well, yes."

"I'm surprised he decided to hire me."

"I was kind of surprised, too," Eloise admitted, flushing. "When I brought up your name I was just making conversation. I didn't intend it as a recommendation." Flustered now, she added quickly, "Oh, not that you aren't good at what you do; I'm sure you are. It's just that you have a different . . . specialty."

I had to smile at the "specialty."

"Listen," I said then, "there was something I wanted to check with John. But it occurs to me that you might be the person I should be speaking to anyway."

"What is it you'd like to know?"

"The morning after somebody shot at John—can you tell me what time he arrived at the office? I need the information for a report I'm preparing for him."

Eloise picked up a large appointment ledger from the desktop and began to riffle through the pages. "Let's see," she said. "That was on a Tuesday, right?"

"Yes, May 13."

"It's just what I thought; John didn't get in until late in the afternoon—around four, I think. He had an appointment at this new development in Cobblestone Lake."

My mouth went totally dry, and my heart forgot to beat. *Could I possibly be on the right track?*

"Where is that?"

"Upstate. In Sullivan County. The builder is a friend of his, and he wanted to talk to John about handling the sale of the units. In fact, John has an-

ther meeting scheduled up there for later on this
week."

"Would you by any chance know the name of the
development?"

"Holbrook Estates. John's friend is Glenn Holbrook."

"This is great. Thanks so much, Eloise. Is it okay if
call you Eloise?"

"Sure, that's my name," the girl responded ingenu-
ously.

"Anyway, the information should help a lot in get-
ing John's itinerary straight for that day. I—" Stop-
ing abruptly, I covered my mouth and slowly shook
my head. After which I bit my lip. I hate to brag, but
t was an inspired performance.

Eloise's eyes opened wider. "What's the matter?"

"I just realized that in spite of John's wanting me
o have the information, he might not appreciate your
iving it out without his permission."

"Do you really think it would bother him?" She
was clearly disturbed.

"I'm not sure, but I shouldn't have involved you—
just in case. I'm very sorry." As if in concentration, I
ut my finger to my cheek and scrunched up my fore-
ead. "But listen, there isn't any reason for John to
nd out I was even here today. I won't say anything
you don't."

Eloise nodded somberly. "Then there's no problem.
'll be just between the two of us."

Chapter 39

The first thing I did when I got back in the car was to check my map of New York State. Which would have given anyone who knows me a really good laugh.

I can't tell you how many times I've been advised that anyone with half a brain should be able to read one of those things. But apparently I'm missing that half. Anyhow, after a couple of minutes of trying to make sense of all those dark red lines and light red lines and blue lines and blue squares and I can't remember what else, I shoved the map back in the glove compartment and headed for the nearest gas station.

I was informed that it shouldn't take more than a couple of hours to reach Cobblestone Lake. But in spite of Chuck's best efforts—he was the gas station attendant—I managed to keep getting lost, so I wound up traveling for closer to four. And I'm not even counting the twenty minutes or so I spent in the Swell Eats Diner on the way to the place.

Well, one thing about being alone in a vehicle for an extended period like that: you have a whole lot of time to think. And that's what I did. And at long last I got a handle on some crucial elements of the case.

I began by examining the startling fact I'd discovered only a short while before, during my talk with Eloise. I'm referring to what John knew of my background. As you're aware, once he'd manufactured that attempted shooting, Trudie tried to steamroll him into bringing in a private investigator. But John recognized that having a professional look into the events of the past couple of weeks could prove disastrous for him. So in spite of what must have been almost unbearable pressure from that harridan he was married to, he held firm for a few days.

Then Eloise told him about one Desiree Shapiro. He must have regarded me as the answer to a prayer—and, unfortunately, I say this in all modesty.

Listen, not only could I boast of having been employed to hunt for somebody's pet boa constrictor, but that sort of thing was actually my "*specialty*." So what were the odds of someone with my credentials posing a threat to a clever fellow like John?

Not only that. I have a feeling the man decided that I could prove useful with regard to the missing Air Force wings, which he very much feared had come off at the crime scene. I mean, he realized that it might be helpful (which it wasn't) if I were to relate to the police that even before they found that pin in Edward's apartment, my client had begun to suspect that someone might have planted it there.

Anyway, you can see that there isn't really much doubt about it. John Lander hadn't come to me because I had the best chance of uncovering the perpetrator, but because he figured I had the best chance *not to*.

Hardly an ego-booster.

I switched on the radio after that, just so I could relax for a bit. But before long, I was back to ruminating about the investigation—I couldn't seem to stop myself. And pretty soon I was ready to abandon the idea of driving to Cobblestone Lake in favor of kicking myself all the way up there instead.

The thing is, I'd been so-o-o perplexed over the fact that Sara Sharp's lover had murdered Edward before he inherited—thereby preventing Sara from becoming an extremely wealthy widow.

Well, I demanded of myself now, *why hadn't it occurred to me that there was one person who wouldn't have derived the slightest benefit from postponing the shooting?* I'm referring, of course, to the individual who was next in line for the money.

This thought quickly led to another. John's affair with Sara could also explain why he hadn't rid himself of Trudie ages ago. Evidently, financial gain alone hadn't been enough of a motivation for him to commit murder. But then he discovers this grand passion for his cousin's wife. And *that,* coupled with the windfall that would accrue to him if Edward went bye-bye, had evidently proved too strong a magnet for someone of my client's character to resist.

It was close to five when, after more wrong turns and missed signs than I can estimate, I arrived in Cobblestone Lake—where I had to obtain further instructions from another kindly service station attendant. Obviously assessing my intelligence, this one even felt it advisable to jot down the very simple directions. At any rate, two traffic lights later I made a right off Liberty Avenue, the town's main thoroughfare, onto a gravel road. The next quick right and I was on the dirt lane that marked the entrance to Holbrook Estates. The endless trip had finally come to an end.

The homes here—there were about two dozen of them—were set quite far back on the tract and appeared to be in various stages of completion.

Driving closer to the construction, I spotted a level area that was evidently functioning as a parking lot. Approximately fifty feet from the first of the houses, it was occupied by a beat-up pickup truck and two fairly new-model convertibles. My Chevy joined them. On getting out of the car, I noted absently that there were only a couple of workmen around, both at the far end of the development. Well, I reminded myself, it was late afternoon. And it was a Friday.

Anyhow, once I was faced with proceeding on foot, I realized how poorly prepared I was for this little adventure of mine. With remarkable absence of foresight, I'd elected to put on a pair of high heels that I have difficulty walking in under favorable conditions. But today, thanks to all that recent rain, I was sinking into the wet earth and pitching so far forward that there was an excellent possibility I'd soon be horizontal.

I was so intent on keeping my balance as I made for the dwellings that I paid very little attention to the other car that was pulling into the lot from the rear. Or to the fact that it was a Range Rover.

I'd covered all of about two yards when I heard a squishing sound. I turned. And eight or nine feet behind me John Lander stopped dead in his tracks.

This was a John Lander I hardly recognized. That amiable and fair-minded fellow I once knew now had the face of an extremely dangerous man. And I'm not being melodramatic, either. Our eyes made contact for an instant—his had narrowed to mere slivers—but neither of us said a word.

I tried to run. Only between the mud and the shoes and a long-standing disinclination to subject my limbs to any exertion, I had little hope of eluding my pursuer. I knew for a certainty that he was moving quickly—and closing the gap fast.

Then two things happened. John attempted to tackle me—at the precise moment I lost my footing. The result was that I landed facedown in the mud and John, with nothing but air to connect to, did the same, winding up right behind me.

I believe the wind must have been knocked out of him, because for a moment he lay there, unmoving. Well, being built a lot closer to the ground than John is—and, consequently, not having had nearly as far to fall—I was relatively unscathed. Almost at once I was able to roll onto my back (although with great difficulty) and push myself up on my elbows (with even more difficulty). Leaning over now, I gathered up all of my not-very-impressive strength and whacked that dirty rotten creep full force on the head with the one lethal weapon I'm never without: my handbag.

The combined impact of the flashlight, cell phone, bottled water, stapler, cough medicine, etc., etc., was enough to knock him out cold.

Struggling to my feet, I made it to my Chevy, only to realize that I was too shaken to drive.

I locked the doors and windows and, my eyes riveted to a still-prone John, got out my .32, which that morning I'd thought it might be prudent to carry today. But then—wouldn't you know it?—I had left the gun in the glove compartment.

I placed it in my lap. After which I got out my cell phone and dialed 9-1-1.

Within five or ten minutes a tall, beefy state trooper was tapping on the windshield. Rolling down the window, I handed him my PI license before explaining that a client of mine had just attacked me and that I'd struck him with my pocketbook in self-defense. The man seemed to find this amusing, not even attempting to conceal a smirk as I pointed to the figure on the ground.

I watched intently as the trooper, who had just been joined by a second officer, hurried over to John. They both knelt beside him, and while I couldn't see exactly what was going on, I assumed they were checking his vital signs.

It wasn't long before trooper number one returned to talk to me.

"You're a very lucky lady," he said. "Were you aware that this guy had a knife in his hand?"

I gulped, then shook my head. "Umm . . . I didn't kill him, did I?"

The trooper was smiling in encouragement. "He's coming to now. So the answer's no."

"That's too bad," I mumbled—right before I fainted.

Chapter 40

John Lander was arrested for assault immediately following that terrifying confrontation at Cobblestone Lake. Six days later he was finally indicted for the murder of his cousin Edward.

My old friend Fielding and I had had a number of brief telephone conversations in the interim. Then a few days after the homicide indictment he took me to lunch at the Palm, a wonderful scarred-wood-floor, no-frills, guy-type steakhouse in the East Forties. Evidently this was a thank-you for my contribution to John's finally winding up where he belonged. In addition, Fielding seemed anxious to compare notes—*and* have the opportunity to bawl me out for what he considered my thoroughly irresponsible behavior.

Even before our shrimp cocktails, we started to rehash the case that had until recently occupied center stage in both our lives. The postmortem continued through our sirloins and mashed potatoes, extending well into the cheesecake and coffee. Now, as you're well aware, normally I'd have preferred to wait until we were through eating before entering into a discussion on things like murder and attempted murder—particularly when that attempt had been on my person. In this instance, however, we were talking about an evil, manipulative scum's being brought to justice. Which, if anything, acted as a flavor enhancer.

Of course, I wasn't crazy about Fielding's kicking

things off with a lecture. "Whatever possessed you to go to that development alone like that? You should know better."

"I do. Honestly, Tim. But when at long last I figured out that it was my client who killed Edward Sharp, I was just so anxious to help you apprehend him." Fielding raised both eyebrows at that one. "And as I said on the phone, I had this vague notion that he might have buried the gun up there. But I saw it as a real long shot, I swear. Besides, I took precautions."

"Yeah? Well, go on. What's your idea of 'precautions'?"

"Number one: I had my gun with me."

"So I understand. And then you proceeded to leave it in the glove compartment of your car, where it was absolutely useless."

I could feel my cheeks burn. "I admit that was careless. But there was no real reason to anticipate any trouble. Which brings me to precaution number two: I only went to Brooklyn Heights that morning once Eloise—John's secretary—informed me that he wasn't expected until two o'clock. And number three, I got her to agree not to mention to him that I'd been there. Of course," I grumbled, "she turned out to be quite a stand-up little girl. As soon as John starts questioning her, she rolls over and gives me away, obviously spilling a lot more than was necessary."

Fielding clucked in mock sympathy. "You have every reason to be pissed. She owed you her allegiance on the basis of your close, long-standing friendship." And now he regarded me sternly. "Listen, Shapiro, you can't afford to bank on everybody's behaving according to your script. Something else you ought to have discovered way back."

"You're right," I responded meekly.

I should mention that by then both Tim and I had learned that John's last appointment that day had been canceled and that he spotted me walking out of the building when he unexpectedly returned to his office.

"Anyhow," I continued, "I realize that I could have worked things out a little better. But when I finally recognized my client for what he was, I reacted viscerally. I mean, I got mad as hell—probably as much at myself as at him. God! What a wonderful judge of character I'm not! I believed he was *such* a decent person."

"That's what you get for not paying attention to your uncle Tim," Fielding teased. Then he noticed the look on my face. "Listen, Lander was good, really convincing. If we didn't have what we did on him, I might have bought into his act myself."

"I doubt it. I am *such* a patsy."

"Will you cut it out? Anybody can be fooled, and you know why? Because nobody really knows another human being."

"Thanks," I said, touched by this attempt to console me. It was a side of Tim I didn't see very often.

"There's something I'm a little uncertain of," he brought up at this point. "As I recall, when we talked the other day you told me that during that entire two-hour trip upstate, you didn't have even the slightest suspicion you were being followed. Did I get that straight?"

I couldn't see any reason for apprising him that the drive had taken almost twice as long. "Yes, you did." And then in an attempt to erase his nonplussed expression I added, "I'd never laid eyes on that car before, though. The one time John had given me a lift it was in a black sedan." I also didn't feel it was important for Fielding to know I was aware that John owned a Range Rover, as well.

"Let me ask you this," he said, moving on. "What gave you the idea that Lander might have ditched his gun at that development in the first place?"

"I keep trying to make you understand, Tim. It wasn't that I actually *thought*—"

"Yeah, yeah. I stand corrected." And in a voice dripping with sarcasm: "I'll rephrase that. What made you entertain the extremely vague possibility that the man could have disposed of his weapon at Holbrook Estates?"

"I don't really know," I answered, ignoring the tone. "No, I take that back. I guess I do. The thing is, I'd tried reaching John at his office one day, and Eloise told me he was at a construction site. This was before I finally concluded that it was my own damn client who'd blasted Sharp.

"Anyhow, once I hit on the truth, it occurred to me that the gun had never been found; otherwise, by then John would have been charged with the crime. The other thing I figured was that it had still been in his possession on the night someone supposedly took a shot at him. After all, he had to assume that you'd try to find the bullet, so it would have made sense for him to actually fire the weapon." I looked at Fielding for confirmation.

He interpreted the look correctly. "He did fire it, and we located the bullet in some hedges. That bullet—along with the one in Edward Sharp's chest—came from the 9-millimeter semiautomatic we've since recovered. Which, as you already know, is registered to a fellow named John Lander. By the way, you *were* aware that our boy owned one of those babies, weren't you?"

"As a matter of fact, no."

"Why am I not surprised that he didn't share this with you?" Fielding remarked cynically. "Evidently Lander owned a jewelry store at some point, and after being robbed twice, he got the weapon for protection. Naturally, he insists it was stolen years ago—although he never bothered to file a report to that effect. But as you were saying . . ."

"What *was* I saying? Oh, I remember. By the time my upstanding client resorted to staging that phony shooting, things had become kind of hot for him, so it would have been really foolhardy to continue hanging on to the gun. *I* figured that *John* figured he'd better dump it. *But where?* I asked myself.

"It seemed doubtful to me that he'd discharge the weapon right in front of his home and then immediately hop into his car so he could fling it into the Hudson River or someplace. What if someone noticed him take off like that? Besides, that Wednesday breakfast slipup of his must have wised John up fast; he started playing things pretty cagey from then on. And for the victim of an attempted homicide—as John professed to be—the natural thing to do would be to rush into his building. Maybe ask the doorman if he'd seen or heard anything, too."

"Which is what our guy did," Fielding put in. "We checked."

"At any rate, I believe it's likely that John had the gun in his briefcase the next morning when he and Trudie went to speak to you about the alleged attack." Tim scowled. For some reason even the thought of this appeared to irritate him. "Or maybe," I amended, "he'd concealed it in his car. I had reservations, though, about his attempting to ditch it in a crowded city in broad daylight. *That's* when I recalled Eloise's mention of a construction site. In his business, I reasoned, John must have frequently spent time at new developments. And just think about it, Tim. You bury the evidence in the ground right before the house is erected, following which it gets covered with a few tons of cement or whatever they use. And then—look, Ma!—I'm clean."

Fielding stroked his chin. "So you went to Lander's office that Friday to interrogate his secretary as to whether on the day after the staged attack he'd been at a location that would fill the bill."

"Exactly. At that juncture he must have been itching to lose the murder weapon. Still," I emphasized, "I only talked to the girl on the off chance that he *might* have visited some sort of construction on the heels of his little stunt."

"All right, but tell me this, Shapiro. What were you supposed to accomplish up at that place, anyhow? Did you plan on digging for the gun with your fingers?"

"Don't be such a wise guy. I was just checking things out. I wanted to satisfy myself that there was even a possibility that my client had chucked it there."

"And how did you plan on determining this?"

"Look, if the homes were already at the wallpapering stage, I'd have taken this as a fairly good indication that I was barking up the wrong tree." And now I put down my fork and leaned back in the seat. "It turned out I hit pay dirt, though," I proclaimed, smiling smugly.

Fielding also put down his fork and leaned back in the seat. "Well, not quite," he said softly.

"What do you mean?"

"It seems all the foundations had already been put in by the time Lander elected to dispose of the gun. Naturally, we had the area thoroughly searched anyway, with the assistance of the law-enforcement people up there. Nothing doing, though."

"But I assumed—" Confused, I broke off. "So where—"

"Hey, us dumb cops can have a productive thought, too, on rare occasions. The name of that town is what, Shapiro?"

"Cobblestone Lake. But how does that—" I stopped abruptly, having just answered my own unfinished question.

"You got it. The lake itself isn't very big, but it's only a few miles from Holbrook Estates and in a pretty isolated spot. Not a bad choice for unburdening yourself of a hot piece of property if you happen to be in that neck of the woods. Anyway, we had a team of divers go down and have a look around. And on the second day—whaddaya know? We discovered that this is just where that little sucker had been hiding."

"Then I was actually way off base," I pouted childishly.

Tim reached across the booth and playfully punched me in the arm. "Are you kidding? If not for you, who can say if we'd ever have wound up with that gun—in fact, we probably wouldn't have. Besides, you'd have thought of the lake yourself. Even old Johnny Boy was fairly certain of that."

"What makes you say so?"

"Listen, considering his actions that afternoon, he must have been damn spooked by your going to that development. He obviously realized that if you could figure out Holbrook Estates, it wouldn't be long before it dawned on you that right nearby was another handy receptacle for incriminating evidence."

Suddenly my dear friend (and sometime antagonist) was glaring at me. "Which is not to say you made any use of the sense you were born with when you hot-footed it up there the way you did. You came *that close* to getting your throat slit, for crissakes. And if I'm not mistaken, you're the one who's always mouthing off about our sharing, right? Well, there couldn't have been a better time for it. But no, you went and—"

"Believe me, I had every intention of going to you with this if I decided it was a viable location." And now, since it looked like this dressing-down Fielding was treating me to might still have legs, I concluded that it would be an ideal moment to pose a question of my own.

"I have to know something, Tim. Why were you so positive all along that my client was the perp—aside from the inheritance business and finding those wings at the crime scene, that is."

"'*Aside,*' did you say? Listen, Desiree, I wouldn't call either of those things exactly irrelevant. And I seriously doubt if *you* would—if the guy hadn't been your own client. But as it happens, there was more. Early on in the investigation Norm and I had a conversation with the Sharp housekeeper."

"I didn't even know there *was* a housekeeper."

"She comes in a couple of days a month. At any rate, the woman—a Mrs. Clavell—could hardly wait to engage in a little gossip, and she provided us with what turned out to be a very interesting lead. Apparently she'd overheard Sara Sharp arranging to meet someone after class this one week. Sara sounded very cozy with whoever was on the other end of the line, too. According to Mrs. Clavell, that is—who, incidentally, claims that even before this she was all but certain her employer had a lover."

"How did she come up with that?"

"Evidently this housekeeper is better than a lie detector—she insists that she can tell just by looking at a person's complexion if they're engaging in a little hanky-panky. The truth is, Norm and I had her pegged as something of a cuckoo bird. Still, we felt it might be worthwhile to follow up and see if, in addition to everything else, our number one suspect was Mrs. Sharp's paramour."

"*Paramour?*" I echoed with a smirk.

Fielding chuckled. "It's Norm's word, but I've gotten kind of fond of it myself. Say, do you want me to fill you in on the rest of this or not?"

"I certainly do."

"Okay, so we got our hands on photos of Lander and Sara Sharp and began showing them around the neighborhood of the pottery school. Both the owner and a waitress at one of the coffee shops down there positively identified the two of them. Said they'd come in a number of times.

"Now, add the affair to the money motive and the

wings, and I'd say things were looking damn good
for Lander—or damn bad, depending on where you're
sitting. Incidentally, we may soon have another piece
of evidence against the guy.

"The night of the shooting we found some brown
hairs not far from the body. Well, Mrs. Sharp's a
blonde, and the victim was almost completely gray. Of
course, the hairs could have belonged to almost anyone else, but they could also have come from the
killer. So the gun wasn't the only thing we were after
when we searched the Lander place.

"At any rate, even though the weapon was no
longer in Lander's possession by then, at least we
didn't walk out of that apartment empty-handed. We
took a few samples from that son of a bitch's hairbrush. And while we haven't gotten the DNA back
yet, it wouldn't surprise me if it matches the DNA of
the hairs at the crime scene."

"Well, suppose it does. You still wouldn't have indicted my client if you hadn't been able to turn up
the gun." It was half question, half statement.

"That sort of thing isn't my call. But without that
baby the case against John Lander would be pretty iffy.
Look, the DA made the point that Lander could claim
that in an attempt to frame him for the shooting, the
hairs had been taken off his jacket and planted at the
victim's apartment, just like the wings. Now that we have
the weapon, though, everyone's feeling confident—real
confident—about the chances of a conviction."

"Thank God you found it," I murmured.

"*We* found it," Fielding maintained gallantly. A moment later he took a final sip of coffee, then put down
the cup and regarded me solemnly. "Oh, by the way,
there's one thing I'd like you to do for me."

"What's that?"

"I imagine it must be force of habit, Shapiro. But
please. Stop referring to that rotten scuzzball as your
client."

Epilogue

Five days after my lunch with Fielding, Uncle Victor died at his home. They say he went peacefully, in his sleep. He expired without ever learning that his favorite nephew had been murdered—or that another of his nephews had been the executioner.

So the old man's will was never changed.

Apparently, however, it's against the law for a convicted felon to inherit—and I can't imagine that John won't be convicted. But as to who *is* entitled to those megabucks, this appears to be sort of muddled.

I've already spoken to three different attorneys regarding the disposition of that money—and received three different responses. One lawyer was of the opinion the windfall would pass to the person or persons next in line according to the terms of Victor's will—in other words, the twins. A second refused to even venture a guess. And a third felt it was likely that the family of the victim would benefit from John Lander's handiwork.

And while we're on the subject of the victim's family, Sara called me when she heard about the arrest. At first she had a great deal of difficulty coming to grips with the fact that John was her husband's killer. Then when she finally accepted the truth, she was inconsolable, insisting that she was as much to blame for what had transpired as her former lover was.

"My affair with John led to Edward's death," Sara

insisted. "If I hadn't . . . hadn't done what I did, my
husband would be alive today."

I tried to convince her that Edward became a potential target the instant he was named his uncle's principal
beneficiary. But although she eventually calmed down,
I think it was because the woman had worn herself
out. Not because she bought into my argument—one
I wasn't even certain I believed myself.

At any rate, if she does come into that bundle, I
doubt that Sara Sharp will be able to derive any pleasure from it. At least, not for a very long while.

As for Victor's other relatives, the only one to contact me aside from Sara was Scott Riley, who phoned
for the gory details—doubtless the very second he got
the news.

"Well?" he challenged in that prissy manner of his.
"Who warned you from the get-go that John was the
culprit? Tell me that, Desiree." I was all set to remind
him that he'd also suspected David Hearn for a time,
but he sailed right into his interrogation.

How did it feel to discover that my own client was
the individual I'd been seeking all along? (I could picture Scott smirking and rubbing his hands together as
he put this to me.) Had I ever had any suspicions at all
about John? What evidence did the police have against
John? And then my absolute favorite: Was it true what
everyone was saying? Did John Lander *really* attempt
to drown me at Jones Beach?

My answers were terse and honest—for the most
part, that is. "Lousy." "Only toward the very end."
"I'm not at liberty to say." Even my handling of that
last, off-the-wall question was—if you'll grant me a bit
of a stretch—not untruthful. Although I admit that I
wasn't above playing a kind of head game with that
insufferable little snot.

I began by making him endure an extended pause.
After which I went into my histrionics. "Oh, dear. How
did you happen to—?" A shorter pause. Then, with a

throb in my voice: "Please, Scott, swear to me you won't mention that again—to *anybody*."

Well, you couldn't call this a lie, could you?

Anyhow, immediately following Scott's promise to me (a promise I was sure would be in effect only for the duration of our conversation), he seemed pleased at being the first to inform me that Trudie Lander was considering joining a nunnery. Which, from my knowledge of that lady, I can state unequivocally had about as much validity as the Jones Beach rumor.

Right before the call ended, Scott griped about his sister and David Hearn continuing to be an item. Which did not make me any too happy, either. Let's say Shawna *did* get half of Uncle Victor's estate; I still hated to think of anyone as likable as David being saddled with someone like *her*. I mean, I could certainly find him a girl who was a lot better suited to him. Maybe when he and Shawna broke up—I try to think positively—I'd introduce him to this young lawyer who sometimes stops in at the office to see Pat Sullivan (you know, of Gilbert and Sullivan). She's Pat's niece, I believe, and she's charming and very attractive. Well, except for her teeth. But then, David has a very good dentist.

Closer to home, things have been pretty uneventful lately—although considering recent occurrences, I don't suppose I should knock "uneventful." But just to bring you up to date, Jackie's still on speaking terms with Derwin. Pop—thank heaven—continues to see that Florida divorcée. And my nervous Nellie of a niece persists in conjuring up one wedding-related crisis after another—and manages to survive them all.

As for me, I was involved in a brief investigation a couple of weeks back—a runaway teenager who I was fortunate in tracking down in Pennsylvania, unharmed. Since then, though, I've been, as we say in the theatuh, "between engagements."

Of a more personal nature, only the other night Nick Grainger and I had an unexpected meeting in the laundry room.

I was just taking my stuff out of the dryer when he walked in. Once again that short, bony frame and those sexy buck teeth turned my knees to jelly.

He greeted me pleasantly, and then looking uncomfortable, he said, "I . . . uh . . . wonder if you'd do me a favor. I was using that same dryer about an hour ago, and it's possible something of mine may be mixed in with what you have there. Do you . . . would you mind checking?"

"Of course not." I set the load down on the folding table—and immediately spied the white silk boxers with the red hearts all over them. Clearly an item not my own.

"Would these be what you're referring to?" I asked, extending the shorts between my thumb and forefinger.

Nick, his face now redder than those red hearts, practically grabbed for the things, quickly tucking them under his arm in a not entirely successful attempt to conceal the source of his embarrassment. "A friend gave these to me as a gag, years ago," he mumbled with a pathetic try for a grin.

Well, the print *was* kind of faded, and the shorts *did* look a bit frayed. And what was past was past.

Quite uncharacteristically, therefore, I decided not to waste any energy speculating about the donor, opting instead to regard the commingling of our laundry as a *sign*.

I don't suppose I should count on it, though, my intuition being what it is.

So, like Uncle Victor's fortune, where this goes from here is really anybody's guess. . . .

Desiree's Orange Chicken with Almonds

2 tbs. slivered almonds
small amount of butter
1/3 cup orange juice
2 tsp. honey
1 tbs. soy sauce
1 tsp. grated fresh ginger
1 1/2 tsp. arrowroot or
  cornstarch
2 tsp. vegetable oil
2 cloves of garlic, minced
2 tbs. sliced scallions,
  white part only

1/2 tbs. fresh orange peel,
  slivered
1 lb. chicken breast,
  boned and skinned,
  cut into 1" × 2 1/2"
  pieces
salt and freshly ground
  pepper to taste
1 1/2 tbs. chopped scallions,
  green part only

Sauté almonds in butter until lightly browned. Drain on paper towels and set aside. Whisk next 5 ingredients in a small bowl until mixture is smooth and set aside. Over high flame, heat oil in wok or large skillet. Add garlic, white part of scallions, and orange peel. Stir-fry one minute. Add chicken and stir-fry until chicken loses its pink color—about 3 minutes. Stir orange-juice mixture and add to wok. Stir-fry until liquid has thickened and chicken is cooked through. Season with salt and pepper; then add green part of scallions. Sprinkle with slivered almonds.

Recipe serves 2 generously and can be doubled.

**Here is a preview of the next
exciting Desiree Shapiro mystery,
coming in early 2003 . . .**

Ellen's bridal shower.

It has to be really, really special, I'd been reminding myself from the instant the planning began. After all, this was a very important day in the life of my favorite (and only) niece.

And special it was.

This had nothing whatever to do with the ambiance—although you couldn't have asked for a setting lovelier than the Silver Oaks Country Club. With its stately colonial-style mansion set high up on a sweeping, impeccably groomed front lawn, the place looked like something straight out of *Gone with the Wind,* for heaven's sake.

It had nothing to do with the food either—even though my cohostess, Allison Lynton—the prospective bridegroom's mother—and I had agonized over the menu options for hours. And every dish—from the filet mignon and salmon Florentine to the three dessert choices—was very tastefully prepared, too. As it turned out, our painstaking efforts and the kitchen's expertise went equally unappreciated.

And it certainly wasn't the gifts that made this event so memorable. All of that extravagant silver and china and crystal, in company with the requisite cookware and toaster-ovens (there were three of these), remained in their beribboned wrappings, unopened. Not destined to catch so much as a single light ray on this sunshine-y late August afternoon.

No.

What *did* make this an affair that no one who attended is likely to forget was something horrific, chilling—*unimaginable*.

And it happened right in the middle of the salad course.

Suddenly, the woman seated directly across from me dropped her fork and pitched forward on her elegant, damask-covered chair, uttering strange, guttural sounds and snatching frantically at her throat.

And at that moment, Ellen's bridal shower turned into a death watch.